Little Faith

ALSO BY MICHAEL SIMON

Body Scissors

Dirty Sally

Little Faith

A Novel

MICHAEL SIMON

VIKING

VIKING
Published by the Penguin Group
Penguin Group (USA) Inc., 375 Hudson Street, New York, New York 10014, U.S.A.
Penguin Group (Canada), 90 Eglinton Avenue East, Suite 700, Toronto, Ontario, Canada
M4p 2Y3 (a division of Pearson Penguin Canada Inc.)
Penguin Books Ltd., 80 Strand, London WC2R 0RL, England
Penguin Ireland, 25 St. Stephen's Green, Dublin 2, Ireland
(a division of Penguin Books Ltd)
Penguin Books Australia Ltd, 250 Camberwell Road, Camberwell, Victoria 3124,
Australia (a division of Pearson Australia Group Pty Ltd)
Penguin Books India Pvt Ltd, 11 Community Centre, Panchsheel Park,
New Delhi – 110 017, India
Penguin Group (NZ), Cnr Airborne and Rosedale Roads, Albany, Auckland 1310,
New Zealand (a division of Pearson New Zealand Ltd)
Penguin Books (South Africa) (Pty) Ltd, 24 Sturdee Avenue, Rosebank,
Johannesburg 2196, South Africa

Penguin Books Ltd, Registered Offices: 80 Strand, London WC2R 0RL, England

First published in 2006 by Viking Penguin, a member of Penguin Group (USA) Inc.

10 9 8 7 6 5 4 3 2 1

Publisher's Note
This is a work of fiction. Names, characters, places, and incidents either are the product of
the author's imagination or are used fictitiously, and any resemblance to actual persons,
living or dead, business establishments, events, or locales is entirely coincidental.

LIBRARY OF CONGRESS CATALOGING IN PUBLICATION DATA
Simon, Michael, 1963–
Little faith : a novel / by Michael Simon.
p.   cm.
ISBN 0-670-03790-7
1. Reles, Dan (Fictitious character)—Fiction. 2. Police—Texas—Austin—Fiction.
3. Austin (Tex.)—Fiction. 4. Jewish men—Fiction. 5. Jewish fiction. I. Title.
PS3619.I5625L57 2006
813'.6—dc22   2006044732

Printed in the United States of America
Set in Horley Old Style MT
Designed by Daniel Lagin

To Jeffrey Robles

Freedom is about authority. Freedom is about the willingness of every single human being to cede to lawful authority a great deal of discretion about what you do and how you do it.
                    —New York City mayor Rudolph Giuliani
                    April 1998

We are the national laboratory for bad government.
                    —Molly Ivins on the Texas state legislature
                    March 2005

Part One

||||||||||||||||||||||||||||||||||||||||

MAL SUEÑO

APRIL 11, 1995

Yellow light from the bathroom played on her small breasts as she lay on the coverlet, her belly rising and falling. She gurgled in the dark room.

He felt strangely peaceful considering the circumstances. Fear and shame, the guiding forces of his life, had been purged in a few joyful moments. Now he felt tall and strong and peaceful. Part James Bond, part Buddha.

"Mama?" she said, her voice weak and thick with sleep.

"She's not here." Outside, a car rolled up the gravel alley.

"Call Mama." She furrowed her brow like a serious infant. Baby face, soft skin, shivering in the warm room. The little cherub who brought him peace.

He spoke in lullaby tones. "You called. She wasn't home. You got me."

An empty Valium bottle lay on the worn braided rug by her single bed. He put it on the nightstand. It was time to go.

In the tiny bathroom, he wet a washcloth, then wiped any surface he might have touched: the faucet, the pill bottle, the doorknob. He was about to leave when his shoe hit another pill bottle.

"Jesus," he said. "How many of these did you take?"

Her head arched back and she choked for air.

In a rush his blood pressure shot up and all his fear and shame came back, all his self-loathing, as it hit him: She could die! She was full of his DNA. He'd be charged with rape, maybe murder. Arrest. Court. Prison. Hell.

He stumbled into the bathroom and ran hot water into the tiny claw-foot tub, then stepped back to the bed. He had to lean close to hear her breaths, short and shallow. He settled his arms under her neck and knees and hoisted. She hung like dead weight, collapsing in the middle. He strained to hold her up.

He moved sideways through the bathroom doorway and lowered her into the tub. She gasped from the hot water and again when her head hit the enamel. He turned on the cold, swished the water around, raised one of her eyelids. She stirred but didn't register him.

"Oh God!" he muttered. "Oh God oh God oh God."

The water rose to her chest and he turned it off.

Find the washcloth. Where's the washcloth? Wipe the tub. Wipe the floor where he stepped. Wipe the pill bottles.

He heard her throat catch again and he watched from the archway. She began to tremble. Then she began to quake. She was having a convulsion, a seizure.

"Oh God," he cried, softly as he could.

Then he wiped the doorknob with the cloth, stepped out, closed it, wiped the outside, hit the rickety wooden steps and ran down, down, down.

2.
||||

An explosion of whoops and cheers rolled over me and crashed against the walls of the banquet hall at the Austin Convention Center as each name was called and a trophy was presented to each of a hundred officers for outstanding duty, perfect attendance, aboves and beyonds, and he waddled up to the podium on fat legs and waved to his thousand friends, blushing with gratitude for the career that saved him from life as a laborer or a thug.

"Carl Milsap!" Sergeant, Narcotics. Cheers.

I made it through the crowd to the right of the tables, to the bar, run by half a dozen young actresses in tuxedo shirts and vests, mixing drinks and smiling with apprehension at the cops' advances. Someone was bragging about an arrest, the kind of conversation he couldn't have with his wife. "We got these two mullets," a funny word for junkie, "in cuffs and one of 'em screechin', 'You cain't do that, I got my rights!' So I kick his legs out. . . ." I ordered another margarita for myself and a kamikaze for my girlfriend and noticed James Torbett standing by the wall just beyond the bar, surveying the room. We'd worked together on Homicide for a few years and forged something like an alliance. I took my drinks and joined him.

Without glancing at me, he said, "You shouldn't drink with both hands, Reles."

I weighed the two drinks. "I can never decide." I scanned the room for Mrs. Torbett, but the only other African Americans I spotted were a few patrols and their wives. "Where's the missus?"

"I don't bring her to these things."

I spotted my girlfriend, Jessica, sulking at our table. She came along for the event, mostly because she thought I didn't want her to. But the absence of a female companion would have looked more suspicious than the presence of an unusual one, even Jessica. I'd had a few too many free margaritas and didn't care one way or the other.

"Luis Fuentes!" Sergeant, Homicide. Cheers.

I tried to imagine what some of the awards were for. Most improved? Fewest prostitutes solicited? Least weight gained?

"How do you figure they make these decisions?" I asked. Torbett deadpanned me. We knew how. We just weren't allowed to say it. The Family.

The Family was a secret affiliation of powerful crackers, a controlling force in the department helping its own to secure promotions and avoid prosecution. Hardly anyone got promoted who didn't have a Klan pedigree and a lip full of chewing tobacco. You couldn't fight the Family, you couldn't even prove it existed. But I knew I wasn't a member and neither was Torbett.

I shrugged. "What are ya gonna do?"

Torbett wasn't the type to give much away, but I saw a shift in his face.

"What?" I asked.

"Nothing," he said. "Just . . . thinking."

The dais table at the front of the room framed the upper brass as a modern *Last Supper*, only with no Jews. (God, in the form of Chief Cronin, hovered invisibly—he didn't show up, he was nowhere and everywhere.) The rest of the crowd sat at a hundred round tables with twelve chairs each, forcing social interaction a lot of us could have done without. I moved back to Jessica, now dipping her feet into a conversation with husky, thirtyish Jeff Czerniak (pronounced CHER-nik) from Organized Crime, to her left. Czerniak, a high school wrestling champ with muscle under his fat and a hyperpituitary jaw, was half smashed and absently holding his neglected wife's hand. He followed along Jessica's reasoning as if she were flirting. She wasn't.

"What made you become a cop?" she asked, her voice high-pitched enough to have a doll-like vibration that made people think they were speaking to a child, but a lack of highs and lows that made her sound like a child at her parents' funeral.

"Fight crime," he said. "Keep creeps off the street!"

"Define creep."

Liquor had put to rest the part of Czerniak that kept him from panting at another woman's breasts in front of his wife. The hurt in young Mrs. Czerniak's face told me it wasn't the first time she'd been through this. Czerniak didn't have the looks or the smoothness to score with every woman who crossed his path, but he was a drooler.

The front tables where we were, closer to the dais, were infested with administration, detectives and their wives. Farther back, the blue knights crowded closer together in full dress uniforms, bloated faces reddened from the department-funded liquor. The banquet wasn't a regular event but a major public relations turnaround, an orgy of self-congratulation meant to jolt the department from the inside, radiating outward as far as the press——and, God willing, the public—to counteract the bad hype that came down in the aftermath of the Salina Street incident. Responding to a bogus call about gang activity, eight cops busted into a children's Valentine's Day party, manhandled children and beat and arrested adults, some still pending trial.

"Harland Clay." Lieutenant, Organized Crime. Cheers. Greasy hair, ruddy face, tobacco juice staining his drooping mustache, Clay had made his name in Narcotics, blending in with the suspects.

I spotted Torbett loping grimly across the floor. I knew that, from a back injury he'd sustained at the hands of another cop, each step caused him pain. And I knew his wife wanted him off the force. Pressure from every side. I saw him greet a younger black detective—Torbett had been the first——talk briefly with him and shake his hand.

The speaker called out several more names, none of them mine. My record had been clean for years, sometimes outstanding. But it had a few old minuses on it. If they gave me an award, that was bad news. It would mean they wouldn't read my name on the list of promotions.

Czerniak was explaining crime to Jessica, his reddened eyes drifting again in the direction of her blouse. "Without the police you'd have anarchy."

She said, "What do you have *with* the police?"

"How's that salmon?" I asked, tapping her bare shoulder. "Any good?"

I didn't blame Czerniak for the path of his eyes. A young twenty-five, Jessica still had a youthful tone. She dyed her natural blond hair Cadillac black to keep from being exploited, she said, surrendering the social advantage of blondness for the emotional distance of a young Lizzie Borden. But her thin hips and waist ballooned out to an ample bosom. She wore outfits that stretched the bounds of what most people called decency, low-cut silks and knits that obscured the color, but not the shape or detail, of her nipples. What passed for her blouse tonight had probably been designed as underwear, a white silk tank top with lacy trim, highlighting pale, baby-soft skin. Men stared and she insulted them, and often as not I had to swoop in to save her. I blamed this on the age difference. When I joined the force back in '77, Dark Jessica was in grade school. Even now the years between us as well as the size differential made our pairing look like a computer mistake. Luckily her screaming and crying jags and suicide threats were growing to dominate our relationship, and our sex life added up to slightly less than never.

"And now to announce promotions . . ." A wild roar rose up and shook the light fixtures. "Assistant Chief Ron Oliphant!"

Again cheers as the black assistant chief, hired from out of state, took the podium and smiled with pride. If he'd ever been shaken down by a white cop, it hadn't happened in Austin. "Every day," he began, "a police officer risks being shot, stabbed, busted or sued." He babbled about pride in the department, inclusiveness and the new East Austin substation—the branch police office in Austin's Spanish ghetto. It was April 11th, so he made a joke about taxes. Ha ha ha, sir.

"I want to remind you," Oliphant went on, "of the memorial service for those killed in the Waco fires. I know some of you are driving up. Keep in mind that you'll be representing the police department. You should be on your best behavior. We had some incidents last year, a few officers brought their guns, they were drinking. . . ." He trailed off. The chatter didn't raise or lower in volume. "Now for the promotions!" he said. More whoops and cheers.

Lieutenant Pete Marks, who had headed Homicide since before Czerniak and I got transferred off, approached our table and stood over Czerniak and Jessica, a hand on each of them, most notably on Jessica. Not having that many opportunities to touch Jessica's bare skin myself, I wasn't inclined to afford the opportunity to Marks. I jumped up to greet him, putting my body in the space where his had been and forcing him to step back.

"Marks! How the hell are ya?" I pumped his hand. "Hey, looks like a lot of your guys were in for honors tonight."

Before Marks could respond, something like a bird chirped from his jacket pocket. He unearthed a phone and clicked it on. "Yup."

Jessica asked, "Can we go?"

At twenty years on the force, you have the option of retiring. For its long investment, the department has reason to offer you something to keep you there: a promotion, a command, even an interesting transfer, say, to Organized Crime. At eighteen years and counting, I was shooting for a promotion. I'd been senior sergeant for a while, a nominal promotion from sergeant, while others leaped over me to lieutenant and commander and more. I wasn't a Texan or even a southerner, and I didn't fit the mold. What I was, was a six-foot, New York–born, ex-boxer Jew, with a Mafia grunt father whose thumb-breaking career had kept me out of the FBI. I'd kept my boxer's physique, but my already prominent schnoz had been busted twice in fights, and I'd collected an assortment of scars and other injuries in the course of my career. While I might have fit right in in my home town of Elmira, New York (if not in the mob hangouts, at least in the prison), all my years in Texas hadn't made me one of the boys.

But I couldn't drop the idea that, in the midst of all the dirty promotions, rewarding insiders for doing anything besides what they were being paid to do, there had to be room for me. It wasn't because I deserved it. It was just that, besides my job, I didn't have anything else. I needed it.

Marks said to the phone, "Of course it's an overdose. File it. We ain't leavin' the banquet."

I scanned the room. A hundred white tablecloths, a thousand cops in various states of intoxication. A thousand spouses. Food, waiters in white jackets, girl bartenders, more class than the rank and file had ever experienced firsthand.

Jessica was arguing with Czerniak, in her dark monotone. "You barrel into a room like you own the place, you have no sense of people's humanity . . ."

Oliphant announced, "Sergeant . . . Charles Pickett!" Street Response Unit. Cheers as a young patrol paraded his uniform down an aisle for the last time, waved and smiled.

I murmured, "Reles. Me. Reles. Dan Reles."

"Sergeant . . . Donald Boyum." Sex Crimes. Cheers.

Reles. Rhymes with jealous.

Jessica: "Lots of jobs are more dangerous than yours. More bus drivers were killed in the line of duty last year than cops. You shouldn't think of yourself as a hero."

Rhymes with tell-us.

"And finally a man who has served the department long and faith-fully. Promoted to the rank of lieutenant and taking command of the Division of Internal Affairs . . ."

My breathing halted. The crowd hushed. Everyone wanted to know who the new IA head was. Who polices the police?

Reles, Reles, Reles . . .

Oliphant said, "*Lieutenant* James Torbett."

A thousand jaws dropped as the first black detective became the first black lieutenant of Internal Affairs. Not one of the boys. Not a team player. A straight arrow. Torbett crossed the room, buttoning his jacket, greeted Oliphant with a solemn handshake and took his plaque, then turned to the silent audience.

Somewhere in the machinery of upper administration, there was a decision maker who wasn't corrupt. Or so I thought.

The comedy of the convention center wasn't that it was built to serve thousands in the middle of downtown but that they forgot to account for parking. It was symbolic of Austin's growth. Bigger! Newer! More! Never mind that the streets and the highway can't accommo-date the number of cars. Never mind epic traffic jams. Don't worry about pile-ups at the airport; it's a beautiful town, it's worth circling over for a few hours. By the mid-nineties our growth was unparal-leled. Motorola reported a 25 percent growth in first-quarter earnings. The Austin-based Schlotzky's sandwich chain was planning to go public. And with the new governor in place, decades-old environ-mental protection laws disappeared by the dozen, treating the city to a plethora of unfamiliar industrial sounds and smells.

I wore a lightweight wool-blend suit, dark blue, that had been tempting moths in my closet between formal occasions for some time but was just about right for the cool evening. Jessica and I walked side by side, two steps apart, up Red River Street, looking for my car. I favored my right leg, owing to a knife injury to the left. It was something I tried to hide, except now as I loped along, fuming. I couldn't blame Torbett for getting promoted when I didn't. I couldn't say he didn't deserve his promotion, because he did. I just didn't think he'd get it.

Jessica stepped next to me, nearly a foot shorter and seventy pounds lighter, in a ratty, oversize sweater she'd pulled on over her tank top, and a vintage-store striped skirt, a suicidal poet. Jake Lund said she looked like someone I picked up in Germany between the wars. Couples passing us on the sidewalk looked back and forth between us, the boxer and the waif, wondering what the hell we were doing together. It was a legitimate question.

I stewed over Torbett's promotion.

"How can you deal with that awful man?" she asked.

"Who? Czerniak?"

She said, "You're not paying attention."

"No, it's just . . . I been there eighteen years. I lost . . . ." I was thinking about Rachel, but I didn't say so. I just kept stewing: I'd been there eighteen years. I'd lost my best friend and my girlfriend. I'd been blackmailed, set up, shot at, stabbed and bitten, and half the time by cops. I didn't have anything to show for it. I said, "I just want my fuckin' promotion."

She said, "You should quit." I must have chuckled, because she said, "What? You think I'm stupid?"

"No, it's just . . ." I knew it was a mistake when the words escaped my lips: "Someone has to pay the rent."

That was all it took. Between the tears, mostly all I heard were the words "I can't." "I *can't* work! You know that! You don't understand!"

I have historically displayed what people describe as a rage problem, which has resulted, over the years, in several bodily injuries to others and, arguably, one or two deaths. My temper or my work as a cop (it's hard to separate the two) also caused the end of my relationship with Rachel. I'd had four years to think about that, whether it was the moodiness or the late-night calls from HQ or a few other unfortunate incidents that drove her away. But I swore to put a lid on my temper and keep it there. I'd be generous and caring, no matter what, to make up for how I screwed up with Rachel. I'd live a life of atonement, at least as far as women were concerned. And the next woman who showed up in my life after Rachel would get the devotion and concern and patience I should have shown Rachel, who deserved it. Jessica got away with a lot.

I allowed myself one angry breath through my nose. "No, baby," I said, low and without integrity. "I understand." I reached for her. She pulled away.

"You don't. I was abused and mistreated—"

"I understand. It's okay. You don't need a job." I still felt my insides bubbling.

"You go do your important work—"

"Jessica, please." I got my arms around her. "You can stay home and . . . write." She talked a lot about her poetry, but I'd never known her to actually work on it. "And, you know, be a . . ." I tried to think of the right word. Housewife? Stay-at-home mom? No wedding ring, no kids. "Kept woman" mostly fit the bill. But that would imply sex. "You could stay home and take care of the house."

At this she broke away and stepped off the curb, into the path of traffic. Two women came out of a bar and witnessed Jessica shouting, "All you want is a maid who puts out!"

I would have settled for a roommate who did her own dishes.

I yelled, "For Christ's sake, Jess, get out of the street!"

"Don't tell me what to do!"

"Miss," one of the women said, "should we call the police?"

Jessica went on. "I don't want to see you or talk to you . . . or . . ." Her imagination failed her. She snorted and walked northward, against traffic. She would at least see the cars coming.

I said, "Where are you gonna sleep?"

"You can come with us," the other woman said.

Jessica said, "Fine!" She joined them, and the three of them passed me, heading south with a dirty look in my direction, me the wife beater. I tossed up my hands and watched, marveling, as Jessica walked down the street between two strangers who had earned her trust more than I had.

Still shaking my head, I looked up to the sky. Between battered clouds a moon shone, waxing at 80 percent. A nearly full moon and most of the police force including me was drunk. It would be an eventful night. Jessica had suddenly dumped me. I'd screwed up on the atonement front.

I found my car, a rebuilt '83 Chevy Caprice I'd had painted a cool blue for a fresh start, one I needed. I drove under the overpass at Fifth Street, then headed up the raised level of Interstate 35 with the windows down and the cool breeze blowing through the disappointment of my career and my personal life as I rode past the dome of the capitol building.

In the early 1990s, the lady governor of Texas conducted a noncommittal first term, marked more than anything by her veto of a concealed-weapons bill. The bill would have allowed you to carry a handgun nearly anywhere in the state. Undaunted, maybe excited, by the prospect of gunfights at Wal-Mart, Texans voted to replace her with another professed ex-drunk like herself. He shook hands, kissed babies, posed in cowboy hats, wrapped himself in the flag; he ran on a platform of more jails, longer sentences, less government, less welfare and more executions. But where the lady governor had been saved from drunkenness, famously, by an anonymous program she mentioned to the press every chance she got, he had been saved by Jesus—through His personal messenger, the founding televangelist Billy Graham—christening, in an unholy manner, the most prominent of open marriages, a sanctioned three-way between Jesus, politics and television.

Riding into town from the Northeast on a horse paid for by his father's rich friends, the new governor boasted an impressive résumé: He struggled in school, barely worked an honest day in his life and never ran a business without running it into the ground. Not long after his 1995 inauguration, Texas, formerly distinguished by its social programs and environmental protections, would lead the nation in toxic releases, cancer risks and percentage of residents without health insurance. Talk about growth, we got growth. Highways were packed, small businesses were driven out by chain stores, and as the punchline, the capital city of Austin expanded its borders in anticipation of the 2000 census, just to make a sudden jump in population and the audacious claim, "Now we're bigger than Boston!"

Austin won favor with prominent national magazines, earning placement on their "Top Ten Places to Live" lists, prompting an influx of the mildly discontented. Like the post-WWII outpouring of pilgrims from the cities to the suburbs, only slower and more polite, people traveled from around the country, from New York and Orlando and St. Louis, to Austin, for the promise of a fresh start, new homes and clean air. Two out of three ain't bad.

I rolled off the highway at Airport Boulevard, thinking about Jessica and the two women from the bar and, if they decided to spend the night together, the disappointment that was in store for all three of them. And I realized that, with Jessica leaving, my life would be losing roughly nothing.

Winding through the confusion of traffic under the half-built Koenig Lane overpass, I turned right, away from my own house, and headed toward the address I had memorized and tried to forget, on lonely nights. A place where I thought I might get a little comfort, or not, thinking what a bad idea it was as I crossed the tracks of the Austin Northwestern Railroad and pulled in front of the house on Hammack Drive and parked. What the hell. I was single. By the time I reached the front door, she'd opened it, significantly filling out a floor-length green silk robe. Her eyes were still the same burning green, her hair still black with unlikely red tips. The years had been kind, but not too kind.

"How'd you find me?" she asked. She knew how. I was a cop. "What do you want?"

I didn't answer right away. Finally I said, "A friend?"

She'd have been within her rights to curse me out. I saw her chew it over. She said, "Same price either way."

It made me sick that the only way I could get sex, or even comfort, was by paying for it. But I nodded. She turned and walked into the house, dropping the silk robe to the carpet behind her, where it trapped a puff of air like a parachute, and she swayed, nude, out of the living room.

3.
ⅲⅲ

I lay on my back on heavy, dark cotton sheets, under a spongy blue blanket of unnatural origin. Everything in the room had come from a superstore. None of it looked like the home of a hooker.

She lay on her side, her head on my chest. My arm curled around her neck and I stroked her hair.

"Is this what you wanted?" she asked.

"It's better," I said. "Do you mind?"

"It's okay." Some time passed. "I can't ask you to spend the night."

"I understand," I said, and threw off the blanket.

"You don't have to go now."

"I should."

"I just . . . I don't want any trouble with the neighbors. I saved for this place for a long time."

"That's cool," I said, pulling my pants on.

"I'm retired now." She eyed the ceiling. "Semi."

"What do you do with your time?"

She took a moment. "What does *that* mean?"

"I'm serious."

"I have friends!"

I nodded. "I don't."

She'd sat up. Light rolled in from the living room. She noticed the path of my eyes and pulled the blanket up over her breasts.

"I'm saving to have them hoisted," she said.

"They're fine." I put my jacket on, left money on the dresser, what I knew from Vice was a typical call-girl rate plus tip. And not so much that I couldn't afford to come back.

As I headed out of the bedroom, she said, "Good night, Tonto." Tonto was a nickname she knew from way back, when I was a young detective under an older detective's wing. Once, I interrogated her. Once, she sold me out. And still I didn't have a place I could go where I could count on a warmer reception. Not even home.

I said, "Good night, Vita."

I drove down Airport Boulevard, past the monolithic cement columns that the Koenig overpass would use to tread through Hyde Park, following the interstate frontage road to Thirty-eighth Street to my house.

ⅢⅢⅢⅢ

I first came to Austin when I was fifteen, leaving my home in Elmira, New York, in the middle of the night when my father woke me with the information that he had fallen out of favor with the Big Boys and that we were leaving the state, *now*. My mother had walked out years earlier, with the promise that she was leaving my father, not me, though I never heard from her again. Her family had disowned her for marrying a Jew—they didn't care that he was a mobster. His family, including an ex-wife and two kids, were having nothing to do with either of us. So Pop and I arrived in Texas as a duo. I had a few laughs as a high school hoodlum, then joined the army, saw the world, came back to Austin for college, married my college sweetheart. I got turned down by the FBI, nixing my ambition to get revenge on the Mafia for destroying my family. Joined the police. My wife left. I fell in love with my best friend's wife, Rachel. He died, we shacked up. She split. Four years later I still rented a house—the house Rachel had lived in with me—catercorner from the one where she'd lived with my best friend. I only thought of her when I saw their house, when I saw our house, when I saw our bed and when I breathed. Like an idiot I'd passed up the chance to marry her. If I'd played my cards right, I could have had a long and happy life with the woman of my dreams. Instead all I had was my job.

It was 1:30 A.M. when I got home, and Jessica greeted me at the door in her flannel jammies, with no acknowledgment that she'd broken up with me barely two hours before. I was too tired to bring it up. She handed me a chalk drawing on a rectangle of construction paper, torn at the edges. The gray chalk smeared my fingers. Jessica bounced on the balls of her feet, saying, "Look what I drew you!"

Jessica had her moments. I tried to put aside that they were always moments of acting like a sweet kid. She didn't have too many moments as an adult.

"What is it?" I asked. What I saw was an oval in seven shades of gray, on a nearly black background. An egg floating in space.

"It's the cosmic egg."

When I first met Jessica a few months earlier, she had been thrown out, she said, by her abusive boyfriend. She moved in with me. We had incredible sex, for two weeks. Then restrained sex occasionally, me trying to hit all the right spots without hitting the thousand or so that would set loose some old trauma. Then that fizzled, too. There wasn't much that occupied her life, though she was often tired. She didn't have a job or money, or any desire to cook, clean or even be independent. Desolation brought us together and kept us that way, a union built on loneliness. I would have thought two lonely people together would be less lonely, but the math didn't work that way. I knew that she'd previously gone by the names Lizzie, Snow, and Jocasta, after the mother of Oedipus. (If I needed help deciding not to have kids with her, that would have clinched it.) I made it a point never to ask or research her real name. I did that once to Rachel, with unfortunate results. As it turns out, people take it personally when you investigate them.

What I'd learned about *Rachel*, years back, was that she'd had trouble with the law in Houston, that she'd killed a guy in self-defense, that she hadn't been arrested for it. I learned also that her Social Security number had a New York State prefix, though she always said she was from Chicago. We never discussed the discrepancy.

Jessica took the drawing. "The cosmic egg rose from the ashes of Eve. It drifted into the stratosphere and when it was ready, hatched the first lesbian."

"Something you wanna tell me?" The phone rang. "It's beautiful, thank you." She reached her arms around my neck and liplocked me, an intimacy we hadn't shared in a while. I thought for sure she'd smell

Vita on me, but she didn't. The machine picked up, *"Please leave a message. . . ."* and beeped.

"Captain Action, it's Jake. Pick up."

I pulled gently from Jessica and reached for the phone. "Yeah."

"Got a hot tip. You're in line for lieutenant."

I asked, "Didn't you get a hot tip before?" It was Jake who'd told me I was in line for promotion. A dedicated desk jockey, Jake had hid out in the squad room for years until the brass discovered his talent for computer and telephone research and moved him into administration where he belonged.

"Girl, eighteen, rents an apartment over a house. Landlord comes home, smells something's up, goes in. She's in the tub, drowned."

"Accident? Drugs?" Jessica was kissing my neck.

"That's what the patrols thought. Empty pill bottles. They called Marks, and he wrote it off without coming to the scene. He didn't want to leave the banquet, and he didn't want his boys leaving either. But the patrol at the scene found semen on her bedspread. He called us, and I'm calling you."

Jessica was working on my fly. She'd decided that I was better than independence and that she had to do something once in a while to keep me from tossing her. But her timing was off. I took her hand.

"Why?" I said to the phone. "I'm not Homicide." They'd transferred me to Family Violence a couple of years earlier, which made as much sense as anything.

"I'll clear it. Ace this and you'll show up Marks for his fuckup. Put you in line for a promotion you richly deserve."

"Jake . . . why are you doing this?"

"You saw those promotions go to those dumb rednecks."

"And Torbett," I said.

"And Torbett. God knows what they want from him. The Family's got most of that locked up."

I'd practically never heard the Family mentioned by name before, and I worried that someone might be listening in to Jake's phone.

"So?" I asked.

He said, *"They have the Family. You have me."*

It was nearly 2:00 A.M., and the shift had changed by the time I stepped into the formaldehyde chill of the morgue, still in my banquet suit, fluorescents shining down on a room of gurneys and file drawers. Three new guests, one named Faith.

The graveyard-shift attendant pulled the sheet away. Faith Copeland, eighteen, white, female. They'd found her in the tub. Thin body, but a face bloated with water, giving her the round look of a girl with baby fat. She read younger than eighteen. Pale blond hair combed back. I ordered the body sent to the medical examiner and drove to Faith's home.

Drowning is a bad way to go. You struggle to hold your breath, and when the need for oxygen gets desperate enough, you suck in desperately and your lungs fill with water. Homicidal drownings are rare: People will struggle to stay alive. Except in the presence of drugs.

A patrol named Scotto waited for me in the back alley behind Avenue B, at the wooden steps leading up to the apartment. He looked tired.

"I tried to punch out at one," he said. "They told me to come back here and wait for you." He led me upstairs and into the apartment, a humble one-room operation with a bathroom. "No prints anywhere, even hers. They wiped every smooth surface, which knocks out the possibility of suicide." I nodded. "Sorry."

"Go ahead," I said. "What do you think?"

"Department of Public Safety didn't find anything on the rug but gravel, and she could have tracked that up herself. The landlord came home a little after nine, parked in the garage, saw the ceiling was dripping. Knock, no answer, goes in, she's dead in the tub, water splashed around the bathroom. He calls, we show up around nine-thirty." The bathroom had an old-fashioned tub against the wall. The killer would have been standing right in front of it, or kneeling, if he held her under. Scotto showed me the empty Valium bottles, one dated last week. Another from another doctor. "Before we checked for prints, we figured she OD'd and slipped into the water. But . . ."

"Yeah?"

"If she'd meant to kill herself, wouldn't she have been wearing something? People don't like to get found naked. And if it was an accident, why was there water all over? I called Homicide about this, and I got transferred to Marks—"

"And he didn't want to leave the banquet, so he said it was an OD."

Scotto nodded. "And then I saw the bedspread."

A male visitor, Scotto said, had left a sample in the middle of the bed. We guessed Faith was on the bed at the time. DPS had taken the bedspread with them.

I scoped the room. No pocket calendar or personal phone book, but the killer could have lifted those. Small refrigerator, yogurt, granola, vegetables. Vegetarianism as an excuse for anorexia. Crystals and trinkets read hippie chick, close to the earth. Rolling closet. Inside: Office dress, cocktail dress, evening gown. Like a set of costumes. Drawers: makeup, lots of it. Pimple creams. Moisturizers. Like any other young woman, only more so.

"I feel bad," Scotto said as I yanked open the warped wooden drawers of her dresser, one by one.

"Why?" Socks, stockings, panties.

"I was a fan," he said.

"Of what?" That's when I saw her photos.

As it turned out, American popular culture went on long after I stopped paying attention to it. Faith Copeland was once the star of her own TV show, which ran briefly in the 1987–88 season. Her star rose and fell in the span of twenty-two episodes. A series of black-and-white glossy eight-by-ten shots showed her face go from cute (age eight) to less cute (eleven) to desperate. At eighteen she was an old kid, way over the hill by Hollywood standards, living in a Hyde Park garret and forgetting to lock the door.

I found a fat wallet, stuffed with cash-machine receipts, pawn tickets, phone numbers and a credit-card bill. A business card from a cabdriver. One phone number read "Mom," with no area code. I figured local. I called information and got the address, then told Scotto to request Faith's phone records. His jaw dropped.

"Tomorrow," I said. "Go home."

I drove west on Forty-fifth Street, past the state school and the national guard, to the area where the river curved north and wound around to Tanglewood Trail where Faith's mother lived, wondering if I should give this poor woman one last decent night's sleep rather than waking her to tell her that her daughter was dead, the tragedy of what happens to your children when they're out of your care, when I pulled in front of the house and saw the living room light on. I stood at the front window. A flag waved on the TV screen, and Mrs. Lucille Cope-land lay sprawled on the sofa, a tumbler clutched in her hand. She wore a floral kimono. Peroxide-yellow hair burst from her head in curls. She was something once. I rang the bell twice before she got up, staggered to the door and opened it.

"Yes," she said, eyes half shut, absently puffing her curls out with her splayed fingers.

"Mrs. Copeland. I'm Dan Reles."

"Yes?"

"This is about your daughter, Faith."

"Oh," she said. Then she smiled bright. "Are you an agent?"

4.
||||

Sergeant Jeff Czerniak planted his wife at home after the banquet, changed out of his suit and left the house again without even bothering to apologize. He couldn't stay in at night anymore. Once he got the itch to go out, there was no fighting it. He thought for sure the banquet would be enough excitement for one night. His feet told him otherwise.

He drove down I-35 and into East Austin and turned in and out of the blocks around the club, then parked two blocks up Poquito and walked back. He was wearing his deliveryman jacket and matching pants. He figured that, if spotted, he'd look like a working stiff on the prowl, and not like an off-duty cop trying to make rank. The truth was somewhere in between.

These night crawls had become Czerniak's regular pattern. It wasn't that he was such a great cop or so dedicated. The chase gave him a rush. So on a free night, between staying home with his wife, going out with his buddies, and the chase, he always went for the chase. Like it was up to him.

He'd made some easy collars: a john in the act of making a deal with a whore, possession of a few joints. These weren't even worth the booking and the paperwork, hours of anticlimax on a night off. He'd get their license information and use them for stoolies if he could. But he'd caught a few bigger ones. Back when he was on Criminal Investigations, he witnessed a drug deal, a transaction in the street where he was parked. He radioed for backup. Chase the seller or chase the buyer? Can't get both, and there's no law against walking around with money. But a dealer is worth more. He climbed from the car, raising his badge and gun and shouting "Police!" then chased the dealer a block, finally tackling him. Czerniak's bulk threatened to crack the dealer's ribs and made him more willing to submit to handcuffs. The arrest made Narco look dumb, but Pete Marks noticed and mentored Czerniak onto Homicide.

Now Czerniak was on Organized Crime. His prowling could get him promoted. If it went right.

He'd put on weight as a cop, over a naturally big trunk that he'd built up in his football days. His ruddy complexion made him look drunk most of the time, though he was actually pretty drunk now.

He didn't see the surveillance van anywhere in the area. It should have been there. A months-long investigation wasn't taking a night off just for a banquet. Tonight especially, while most of the department was celebrating, while only the lowest of the patrols were out on the street. It was like turning off the lights and letting the roaches have run of the kitchen. Someone should be there.

The one-story brick building housed the club, a gun store and a liquor store. A neon martini glass, fifties style, hung in the club window and lit up the cars in the front lot. Neon spelled out the name of the bar in glowing green script: *Sueño*. Dream. The operation was code-named Mal Sueño, Bad Dream. Boyle, the club owner, was suspected of running drugs and whores out of his club. A bust under the RICO Act required a long investigation and a warehouse of evidence. Czerniak breezed by the liquor store and gun store and glanced into the bar window deep enough to see he'd be the only white man in the club if he went in. He kept walking.

He sauntered past a cheap furniture store and turned, walked around the back of the darkened store and scoped the side of the bar. His heart pounded.

Think hard, Czerniak. Get yourself sighted and blow a big, long case. Lieutenant Clay will bust you down to patrol. Go home now. You're drunk. This ain't the time to make points.

But his feet wouldn't listen. And where was the van? Should he call Clay now? Risk pissing him off after the banquet?

He noticed a Dumpster behind the club. No cars in back. A back
door. The bartender would come out to dump bottles now and again.
People would come out the back way to smoke a joint. He crossed the
alley and stood behind the club.

No windows. Music, laughter. Heart pounding, Go home, Czerniak. You got no audiotape, no video. The back door, a fire exit with
no alarm, not quite latched. Czerniak listened, then pulled the door
open.

No one was there to notice as he peeked in. He stood at the end of
a dark brown hallway; at the other end, he could see the neons from
the front of the club. Jukebox music, R&B and laughter. Like any bar,
the unreal lighting that set up a different universe. All rules of normal
life are suspended. Back here another door, maybe the crapper. And a
staircase leading down. He headed down the steps.

Stupid, stupid, what are you doing? he thought as he dropped
down the steps as softly as his two hundred–plus pounds would let
him. No cameras, no microphones. If they find you, you blow everything. And still he couldn't turn around, drawn by a pulse in his heart
and another in his feet, his stupid fucking feet. A faint light at the bot-
tom of the stairs, another hallway. At the end a single bulb, maybe
forty watts. And to the right of that, a single door, a kitchen-type
swinging door with a round window at eye level. Czerniak could hear
chatter down the hall and more music, something in that room.

As his heart pulsed, Czerniak felt something else, not the excitement of nearly catching a crime in progress, not the fear of fucking up
a big case, of getting found out as a cop, maybe killed. It was the same
jolt he felt the first time he went into a porn parlor at fifteen to look at
girly mags. The ammonia smell of the floors, the perverts in raincoats
and the endless supply of squack, the mother lode of miles and miles
of naked women. Czerniak was a divining rod for it. He could find
anything that had shadows around it: He could sniff out porn hidden

in a church library or a crap game in a small town miles from the interstate. He could find drug dealers in an underground club in a strange city in his first hour. He just couldn't stay away from them. The arrests were just an excuse.

He contemplated this, the refusal of his feet to listen to his brain saying, Get out, get out now! as he stepped to the end of the hall, stood back from the window and adjusted his stance to peek through the dirty glass without being seen, he hoped.

Eureka.

Czerniak swallowed hard. Two white chicks in G-strings tongue-kissed each other, standing between two men, one clamped to the back of each of them. A heavy white man, Boyle, the club owner, sat laughing in a chair. He held a mirror for a third stripper, a small-chested brunette with freckles. If she wasn't underage, she would do till underage came along. She snorted two lines, wiped her nose, hawked it back and swallowed. Then she unzipped Boyle's pants.

Czerniak's heart pumped. His throat buzzed down to his crotch.

While the freckled girl was bent at the waist, a man in a black suit pulled her G-string down and mounted her from behind. Czerniak clapped a hand to his mouth. His knees wobbled. The man leaned forward over the girl, slobbering on her, with his slicked-back hair and drooping mustache, and the man turned toward him, the cock-eyed smile freezing on his face as he caught Czerniak's eyes in the round window and Czerniak realized that he was looking into the face of his commanding officer, Lieutenant Harland Clay.

WEDNESDAY

I woke before the alarm, stiff in the back and shoulders, with a hangover headache like a brain cramp. Jessica breathed soft and regular rhythms, a gentle riff in her throat like a kid with a cold. Her breasts rose and fell, as off-limits to me as they were to any guy on the street. At least I could look.

We'd met one lonely Saturday night in the Continental Club, a retro joint on South Congress. A band I'd come to see played straight rock and roll with an Elvis impersonator fronting. I stood by the side wall sucking a beer, feeling embarrassed to be in a club by myself. I'd taken to wearing a suit jacket and slacks in moderate weather, and I got used to musicians asking if I was a talent scout ("We played at South by Southwest"). I'd kept working out, maintaining more muscle than fat. In spite of my scars, I started getting more attention from women instead of less. I figured it was the suit jacket. It suggested I might have money, or at least a job.

Jessica was sitting at a martini-size round marble table, alone, wearing a red vintage cocktail dress and torn stockings, thin legs crossed, party shoes sitting on the floor by her narrow feet. She'd pinned up her hair under a clump of a black hat with part of a veil attached to it. She had some kind of fishnet glove arrangement on her hands that let her tiny fingers poke through. With these she smoked French cigarettes and gently, theatrically, tipped a Manhattan to her lips. She saw me looking. I smiled because she was so pretty and turned away because she was so young, a kid dressed up in a cluster of affectations, on her way to finding her own personality. But when I looked back at the end of the song, she was still alone and still looking at me.

She had, I learned for the price of a drink, had a fight with her boyfriend. She had not quite graduated from UT. She had delicate hands and big, mournful eyes. She had condoms in her purse.

I learned soon that her skin was soft as a baby's, distinguished from that by a total lack of fat and a stink of French tobacco and ginseng. She was so thin that I could practically put my hands around her waist. At special moments she would clamp her legs around me and we could make love standing up, against a wall, rolling on the rug, in the kitchen, in every geometric possibility. And by the time the possibilities were exhausted, our sex life was pretty much finished and she had moved in.

In spite of the fishnet stockings and cocktail dresses and pillbox hats—an upbeat fifty-year-old wardrobe—she cried often, sulked always and needed consoling. After a few weeks, I suggested she see a psychiatrist and she screamed, so I grumbled and dropped it and never brought it up again. I was lonely and making up for my carelessness with Rachel, and Jessica seemed to need a friend.

I got up without waking Jess and made coffee. The night before, Faith Copeland's mother, Lucille, took the news of Faith's death with drunken equanimity, a bump in the road. A former beauty herself, she looked like she was waiting for vaudeville to come back. I took a guess Faith had paid for the house, before moving into her garage apartment. The father, Russell Copeland, not a fan of show biz, left years earlier and got religion. Lucille gave me his address, but by then it was past 2:00 A.M. and I didn't have it in me to deliver the same message again.

So after morning coffee, with Jessica still asleep, I headed out to Mr. Copeland's house, hoping to catch him before work.

The house was a brick ranch number, low-roofed and spreading out in a few directions ("Let's add a playroom. Let's add a den!"). The yard exploded with bluebonnets, the official flower of Texas and a favorite subject for spring festivals around the state. A woman of about forty answered the door in a housedress and called him. He showed himself in dress shirt and slacks, looking frightened the way folks do when someone tells them there's a cop at the door. I dropped the news. His eyes flooded with tears, not so much like shock but as if he knew that this news would come one day. Then he settled into a sob, then he cried out.

I waited while the second Mrs. Copeland consoled him on the couch. I offered to send a counselor, but they refused. She asked the questions. When? Why? How? I gave the answers I had. Copeland didn't stop crying for an hour. He choked on his sobs, sucked air when he could, finally gave in when his wife poured him a brandy and put him to bed. I looked around the front room. Low ceiling, cheap but respectable furniture, nothing extra. Framed "paintings" of barns and deer. The second Mrs. Copeland came back into the living room.

I said, "Can you tell me anything about Faith? Did she have a job? Friends? A boyfriend?"

"They hadn't spoken in months. Faith and Russell."

"Do you know why?" I asked.

She shrugged. "Money?"

I made it back to the medical examiner's office in time for the autopsy. I stood back as Margaret Hay, ME, limped around the cutting table that displayed the body of Faith Copeland. At Hay's direction a new assistant lifted and twisted Faith while Hay looked her over for bruises or cuts. Hay had done the lifting and twisting herself back when she was a kid of sixty. The years and an injury to her hip had slowed her down a little, but at six feet tall with a leathery complexion, she still looked like a tough old cowgirl.

Hay dropped the hand and had Kato spread the girl's legs.

"Hand me a swab," Hay said as I scanned the jarred organ samples on a high shelf. "Reles?"

"Huh?"

"Hand me a swab." She pointed to the sink and a jar of cotton swabs on long wooden sticks. I handed her one and turned away. Chivalry.

"They found her in the bathtub," I said. I didn't know the exact effect hot water would have on destroying evidence. "Can you get a real sample?"

"Should be. Her fluids can interfere with the typing tests," Hay said. "You'd be better off if you can get something off her clothing."

"Working on it." We had the bedspread.

Hay turned to the assistant. "Scalpel."

After the cutting and the drawing of fluids, the assistant wheeled Faith out and Hay peeled off her gloves and limped to the sink to wash her hands. When she turned the water off, I said, "You know anything about antidepressants?"

She looked at me with suspicion.

I said, "My girlfriend. I think she's my girlfriend. We keep breaking up, but she keeps not leaving."

"Am I your family doctor?"

"Just a question."

"All my patients are dead."

"I'll risk it."

She yanked down a few paper towels and rubbed her hands.
"Symptoms?"

"She doesn't do anything. She sits around all the time."

Hay said, "She needs a job."

"When I say that, she screams."

Hay nodded and offered a second diagnosis that sounded more
final. "She needs a zookeeper."

I walked around the front of the building complex to HQ, headed
through the bustling reception area toward the elevators when I heard
someone hiss my name. "Reles!"

Sergeant Jeff Czerniak was standing beyond the elevator bank,
motioning me toward him like he needed to sell me a watch. I followed him down to the alcove by the auditorium entrance.

Czerniak was a chunk of years younger and less experienced than
me and had landed a plum spot on Organized Crime, my dream gig
short of getting onto the FBI, while I got shuffled off Homicide onto
Family Violence.

He looked flushed and scared. "Can you keep a secret?" he asked.
This is cop lingo for either "I'm stupid" or "I'm pretending to be stupid," and Czerniak wasn't smart enough to pretend.

"Go ahead," I said.

He looked around and leaned close. "I saw something." He waited
for my reaction.

I said, "Yeah, that's great. I'm pressed for time. . . ."

"No, no, listen. You know how we do things on my unit. We target a guy, we're on him for months. I saw someone with him."

"Who?"

Czerniak took five or six steps without moving from his spot. His hands reached for his hair, thought better of it, looked for another place to go and didn't find one.

"Who?"

"Look," he said, scanning the hall. "It's none of my business. Guy parties, what do I care?"

"Czerniak . . ."

"But the subject of the investigation . . ."

I said, "I gotta go."

He whispered something I didn't get.

I stopped. "What?"

Czerniak checked the halls again. "My CO."

Czerniak bowed his head to the floor but raised his eyes to me, embarrassed himself at the shame of what he'd confessed, even though it wasn't his shame. I knew Czerniak's CO, Harland Clay. And I didn't like him. "What are you telling me?"

He seemed to have trouble breathing. Each word, he knew, might be drilling him deeper into hell. "Consorting with the . . . target . . . of an investigation."

Some younger detective walked by us, and Czerniak looked up, caught red-handed. If he'd kept his eyes on me, the guy wouldn't have noticed. Czerniak pulled open the door of the auditorium, peeked in and waved at me to follow him.

In the empty auditorium, I said, "Any chance he was working?"

He shook his head. "Hookers. Cocaine. *Sex.*" He squeezed his eyes shut and slapped his forehead. Then he spat out, "He saw me, I saw him. Consorting."

You're screwed, I thought. I wasn't sorry to know something

on Clay, only that I couldn't use it. I couldn't stab Czerniak in the back.

I asked, "Has he mentioned it?"

"Not yet."

I rolled it over. Finally I said, "Two choices. Tell Torbett in Internal Affairs. He'll start an investigation."

He said, "And everyone knows I'm a backstabber."

"Or," I said, "keep your mouth shut and protect the dirty fucker who put you in this spot."

His mouth twisted up as he considered two crappy options, hell and purgatory. Then he asked, "You won't tell anyone, will you, Reles?"

Two choices. Tell IA and break the police code of silence and maybe get myself killed. Or keep my mouth shut and protect a dirty cop sabotaging the core work of the department. Thanks for dragging me in, Czerniak.

"No," I said. "I won't tell anybody."

"Thanks."

"But you've gotta do something about this. If you don't, what the hell are we all here for?"

He thought about that. "What's gonna happen?" he asked.

"I don't know. But if you stand up to that fuck, I'll back you up."

He looked downward, shaking his head. What was I gonna do for him, or for any cop? How far would one cop stick his neck out for another? And what would it cost him?

I'd already stuck my neck out too far for Czerniak. I just didn't know it yet.

6.
ⅢⅢ

Suzanne cut open the wax-sealed letter with an antique letter opener her father had left her. So few people appreciated the art of letter writing.

The letter was from Edith in the governor's office and had been delivered by messenger. It read:

Dear Suzanne,

I hope this finds you well. The governor sends his best. This is an exciting time for all of us!

As you know, next week the Senate will be taking up Public Utility Reform. There's a lot riding on it, and the governor is concerned that Lieutenant Governor Muller might be, let's say, "exaggerating" his power as president of the Senate. We can't get anything through, it seems. The governor has tried speaking with him, but it's no use. The LG doesn't come from the same world.

When I asked the governor if I could get him anything (I meant lunch), the governor joked, "Something to neutralize Win Muller." It was a good joke, and we all laughed.

I said if anyone knew how to neutralize Win Muller, Suzanne Wade would. The governor smiled, you know, with one side of his mouth, and said, "Suzanne Wade can do anything." Those were his exact words.

Of course we were all joking. Not the part about Suzanne Wade can do anything, but the rest. We would never do anything like that. Still, you know that the governor appreciates your support.

Please make sure this message doesn't get into the wrong

hands. People like to take things out of context. The messenger will wait for your response.

Best,
Edie

Suzanne wrote back:

Dear Edie,

I don't know when I've laughed harder. And you can tell the governor I said so.

Of course we'd never do anything like that. Win isn't exactly a friend, but I'm sure I know someone who can talk to him.

By the by, I'm speaking at a ladies' church group in Amarillo on the nineteenth. They expect over three hundred people, all from the best families, if you know what I mean. I'm sure they'd double that number if I was introducing the governor, instead of just talking myself. It might be good exposure for the governor and help him build support among like-minded people.

If the nineteenth doesn't work, I'm speaking at Park Methodist right in Round Rock tonight at eight. I know it's late notice. But what a surprise guest he'd make!

Suzanne

Suzanne used her private stationery and her own sealing wax, feeling certain she and Edie were among the last real ladies in the world. The response came within the hour:

Suzanne,

Tonight at eight will be just fine. The office will be in touch about security.

The governor considers you a true friend.

Edie

7.
||||

The elevator doors opened onto the carpet of the Fifth Floor, APD Administration. The receptionist buzzed Jake Lund, who gave his permission, and she opened a pine door and led me through (on all other floors, the doors were steel) into the computer lab that seemed to function as Jake's outer office. He greeted me with a big open grin, a kid showing off his new toys. He was wearing a white shirt, black tie and black slacks. His wiry black hair had turned a steel-wool gray on the occasion of his fortieth birthday. Three young civilians, two males and a female, worked on the six computers in the room under Jake's supervision, carrying out tasks that I'd never understand. Not surprisingly, the room had no windows. Never a fan of real life, Jake had found a home.

He led me into his private office, also windowless except for the screens of a desktop computer, a laptop and a TV. An assortment of candies and video-game implements decorated the desk. And there was a couch on which, I guessed, the department would have no complaints about Jake spending the occasional night.

"What do you think?" he asked.

"From here you rule the universe."

"No. Her."

I thumbed at the computer lab. "The girl?" He nodded, all pride and sugared exuberance.

I looked out his office door. The female tech, small and chunky, in her thirties, wore baggy jeans and a Hawaiian shirt. She seemed more like someone's bowling buddy than someone's girlfriend. "Is it serious?" I asked.

He pulled the door shut. "Six months," he said.

Jake had found the perfect woman: a programmer. I said I approved.

"Thanks. Hey, good news. You're official."

"I'm promoted?!"

"No, you're back on Homicide."

I blinked. "I'm . . . You said you were gonna fix it!"

"I fixed it." He laid into a bag of Skittles. "You're still on Faith Copeland, by order of my good buddy Assistant Chief Oliphant, who owed me a favor, and now you're on Homicide, so it makes sense."

"And I'm under Marks, who hates me. Plus I'm making him look stupid for fucking up and signing off the case over the phone."

He grinned, chewing the candy. "Last time I do you a favor."

I found the Homicide squad room empty so I walked down the hall and saw the briefing room door open. Inside, Lieutenant Pete Marks sat at the head of the table, looking administrative, while a detective next to him, a guy I recognized as Gus Highfill, read announcements about unreasonable force, orating in a thick Texas twang.

"Physical force is to be used only to the *ex*tent necessary to sub*due* a suspect and protect the safety of the public. Our research shows that physical force has been used at the same frequency regardless of the race of arrest suspects. In cases where un*due* force is reported—"

The men chanted the universal defense in unison: "I *feared* for my life," and everyone laughed.

I walked in as if I'd never left the squad, and took an empty chair. Marks squinted at me by way of greeting. I was surprised he didn't just growl. The cracks in Marks's angular face put me in mind of Mount Rushmore, but there was a look in his eyes like he'd stared at one too many cross burnings. Four other detectives surrounded the table, most younger than me by half a decade or more. Luis Fuentes from Narcotics, with medium build and military bearing, regarded me with apprehension. We'd had dealings before, and while he wasn't exactly honest, I had nothing against him. But he didn't know that. I nodded to him and the others as they looked me over, and the announcements went on. The reader, Highfill, was a Corpus Christi native with sagging jowls like a hound dog. Next to him was a tall, skinny Aryan with a square jaw and a built-in swagger I could see even while he was sitting. The last was a dark-haired little fat guy with a mustache, a plaid shirt with snaps and, I'd soon learn, an ingratiating tone that would get him nowhere with Marks. If I hadn't seen these last two guys around the building before, I'd seen a hundred like them.

Marks said, "Any questions?" There was one—who's the Jew?—but no one asked it. Maybe they knew I'd been on the squad before for almost a decade. But that was before their time. Marks said, "Dismissed," and in the same breath, "Fuentes. You stay." Fuentes looked between us and sat up in his chair for better perspective. The others cleared out, leaving Fuentes and me opposite each other at the table, Marks still at the head. Marks said, "I'm giving the Copeland case to Fuentes."

"No you're not," I said. Marks's normally concrete features shifted. Fuentes nearly choked.

I added, ". . . Sir. I'm on this case by order of Assistant Chief Oliphant. Chief Cronin can supersede that order. You can't."

Marks was trying to figure out what, exactly, to do now that he'd been defied in front of a witness. I was trying to figure out if I could have made an enemy out of Marks faster than I had, when the door

swung open and a woman strode in. She moved fast but like a tug-
boat: with enough force to topple anyone who bumped into her. Mid-
thirties, about five-six and toned, in a man's corduroy blazer and
black pants, thick black hair rising up and back from Aztec cheekbones and dark skin. She said, "Sorry I'm late. Where the fuck is
everybody? I was chasing this girl's mother but she's dead and the
father's MIA. Who's this?" She was looking at me but talking to
Marks.

Fuentes said, "Cate Mora. Dan Reles."

She nodded. "Close your mouth, Reles."

In the squad room, now expanded and redesigned with room divid-
ers, no couch, but still a coffeemaker and a color TV with cable and
VCR, I found an empty desk. "Anyone using this?" Highfill (with the
hangdog look and the Corpus Christi twang) and the two others in
the room, who I learned were called LaMorte (short, toadying) and
Halvorsen (tall, smug), looked at each other and mumbled in the
negative. I sat down to make calls, sifting through the papers from
Faith's wallet. I put seven or eight ATM slips in order with the not-
surprising conclusion that her bank balance tallied at under zero. Two
pawn tickets for some jewelry I could check out. A few phone numbers on a folded piece of lined yellow paper. The business card of a
cabdriver yielded ten rings and no answer. One number was scratched
under the word "talent." Fuentes came over and shook my hand just
as I finished dialing.

"*Third Coast Talent.*"

"My name's Dan Reles—"

"*My, what a voice!*" she said. "*Do you do voice-overs?*"

I was pretty sure I didn't.

"*We're the largest representative of voice-over talent in the central*

Texas area. Did you know that over three hundred feature films are shot in Texas each year?"

"Three hundred. Wow."

"The Texas Film Commission sends us weekly rundowns on all the shoots in the state, and we plug in our talent pool. Why don't you come in and meet with one of our representatives?"

I took a shot. "I heard that Faith Copeland was with you guys."

"Yes!" she enthused. *"Faith is one of our prize talents."*

"Gee, I'd really like to have the same agent she has."

"Very shrewd," the woman said. *"I'll set you up with Bruce this afternoon. Say, he's got a slot open in half an hour, if you can come right over."*

I walked into the glass-walled offices of Third Coast Talent on Fifth Street near Lamar Boulevard, several blocks west of the center of commerce and partying, and introduced myself to the woman who had answered the phone, an ex-model of fifty or so in a checked dress I got dizzy looking at. She gave me an unlikely smile. "My, how tall!" She was a pro. Commenting on my height saved her from saying I looked like a mob enforcer with bad sleeping habits. She shuffled me into Bruce's office.

Bruce sat in an oversize vinyl easy chair. His hair was graying and curly, and he wore a button-down blue shirt that was fraying at the collar.

"So, Dan," he said, "what kind of work have you done?"

I admitted that I was just starting out.

"We have lots of new people," he said. "I just booked a guy your age for a commercial. Do you have headshots?" No. He handed me a card. "This is our guy. We send all our people to him. Great work, and very reasonable prices."

I let him wind around another five minutes before he came to the agreement.

"You can register with us for three hundred dollars. That's a one-time-only fee. . . ."

All I needed. I said, "Faith Copeland."

"Yes." He smiled. "I represent Faith. Wonderful actress."

"How long has she been with you?"

"Six months."

"Have you gotten her anything?"

He licked his lower lip. "Faith's sort of tough right now. She's outgrown the little-girl thing, but she's gonna grow into her womanhood—"

"No she's not. Faith Copeland was murdered in her home last night. I wonder what you can tell me about her besides she had three hundred dollars."

In a few minutes, we were watching Faith's audition tape on a small portable TV. She was standing in the eye of a video camera in a denim skirt and floral blouse, choking her heart out.

"To live hopelessly, to wait and wait for something to happen—that's not for me. . . ."

"She washed out in Hollywood," he said, "when she was nine. I guess her mother spent the money trying to get her career back."

"Why'd she come here?"

"Austin was home. She hadn't been here since she was little, though, so she didn't know anyone." He sighed. "It's bad for kids. An adult going into acting at least had a life before. Kids don't even remember anything before the cameras. So when they're not cute anymore, everything is a letdown."

"Did she get any jobs here at all?"

He said, "There's work here, but . . ."

"What?"

He teetered his head side to side, yes and no. "Most of the good roles get cast in L.A. We cast extras. Twelve-hour days, maybe five bucks an hour. Once in a while, someone gets a line. That's important. It qualifies them to join the union. And maybe they can put a reel together."

He gave me her stuff, old photos I'd have to sort through, videos of her early career.

I asked, "Do you know anybody else who knew her? Friends or boyfriends?"

"No," he said, "just her mother."

"Did you fuck her?"

That caught him off guard. He made a noise that sounded like "Up . . . up . . ." then finally, "No!"

"You sure?"

"No, I never . . . No!"

"You got her for three bills."

"That's what we do. We provide a service! Jesus!"

I thought he was telling the truth. She wasn't that much of a hot number. Just a normal-looking girl. Her life would have been normal, too, if she hadn't been America's sweetheart for a year. But she had. Which opened up the potential field of stalkers to anyone who'd watched her TV show. I had a lot of calls to make.

And a new squad that didn't like me. But hey, I thought. What's the worst they could do?

8.
ⅢⅢ

Sometime after eight in the evening, Paul Wade found himself again in the front pew as he did at least one night a week at Suzanne's insistence, in someone else's church for some kind of "meeting." Suzanne would be expounding on her own special blend of politics and spirituality, while Paul perched on the cheap padding and shifted slowly against the twisting pain in his upper back. Too much shifting would earn a reprimand from Suzanne. He had to weigh one form of pain against another.

On Sundays they normally attended her church, Suzanne's church. Suzanne's munificent donations had replaced the stained glass, refinished the pews and kept the place warm in winter, against the natural force of heat rising to the reaches of the peaked ceiling. Suzanne's money defied physics.

What was more, it defied God. More than once Suzanne's donations to the church had curbed the content of the sermons. When the minister's discussion of Mary Magdalene veered close to an approval of prostitution, Suzanne raised hell with the board, threatened and bullied, and finally word was sent to the minister. Later, when the same minister refused to preach a sermon on the subject of abortion— not so much because of the subject matter but because it had been dictated by Suzanne herself—she made four phone calls and he was unceremoniously fired. His replacement, a kindly white-haired gentleman who put Paul in mind of Jimmy Stewart, was tamed from the beginning. Suzanne planted Paul on the church council: he was sitting with the council one day when the new good reverend commented, "The church's resources come from God. But"—he nodded in Paul's direction—"Mrs. Wade signs his checks."

Parked left of the pulpit, next to the governor, Suzanne faced the suburban crowd with a balance of warmth and superiority. She dyed her hair a respectable monochromatic dark brown, almost black, sprayed in layers to increase volume, a big dark puff of hair. She kept her makeup basic; she was naturally pretty, and a more ambitious cosmetic regimen would make her beautiful, even at forty-nine. Green eyes, slightly small and doll-like; a broad, expansive smile. But beauty wasn't what she was after. Shapely, if a few pounds north of ideal, Suzanne wanted to look married. That he was part of that illusion was Paul's great misfortune.

The introduction went on, a local woman talking about Suzanne's role as housewife and mother (two kids in college, raised by nannies; marriage devoid of sex, love or even polite respect), a devout Christian (she thought homeless people should be jailed), and a tireless servant to the party. (This last one was the clincher. Suzanne had won the co-chairmanship by slinging a cross at her opponent: The other woman was also a devout Christian, but not nearly as vocally pro-life as Suzanne. Sue painted her as an abortion-loving slut.) Finally the intro finished with, "Mrs. Suzanne Addison Wade!"

Paul arched his back and applauded with the hundred of others, a rehearsed hopeful look in his eyes. He had his own introduction in mind:

Suzanne Addison made her social debut at seventeen, the daughter and granddaughter of Texas developers. At twenty-one she married Paul Wade, a naïve young business associate of her father's, with a degree in engineering and one in business, with his own small oil company and a mistaken notion of the conjugal pleasures marriage held in store. Through the years, Paul grew his small company, finally joining it with a larger company controlled by the future governor, himself the son of a powerful oil family. Through colossal mismanagement the prosperous larger company went belly-up. The future governor and his cronies somehow walked away with millions, while Paul lost everything.

The stress of losing a business he'd spent his life building, along with all his personal assets, kicked in the recessive gene for hair loss. His once-thick shock of auburn hair dissipated to a small, degrading wisp, losing him his personal dignity and over an inch of height. His midsection thickened. More generous women told him he looked like a cuddly teddy bear. That he had been known as a CEO, specifically one who'd gone broke, made employment impossible for Paul to find, save for a little consulting. He would gladly have worked on a fishing boat, but Suzanne had an image to maintain. They lived in her mansion, on her money, and traveled in her circles, Paul taking much "good-natured ribbing" at the cocktail parties of the oil rich, who enjoyed his newly lowered status and never interrupted it with offers of work. He had a job, after all: he was Suzanne's lapdog.

There'd been good years, when he had his own money. They'd had sex, enjoyably if not often, and even warmth and affection, though his memory couldn't conjure the details. There were two lovely children, before the sex fell away to almost nothing. Then a late pregnancy, difficult, and she went to stay with family, prohibiting Paul from visiting. She'd come back drained—a miscarriage. They were devastated. He waited and waited and after months made stumbling attempts at affection. Finally she told him there would be no more sex. She was done with it. But she didn't want a divorce.

They argued long into the night. He said, "If I'm not getting it at home, don't you think I'll look for it someplace else?"

"I don't care where you go," she said, her voice bearing an unfamiliar edge, "but you're not getting it here."

The baby was born dead, she'd said. But Suzanne was born again.

His attempts at philandering were few and painful. Everyone he met seemed to know who he was. And he couldn't shake the notion that Suzanne was having him watched.

Meanwhile their sexless life had given Suzanne purpose. She had a whole agenda to go with it: antiabortion, anti–birth control, antisodomy—a general antisex platform. Abortion fell at the center of it, the linchpin. For years Suzanne had been saying, "Jesus, Jesus, Jesus," and gotten nowhere. Now she just had to say "abortion" and she was a hero. What Jesus had to say about abortion escaped Paul Wade.

At the same time, Suzanne's cherishing of human life seemed to have a short shelf life: She never opposed cuts to welfare or social services or public-school budgets. Her concern for the children of the poor lasted only the nine months preceding their birth, whereupon they suddenly lost value.

And Suzanne rose in the world of Texas politics, all without taking on the stink of feminism. She toured churches talking politics and visited political rallies talking religion. And here she was again, in a church, double-dipping.

"Abortion," she said, trembling, "punishes the child for the sin of the parents."

It was all getting crazier, a little at a time. Once she thought abortion was wrong. Now the unborn babies were going to purgatory—sixty-four undifferentiated cells in a cosmic waiting room. Soon she'd send them to hell.

She started in on the governor. "A devout Christian, a loyal family man, committed to the values . . ." As she went on, waxing poetic in his favor, one corner of the governor's mouth rose in a smug half smile. He didn't know Suzanne very well.

Growing up in the Addison family, Suzanne knew what influence was worth. The Addisons, unlike the Wades, were part of a class of kingmakers. And they wouldn't let their kings forget that.

She weaved around to, "But somewhere, he has taken a wrong turn," and then something about us becoming "a secular society ruled by the rise and fall of the stock market rather than the will of God."

And there she went. Every time she opened her mouth, the content took another step. Once the conservatives were balanced by the liberals. Now the conservatives hung on one side, with Suzanne and the religious right on the other. ". . . programs to support the destruction of the family . . ." The congregation had to go along with her. Could they oppose her? Could they stand up for abortion, for welfare, for condoms, for free sex (or any kind of sex) once she got rolling? Paul had seen, in other churches, a few dissenting faces looking around the crowd for backup, horrified at the crowd's stunning transformation, solemn to fanatic. But there was no fighting the tide, not once she got them going. It was Paul's destiny to sit and watch, until the end of time.

And what could the witless governor do, his tiny eyes shifting at the roaring crowd as she handed over the spotlight, but buckle under.

9.
||||

By nightfall I'd called all Faith's phone numbers and met with her few friends. Who was she? Where did she go? What did she do? Who did she sleep with? Do drugs with? Argue about money with? Who could have wanted her dead?

I'd learned from a second visit to her mother and a tour through her scrapbook that Faith Copeland had entered show biz "at the tender age of nine months" in a baby pageant she slept through. By age four she was doing the beauty-pageant circuit in the South and was twice crowned Little Miss Central Texas. By six she was in Hollywood doing TV commercials. Lucille Copeland showed me a snapshot of a TV spot featuring Faith opposite a singing tube of toothpaste. She's in profile, laughing at the tube's antics. Her nearly blond hair is pulled back in a high ponytail. She is a cute kid.

By eight she had her own TV series, playing a precocious little girl named, of all things, Faith. By ten she was out of work, a past-her-prime former cutie.

Her next career wasn't finance. By the time she died, she'd maxed out her credit cards on food, clothes, makeup and photographs. A pawnbroker on Airport Boulevard told me she'd hocked eight thousand dollars' worth of beauty-pageant crowns and trophies for about five hundred dollars, either in the hope that she'd score some big role and buy it all back or because she didn't know how to go about selling the stuff outright.

Her landlord, an older man living in the comfortable wooden house under her Hyde Park apartment, sat with his wife at their kitchen table as I questioned them.

"How long had she been living here?"

"Six months?"

"Do you have a lease?"

He showed me a half page, typed. She paid three twenty-five a month for a one-room garage apartment with private entrance and bath. Her signature was the only place her name appeared on the form.

"Did she fill out an application?" They looked at each other, shook their heads. "Do you have any paperwork on her at all? References? Anything?"

Mrs. Landlord said, "She was a nice girl. She paid on time."

I asked him twice how he'd found her body, to see if the story matched what he'd told the patrols. The ceiling was leaking in the garage when he and the missus got home from bingo on Tuesday night around nine. He knocked, no answer, door unlocked, she's dead in the tub, and naked. His face whitened as he told the story.

The bingo game checked out.

I checked Faith for arrests and found one: In a moment of financial desperation, she'd attempted to rob a house. When she heard the owners come in, she hid in a closet, where the police found her half an hour later, her fame lowering the charges from burglary to breaking and entering, and getting her a year's probation and fees. She was no more stupid than any other actress her age.

I went back to HQ to get my stuff from my old office—a box of paperwork, a stapler, notes on some old unsolved files—and bring it to Homicide. It was after 8:00 P.M., and there was no one in the homicide squad room but Cate Mora, sitting at the desk closest to mine. The desk I'd been working at was empty so I dumped my stuff into the drawers while she flipped through some papers and talked on the phone. She'd hung up her corduroy blazer on a hook and was leaning back in the chair. She was wearing a shoulder holster, slung with a hefty automatic, a nine-millimeter with a plastic grip, maybe a Springfield, the kind of gun that might inspire comments about its being too much gun for a lady. But who would be stupid enough to make a wisecrack to someone packing a nine-millimeter automatic? She had on a gray stretch shirt with no collar, tucked into her black pants, which pinched tight at the waist, badge on her belt, and black shoes with thick rubber soles good for running and kicking. The shirt gave away an athlete's build, slim but powerful. I was pretty sure she could throw a punch. She was doing phone interviews.

"Did she have a boyfriend?" She talked like an army sergeant, rhythms pounded out like bass-drum beats. Pause. "Any other relatives you can put me in touch with?" Pause. "Uh-huh. Sorry to take your time," she said with very little irony, and hung up, noticing me. "Hey."

"Hey," I said. "What do you got?"

She kept sorting through her papers. "Cold cases. Girl shit. You?"

"Faith Copeland."

"From TV?"

I wondered why everyone had heard of this girl but me. "Rape/murder."

"You on it alone?" she asked.

I told her that the order came from higher up, meaning the Fifth Floor, meaning that there might or might not be any logic to the decision, but so what? And I told her that the good lieutenant wasn't crazy about me, an old grudge that went back so far neither of us knew what started it.

She nodded and said, "I'm alone on this. I'm not complaining."

"Of course not. Hey, you want to get some dinner?"

"Fuck you. 'You wanna get some dinner?' What do you think I am? The squad cooze?"

My mouth hung open on the odd chance some useful words would come out. I managed, "I didn't mean . . ."

"What?"

I pretended I meant it platonically. "Yeah, forget about it." I turned back to my work.

After a silence she said, "I'm . . . *dating* somebody."

She stumbled on the word "dating" like it left a bad taste. I guessed it was not a happy situation. I also guessed that I was not her type, from any angle.

I said, "I'm gonna go get something to eat. Lemme know if I can help you with the girl."

"You too," she said.

And without a second option, I headed home to Jessica.

10.
‖‖‖‖‖

After dinner Sergeant Jeffrey Czerniak settled onto the couch with his wife and a reassuring scotch and water and put his feet up. The scotch did such a good job of calming him that he was suddenly on his feet mixing another. It was less than an hour before he mixed the third, carefully avoiding his wife's eyes as he made it back to the couch. When that was done, his feet had suddenly taken him to the closet, where his hands put his jacket on him before opening the front door and closing it behind him.

It didn't make any sense to him. Sometimes in the morning, it was all he could do just to get out of bed, and that included his days off. If he had to mow the lawn on a Saturday, he might sit in front of the tube for an hour trying to talk himself into standing up. But come night-time he was out of the house and sailing down I-35 before he realized he'd left the couch.

It wasn't even a Friday. He had things to think about: work trouble, wife trouble—he'd be divorced soon at this rate. Whatever was gonna happen with Clay. And still he found himself cruising down East Seventh Street, the second night in a row, deeper and deeper into El Barrio, pretending he was fighting crime instead of being dragged forward by fucked-up instinct, the way a roller coaster is dragged uphill by a chain.

He drove past busted traffic lights, liquor stores, rib joints and bars. He slowed at a red light. A junkie hooker, a white girl with a big belly, lifted her skirt. A thing like an air bubble passed through his heart. He felt a little jolt, a little electricity. A taste. There was more somewhere, right now. He could feel it.

He headed farther in the scant traffic, spotted hoodlums hanging out on the corners. He weaved through side streets. His heart pumped harder, sugar ran through his veins. Close, he was close. Something waited for him, in the dark.

He turned onto Springdale. A one-story industrial brick building stood back from the street. Small, big enough for one store, with a white roof jutting out over the front of the building, three homeless men sharing its shelter. He slowed. Windows boarded. He breathed deep and pulled in. Fifteen or so cars parked behind the building. Bingo.

Czerniak parked and steadied himself. Call for backup, he thought. Check this out with Vice. You can't take down fifteen men. Two other cars pulled in to the lot.

He wouldn't go in. He would just peek. He walked to the back door as if he knew what was going on. His heart was pounding until a kidney punch ripped into him and he fell to the concrete.

They slapped tape over his eyes and kicked at him. Three of them? Four? He reached for his weapon and felt someone yank up his jacket and slip the automatic out of his holster. They'd known he was packing. He rolled over and tried to bounce up, but they were on him again. They kicked his legs out from under him, and he fell to his knees, hard. Someone punched him in the jaw, and someone else shouted, "Not the face!"

And just as fast, they broke and spread away. But he heard something fall to the concrete near him, something metal, the sound of someone picking it up and the rapid-fire *clickclickclick* of a ratchet.

Handcuffs, he thought.

Cops.

11.
⁙

Onan wouldn't have a baby with his brother's widow, so God killed him, which is why you should never touch your privates.

It didn't exactly make sense to Rolo but he couldn't stop thinking about it. He even woke up with the thought. Mr. Leitch had explained it. Rolo had been with the Leitches for two months.

There was one other boy in the room, a white boy who'd been there for a year. He hardly said anything when he was awake. He always made a lot of noise when he settled into bed. Now he snored softly. Rolo looked up at the ceiling.

It was hard to believe it had been two months since Valentine's Day, since the police broke in on Rolo's mother's party and ruined all their lives.

It was just supposed to be a party for her friends and their kids, but somehow there were only four grown-ups, two other kids Rolo's age and a bunch of little kids. Four cousins, three of Mrs. Peña's kids and six kids from the block all got dropped off by their parents like a day-care center. Rolo pouring Kool-Aid and his mom being nice and leading games. And then the police coming in and slamming her against a wall and Mrs. Peña trying to call someone for help and the police spraying her with tear gas. And when it was over, his mom was in jail.

Rolo's dad wasn't around, and he only had one uncle in town, who wouldn't take him in, so they sent him to a foster home until his mother's case went to trial. They didn't have a date yet.

Chuck and Elizabeth Leitch, the foster parents, were very religious. His mother would like that, except they weren't Catholic. They prayed morning and evening with all the kids, like it or not. They talked mostly about hell, never heaven. Rolo asked Mr. Leitch if he could see his mother. Mr. Leitch said they couldn't let children into the jail because men would rape them, and Rolo wouldn't like that, would he? Rolo didn't ask again.

The first night at bedtime, Rolo said he was thirsty. Mrs. Leitch said, "Make saliva and swallow it."

There was this girl, Joyce, who was fifteen, two years older than Rolo and a head taller, who had a white blouse and straight, light brown hair that went down just to her shoulders and was cut across her eyebrows in bangs, and long legs, and she would stand on one foot like a ballerina and bring the other foot up to her knee. Girls liked him, he was told, because of his curly black hair and his big eyes, so dark they were almost black. So he would practice smiling into the mirror with just his eyes, and he was trying the smile out when Joyce was doing her one-foot stand, and she saw him and smiled back. Later that same day, he found her in the cupboard. The cupboard was big, like a room with no windows. Enough canned and dry food, Mr. Leitch said, to last two years. Rolo found Joyce there, and she put his hands on her waist and she kissed him.

Now Rolo got out of bed and went out onto the landing. The Leitches slept in the big bedroom. There was a room for the boys and one for the girls, including Joyce. The landing looked out over the front hall, with a wooden rail that continued down the stairs. A twisted green glass lamp stood on a table in front of the railing. It had what looked like glass wings sticking out of it on all four sides. It was a gift from the Leitches' daughter in Dripping Springs. It was the only thing in the house that didn't look like it was a hundred years old.

Joyce came out of the bathroom. She was in a long white night-gown and socks. He was wearing white pajamas. She looked around to see if there was anyone there, and he thought for sure she was going to kiss him again when she got her mouth close to his ear and whispered, "Cupboard."

She glided down the stairs, sliding on the last step and grabbing at the banister. The rail rattled, and she caught her balance and ran on. Rolo went down the stairs as quietly as he could and followed her into the kitchen. Rolo found the cupboard door and opened it. He could see Joyce in her white nightgown. She flipped on a little night-light, a bulb in the socket, and he closed the door. She smiled and opened the tiny white buttons down to her belly.

Rolo had never seen a girl's chest besides his mother's. And Joyce was tall and thin with pink nipples, and he would have stared at her forever until she said, "Now you."

"Huh?"

"Take your pajamas off."

Hands shaking, he managed to unbutton his top, and then he walked to her. She kissed him, full tongue in his mouth, pushed his pajama top off his shoulders and squeezed him close.

Then she took his hand and put it on her breast. Rolo could only stare.

She pulled back and giggled and buttoned her nightgown. They both kept giggling and shushing each other, and he dressed and followed her out into the hall. He watched from the front hall as she tiptoed up the stairs in her socks and looked around to see if anyone was there. Then she looked over the railing at him and lifted her nightgown, just enough to show her leg. He started to clap but stopped himself in time. She did a ballet turn and lifted one knee. Then she spun again but slipped on the landing floor and toppled into the lamp. He thought she was kidding, but he saw her move in slow motion like a dream, sliding into the lamp, the lamp and the small table crashing through the wooden railing, the railing breaking open and toppling to the floor, Joyce and the lamp and the table falling all the long way to the floor in front of him with a crash.

Upstairs someone cried out, and feet shuffled around. He got close to Joyce, facedown on the broken lamp. She was bleeding. She made a little noise, "gah," and then blood rolled from her mouth, gallons of it.

He heard Mrs. Leitch scream, "Back in your rooms! Back in your rooms!" and Rolo ran back to the kitchen, back to the cupboard, doused the night-light and closed the door.

He sat there in the dark, silently crying, as the police came and asked questions, stayed for hours and then left. And when the house was finally quiet, he sneaked back up the stairs, got his clothes and slipped out of the house.

True story: Guy calls 911. Says he kicked his roommate out, the roommate came back and tried to stab him. "So I shot him."

The 911 operator says, "Is he dead?"

"Just a second."

Operator hears something metal picked up, maybe from a table. Gunshot. Something metal put back on the table. Guy picks up the phone again.

He says, "Yes."

I've heard several takes on this story, mostly from cops as they get drunk and try to make sense out of things. I say the guy in the story had a very specific sense of right and wrong, that had more to do with finishing a job than with, say, the sanctity of human life. But everybody has a set of rules. The trick is to figure out the other person's rules before you break them and wind up getting fired, divorced or shot.

Three of the Homicide detectives—Fuentes, Highfill and Halvorsen—were moving around the squad room when I got there in the morning. I nodded and said hey to everyone who met my eyes. Highfill said, "Something on *yer* desk," and pointed to a manila interoffice envelope.

LaMorte huffed in. "Anyone seen Mora?" We hadn't. He looked at me and stopped cold like I'd just parked my car in the middle of the office. As I settled in to read the file, I got the vibe that the squad resented my making myself at home so fast. I was the new guy, I was supposed to move in slow. LaMorte vanished.

Hay had sent me the autopsy report on Faith. According to the report, the girl downed more than one bottle of Valium and a few other assorted pharmaceuticals, as we'd expected, and they'd been in her system long enough to be absorbed. There was water in her lungs. She'd slipped under the water before she died.

Hay also discovered that Faith's right thumb was broken, dislocated, and it hadn't been set right. Also, between what Hay managed to remove from Faith and from the bedspread, there was enough DNA to send to the Department of Public Safety for testing. I phoned the DPS crime lab and asked for Ron Wachowski.

"*This is Ron.*"

"Ron, it's Dan Reles."

"*Dan, say, you wouldn't believe what I saw today. I got two sets of DNA results—*"

I cut him off before he got rolling. "That's what I called about. Dr. Hay sent you a DNA sample."

"*Good luck.*" He chuckled. "*We're pretty much in demand. We've only been at this a few months and I have a backlog of fifteen hundred cases. Anyway,"* he said, as if it were unrelated, *"what can I do for you? Besides jumping you ahead."*

I said, "Jump me ahead. The victim is Faith Copeland. She was a TV star a few years back, a kid star. Think how good you'd look." Mora walked in and parked herself at her desk, the one nearest mine. I wondered whether the squad was pissed at me for nailing such prime real estate.

"Tempting, but Dan," Wachowski said, *"there are people on death row. Lives at stake. I promise I'll have it done before you go to trial."*

I said, "Don't put me ahead of anyone on death row."

He laughed and said, *"I'll do what I can."* I hung up and hauled out the memorabilia from Faith's showbiz career, photos and videotapes. We all worked in near silence for about twenty minutes, until the bulk of the squad stepped out in ones and twos on different business, leaving Mora and me back to back.

Mora leaned back in her chair and it creaked. "How's your girl?" she asked.

I turned to her. "The same."

LaMorte came back in. "Mora, Marks is lookin' for ya."

She got up.

LaMorte said. "Not now. He went out. Talk to him when he comes back." LaMorte headed out. Mora dropped into her chair and shuffled files again.

She muttered, "Dickhead."

I held up one of Faith's tapes. "You wanna watch a movie?"

We settled in front of the VCR with coffee and notepads, and I popped in the first tape, which was, chronologically, the last. Grown-up Faith doing her monologue for the agent's camera.

"To live hopelessly . . ."

Mora fast-forwarded to the end of the monologue, which had Faith smiling nervously at the camera, wondering if she did good, then white noise.

The next tape showed Faith in acting class, screaming her heart out at some boy and trying to squeeze out tears. Something from a few months earlier had a low-rent TV commercial, Faith with a cheeseball English accent and librarian glasses demonstrating a humidifier by showing the gallon of water it could put into the air in two hours; she drove the point home by tossing the bucket of water in the air and drenching herself before giving the company slogan. This would be Faith's last contribution to the acting profession.

Before that she was seen dancing with ten other adolescents in some kid show. She was acting all happy and perky, but she was no prettier or more talented than any other kid on the block. The cassette was labeled "Mouse Audition." She didn't get the part.

Before that there was a gap of a year or so where the TV show happened, because everyone in the world had seen the show but me. Before that it got scary. Faith had been, at six and seven, a darling of TV producers, featured in a score of commercials that mostly showed her smiling at some father figure or throwing her tiny head back and laughing, like in the spot with the talking toothpaste. And before that she competed in beauty pageants.

Mora and I marveled at Faith's complex routines of twists and turns, up and down runways at age four, made up like an adult, her mother in yellow curls introducing "Baby Faith" (get it?), Faith singing her little heart out with musical offers of services at rates of, for example, ten cents a dance.

Mora said, "I see a pattern."

I listened.

She said, "Men think teenage girls are hot. It's biological, find a younger mate who can bear you more children." Mora had her black hair pinned back, and she was wearing a black silk shirt with her jeans. I tried to pay attention to what she was saying about reproduction. "Look at it. Her mother dressed her up like a whore and still made her look innocent. A baby and a woman, a virgin and a whore. Might give some pedophile just the wrong idea."

I said, "So some guy stalked her for years and waited till she turned eighteen?"

Mora shrugged and popped out the tape. It was labeled "Little Miss Central Texas 1983."

I juggled the numbers. Her DPS ID (issued to Texans who don't have driver's licenses) put her birth in 1977, which made her eighteen at the time of death. But in 1983 she was competing in the category of four-year-olds. Maybe she was small for her age and she was six and her mother lied and said she was four to get her into that category.

I dug out her ID and held it up to the light. It had a thin glaze.

"You have anything sharp, a knife blade, a razor?"

I watched her back as she riffled through her desk and pulled out an X-acto knife. I scraped the ID, bringing up tiny curlicues of plastic.

Marks stuck his head in the office. "Mora, where the hell you been? Get in here."

She jumped up and headed out after him. I kept shaving the ID.

Soon the clear plastic shavings started coming up in color. Faith had diddled the ID, painted over the numbers and changed them. She was born in 1979. She died a minor.

Maybe someone stalked her for years. But he didn't wait for her to turn eighteen.

13.
⫿⫿⫿⫿⫿

Homicide Sergeant Catarina (Cate) Mora weighed in at 130 pounds of lean muscle and built like a brick Taco Bell, as she'd been told by one cop who got a shiner for his trouble. (Her father, who wanted a boy, taught her to punch and shoot. Mora prayed for a little brother to take the heat off. She often imagined him, but he never appeared. Still, the ability to shoot and fight made everything else seem easier. And in the Academy she learned fast that she'd get further if she was loud and brash and foul-mouthed—if she acted like a man.) With her black hair combed back and bound tight, a blazer over black shirt and slacks, she raced out to the scene with siren screaming and touched base with the patrols parked in front of the foster home. A rickety banister and gravity had joined forces and doused Joyce Graaf's light. The EMTs had come and gone, finding the girl unarguably and nonnegotiably dead. The patrols called it an accident, and Dispatch didn't bother to wake anyone up on Homicide. Joyce waited till morning.

The front door opened on a tall, slightly stooped man of no more than seventy, with a heavy brow and pallid skin. A man who had no business running a house full of kids. "Mr. Leitch? I'm Cate Mora with APD Homicide."

He jolted. "Homicide?"

"We handle homicide, suicide, accidental death. . . ."

He nodded and led her in. Outside and in, the building looked like an old-fashioned farmhouse: Two full levels, two chimneys, wood-frame windows. Bare wood floors. The front landing bore evidence of Joyce's fall: the banister supports, the tiny shards of glass, the bloodstains. Leitch led her into the kitchen and sat with her at the table.

"Nice place," she said as she noticed a boy and two girls watching her from the doorway. She smiled with effort. They had woken to find one of their own dead.

"I built it," Leitch said, with neither pride nor humility. He was looking her over. The look said, *Whore!* but he kept his mouth shut, which was wise. It was his banister that had allowed Joyce's fall.

Mora asked what seemed like the right questions. It was her first hot case—the others had been gathering dust for months or years—and even if Joyce's fall was an accident, she could use the case to make points.

How long had Joyce lived at the house? Was she in touch with her family? Was she depressed? Did she have a boyfriend?

Mora inspected the steps and the railing, what was left of it. She couldn't see charging him with negligent homicide on account of a railing, but she couldn't rule it out. Finally she asked if she could talk to the other kids.

"Can it wait?" he said. "They've been through a lot."

Mora said she understood. As she stepped out the front door, she said, "How many kids are in the house?"

"Five," he said. "Well, four."

"Four?"

His cheeks twitched in succession. "Three."

"Maybe you should count."

He said, "We had five. Then Joyce . . . fell. One of the boys . . ." He struggled for the words. "Ran away. Last night."

Mora stepped back inside. "What was his name?"

14.
ⅢⅢⅢ

Lieutenant James Torbett wasn't fool enough to think he'd been awarded his auspicious command out of appreciation for two decades of service. Or because they felt it was time to acknowledge African

Americans for their hard work. Or in compensation for the life-changing injury he'd received at the hands of an APD patrol four years earlier, the nightstick blow to the spine that caused him near-constant pain, spasms that began in his upper back and shot up into his neck, radiating outward. (When they'd brought the patrol before the board of inquiry, he insisted he didn't know that Torbett was a cop, saw him reaching for what could have been a gun. And the patrol articulated the cop's universal defense: "I feared for my life." Torbett filled with hatred every time he felt the twinge, then had to check himself, forgive and move on.) And they didn't promote him in appreciation of his service in supporting a society that offered his son nothing more attractive than a career in the military, where he, too, would help prop up the system that hated him. No, they gave Torbett the job as a public gesture, a minority in a high position, to dull the public heat from the Salina Street incident, the most recent blot on the record of the department itself. Internal Affairs, everyone knew, had been gathering testimony and evidence and had enough to convict the officers involved. But the Fifth Floor couldn't publicly back down and admit wrongdoing. So in a frenzy of bad decision making, they sat on the testimonies, kept the victims in jail and struggled to spin the event, to make the department look like heroes against all evidence and reason. And they'd give the job of internal inspection, the one who polices the police and makes them look bad, to Torbett. And they'd make him look bad.

But Torbett had a plan.

Reles gave him the idea at the banquet. The Family, the secret fraternity of corrupt and dangerous cops, ruled by self-interest and hatred, controlled everything. They controlled hirings and promotions, they saved the dirty cops from serious discipline, they protected the department's most lazy, immoral and corrupt. What are ya gonna do? Torbett would take advantage of his position. He had a license to communicate with any member of the department individually, to build an alliance of the moral and principled, just as there was an alliance of the greedy and shameless. Exactly how this organization within the department, this "alternative Family" would operate, was still a mystery. Anyone knew that a movement built on morality was a tougher sell than one built on graft and abuse. But he had already started building at the banquet, making contact with one young detective and a couple of outstanding rookies who hadn't had their ideals beaten out of them yet.

Like an interrogation room, the IA interview room had no humanizing elements. Fluorescent lights shone between white cardboard ceiling tiles (they were once asbestos). At 11:00 A.M. exactly, two women entered, one with a tape recorder, the other a stenotype machine, and sat. Torbett asked if they were ready and called in Czerniak.

Torbett greeted Czerniak, shook his hand, made all efforts to put him at ease, which included suppressing the grimace that came to Torbett's lips each time his back spasmed, an event that happened today at intervals of seconds rather than minutes.

"Please have a seat, Sergeant," Torbett rumbled, and Czerniak sat at the table, the woman with the recorder to his right. Torbett sat opposite Czerniak. The young woman operating the huge recorder flipped it on with a prominent click that made Czerniak flinch.

Czerniak's eyes flicked between the faces in the room. The skin around his eyes was reddened, irritated. And his eyebrows were half missing.

Torbett asked, "What happened to your face?"

Czerniak said, "My wife doesn't like this." He pointed to a furrow between his eyebrows. "She put tape on it last night. I tore it off this morning, and look what happened." He forced a laugh, but no one joined him.

Torbett nodded. "Now, tell me what you told me yesterday."

Czerniak said, "No lie detector?" with half a smile.

Torbett said, softly, "Why would you lie? You approached the Sueño nightclub Tuesday night."

"I was drunk," Czerniak said suddenly. "Did I tell you that?"

Torbett's back seized. He tried to hide his reaction. "No, you didn't."

Czerniak said, "From the banquet . . ."

15.
||||||

It was sunny and clear out and nearly lunchtime when I got to Mr. Copeland's house. The second Mrs. Copeland, Gloria, greeted me at the door, wearing a short-sleeved green dress, too formal for most homes and too ugly for anywhere else. Five similarly dressed women lined the living room. Two wore aprons and brought coffee and cake in from the kitchen. I wore a jacket and slacks, but their eyes widened at my appearance just the same, a gangster come to rob the church. Gloria Copeland thanked me for keeping the incident from the press. (A friend in Public Information had made a couple of judicious spelling errors in Faith's name; the press had enough on APD to keep them busy until the errors were corrected in a day or two.) Gloria had already made the necessary calls to have Faith picked up by the funeral home. The funeral would be Saturday morning. She gave me the address. I wondered if Faith's mother would show up. I asked to speak with Mr. Copeland.

One feature of even the smallest suburban houses is that, once the children are gone, there are extra rooms. Copeland had turned one into a sort of study. He sat in a chair with tweed cushions, an afghan over his lap. An olive green rug covered the floor, and paneling coated the walls. He stared at a television set on a wooden stand, though there was no image on the screen. There was a straight-backed kitchen chair with yellow vinyl coating. I pulled it close and sat near him.

"Mr. Copeland."

He nodded.

"We met. I'm Dan Reles. With the police." No arguments. "Can you speak?"

He swallowed. "Why?"

"How old was Faith?"

He said, "Sixteen."

Okay, I thought. On the same page. "Why wasn't she living with her parents?"

He saw something on the TV screen that made him angry, and his eyes bloated with rage and tears. "Her m–mother. Treated Faith like she wasn't pulling her weight."

"Why didn't she come live with you?"

He gestured to the door the second Mrs. Copeland had exited from. "She didn't like Gloria."

"Do you know if she had a boyfriend?" I asked. "Or if someone was following her?"

The imaginary people in the dark TV screen were pissing him off. His eyes reddened, and I realized I'd gotten everything from Mr. Copeland I was likely to get. In the living room, Mrs. Copeland made an offer of coffee and cake but her heart wasn't in it, and she looked relieved when I took my Semitic nose and left. In the car I looked over Faith's file, including what I had on her one arrest and trial for breaking and entering. While a lot of details were lacking—there's no classification for "charges dismissed on grounds of stupidity"—the file included the name of her lawyer, one Alan Anderton, a low-end defense attorney I'd crossed paths with before.

I tracked Anderton at the criminal court building. A guard pointed him out as he emerged from a courtroom with a briefcase, an armload of files and a twentyish Latino defendant with moussed hair, shiny nylon shirt and slacks and dancing shoes. A problem young people have dressing for court is that their only formal clothes are what they wear to go clubbing. Anderton was razzing the guy.

"You do not smile at the judge. You do not buddy up to the judge."

Anderton wore a light gray Sears pinstripe, a mustache and a sunburn, a Texas hazard even in April. I walked up to him. "Alan."

He pasted a smile on long enough to say, "Hey, good to see ya," then let it drop and kept walking. "We have one more chance," he was saying when I gave chase and got in front of him.

"Alan, I'm Dan Reles." I badged him. "It's about your client Faith Copeland."

"What did she do?" he asked.

"She's dead."

The club kid stared, wondering if throwing in with Anderton was that much of a risk. Anderton turned to him and said, "Call me tomorrow. Get a suit. Salvation Army is okay."

The kid walked down the crowded hall. Anderton shouted after him, "Don't steal it!" but I don't know if the kid heard. Anderton led me into a break room with two wood-veneer conference tables, a watercooler and a pair of vending machines. A few jurors sat scattered around, reading newspapers and paperbacks.

I asked what he knew about Faith. He recounted the story of her bungled burglary.

I said, "Did you know she was only sixteen?"

"She was an emancipated minor. Something about her mother and money Faith made."

"Did she try to get her money back?"

"There was a story about a lawyer in L.A. before they came home to Texas. But her mother proved that she only took what they needed to live on. And the money was gone. The house should have belonged to Faith. Why?"

"I don't know," I said. "I'm trying to figure out who she was."

He thought for a moment. "Figure this," he said. "She was a deadbeat. A sixteen-year-old kid who should have been dreaming about Hollywood instead of remembering it. She couldn't go back to school. She'd barely ever *been* to school. Maybe she went to a few classes, I don't know. But she didn't know how to do anything except look pretty, and man, she wasn't that pretty."

I thanked him. As we headed out, I asked, "Did she ever pay you?"

He said, "Yes."

"How?" He thought for a moment. I said, "Her parents?"

He shook his head.

"Well?"

Finally he took a deep breath and said, "I believe she found another venue for her performing skills."

16.
⁗⁗

The muscles in Torbett's back clamped onto his spine. Torbett tried to will them into a state of relaxation but it was no use. He went on with the questions.

"You had a few drinks at the banquet," he said.

Czerniak said, "I was drunk. I shouldn't have gone out alone."

"Then what happened?"

"I drove to the club and parked. I walked around. There was no van. It was supposed to be there."

"Why?"

Czerniak said, "It . . . it was supposed to be in the area every night until the case was closed!"

Torbett said, "That's fine," in his most calming tones. "Then what happened?"

"I parked and walked around the club. There was no one in back, so I went in the door. I wasn't authorized. I had no backup. There were no cameras. I could have blown our cover."

It seemed to Torbett like a lot of confessing for a man in a world where no one confesses anything.

"You didn't," Torbett said evenly. "You were trying to solve a case. What did you see?"

Czerniak, sweating, looked at the two women recording his words. "There was a party in the basement. I saw it through a window in the door. The window was hazy, like I said, and it was dark. Anyway, there were these strippers. I guess strippers, they were wearing G-strings. But they were . . . doing the guys."

"Did you recognize anyone?"

"One of the guys was Boyle."

Torbett said, "The subject of the investigation?"

"It was his club. The other . . . well, I thought it was Lieutenant Clay?" He said it like a question.

Torbett looked him over. "You *thought* it was Lieutenant Clay?"

"Now I'm not so sure."

Torbett leaned back. "You're not sure. You were sure yesterday."

Czerniak twitched. "Yeah. Yeah, but I was drunk."

"Yesterday?"

"No, Tuesday. You're confusing me."

Torbett raised his voice two notches. "You were certain you saw Mr. Boyle. Yesterday you were certain you saw your superior. You know Lieutenant Clay's face better than Mr. Boyle's."

Czerniak seemed ready to jump from his seat. "Look, I said I was drunk. It was dark. Maybe it was Boyle, maybe not. I just don't know if it was Lieutenant Clay."

Torbett said, "But it might have been."

"No," Czerniak said. "I'm sure of that now. It wasn't Clay."

"How do you know?"

"His face was . . . different. Thinner. Darker."

Torbett thought hard. Second day on the job. Zero training. Same techniques you use on suspects. As the first black detective, he'd been the most hated man in the department. As the head of IA, and also black, he was probably the most hated man in the department's history. Time to back off.

"Ladies," he said, "we'll end here for now."

The two women left with their machines, closing the door behind them. Torbett slid his chair close to Czerniak's side. He placed his hand on Czerniak's shoulder. Czerniak stiffened.

Torbett said, "There are a few holes in your story, a few inconsistencies. But I know one thing for sure." He leaned close to Czerniak's ear and whispered.

"You're lying."

17.
||||||

I stopped at the tail end of the lunch rush at a tiny campus-area bank that changed owners every year or two, asked for a manager, showed him Faith's ID, explained the situation and hit him up for account information.

He wore a somber black suit and a matching expression and said that any account information would have to be requested in writing by a judge.

I explained, politely, that Faith had been raped and murdered thirty-six hours earlier and the more time that passed, the less likely we were to find the perpetrator. Not an unreasonable man, the manager asked if I had any information on the account. I gave him an ATM receipt.

He said, "Do you have the checkbook?"

I didn't. It hadn't showed up in a search of her home, demonstrating the likelihood that the killer made a quick sweep of the apartment, took the checkbook and her calendar if she had one and missed her wallet.

He found a computer terminal at an empty desk, typed, waited, typed, waited and finally showed me a ledger on the screen. The most frequently appearing term was "INSUFFICIENT FUNDS." I asked what deposits had been made. He scrolled up and showed me a deposit, check, three thousand dollars.

"Where'd it come from?" I asked.

"The screen doesn't show that."

I stared him down until he realized there was one way to get rid of me. He disappeared into the back offices for a solid twenty minutes, returned with a sheet of business paper and handed it to me. I gave him my card and asked him to call if anyone tried to pass one of Faith's checks.

Outside in the spring sunlight, I looked at the page he'd given me. On it the sole image was a shrunken photocopy of a check made out to Faith Copeland in the amount of three thousand dollars, two weeks back, from a company way down on Ben White Boulevard, bearing the unlikely designation Red Rose Raw.

18.

Cate Mora ran by Child Protective Services. Caseworkers were notoriously overworked. A few years back, a typical caseload was thirty kids, which meant nearly weekly visits to all of them and some kind of supervision. Then cutbacks doubled caseloads, then tripled them. Now a typical caseworker was responsible for over two hundred children. Visits could be months apart. And time had proved that anything could happen to the kids between visits. Anything.

The runaway boy's caseworker, an overweight white woman with bobbed red hair and flaccid eyes, met the boy once when she dropped him off with the Leitches. His name was Rolando Ortiz. Latino, thirteen years old. The caseworker described him as small, sad and timid. He entered the system on Valentine's Day when his mother was arrested in the Salina Street incident, which Mora, the caseworkers and most of Austin knew about. God knew why the woman was still in jail. A single mother, her only child had been remanded to foster care. He went by the nickname "Rolo."

The Leitches were elderly, retired and empty-nested. They showed Mora Rolo's room (two beds, desk, chair), the refrigerator (plenty of food), the clothes they'd purchased for him. He'd been no trouble at all. Quiet, kept to himself. They'd had dinner with him last night. He seemed fine. He went to bed. He was gone by morning.

Between dinner and breakfast, Joyce Graaf fell through the railing.

The two girls who roomed with Joyce woke to the crash. They ran out onto the landing, along with the boy who roomed with Rolo. Mrs. Leitch shooed them all back to bed. The boy noticed that Rolo wasn't in his bed. Mora took the boy aside.

"Why didn't you tell someone?" she said.

"Nobody asked."

Mora visited Rolo's school and spoke to his teacher. He'd stayed at his regular school after his mother's arrest. Yes, he seemed different, withdrawn. No, he hadn't been acting out. He was very sweet.

Mora made it to the county jail, locked her weapon in one of the small lockers, heard the steel doors slam and lock behind her and asked for Mrs. Carla Ortiz. A guard let Mora into the cell block and the small cell where Mrs. Ortiz sat and looked up, a tiny woman in foolish green coveralls, holding a photo and a rosary. Mora put her at under five feet, round face, less than forty but with the bearing of a much older woman. The guard locked them in and Mora introduced herself in Spanish.

Suddenly tears flowed from the woman's tired eyes and a flood of Spanish from her lips, a challenge to Mora's assimilated ears.

It was a Valentine's party. There were children at the house, and neighbors. She named them all. The police came in. They said someone called about gang activity. They pushed her against the wall. She had a black eye. It faded. They took her away in the car. She couldn't get to a phone. She'd had four babies before Rolando. All of them died. His father left them. Rolando was all she had, all she would ever have. There was no one to take care of her baby, her little one. *"Mi'jo!"* she kept crying out. *"Mi'jo!"* Mrs. Ortiz had been told later that the state came for him. He was in a home. Where? Why was she in jail? They gave her a lawyer who wasn't good for anything. Wouldn't somebody help her?

Mora checked herself. The jails were full of victims and people pretending to be victims. She couldn't put her heart out to all of them. She chose her words carefully, then translated them into Spanish.

"Last we heard, Rolo is fine. He went to a foster home. But he's not there. I think he ran away." Mora hoped to God he ran away. *"Do you know where he would have gone?"*

Mrs. Ortiz let out a stream of tears at the notion of Rolo out on his own, then gave Mora addresses: Two friends on the block and another friend nearby. Also his only relative in town, his uncle. Mora called for the guard.

Mrs. Ortiz handed her the photo she'd been holding. That and the rosary were the two items she'd managed to keep when they locked her up. As the guard opened the cell, the woman reached up to Mora as if to whisper a secret. Mora leaned down. Mrs. Ortiz pressed her cheek against Mora's, a warmth she'd seldom seen outside of the women in her family.

Mora stood up fast and walked out, past the guard. She held back a tear as the cell door clanged shut behind her.

Maybe Rolo had something to do with Joyce's death. Maybe he got angry and shoved her. Or maybe he just saw something and was afraid. And now he was a kid alone on the street.

As she headed back to HQ, she knew she'd made a decision. She'd find Rolo.

She'd find him alive.

19.
⁙⁙⁙

Way down on Ben White Boulevard, I stepped into the lobby of a new sandstone office building and felt humbled by its size. My footsteps landed on a marble floor, echoed up into a cathedral ceiling and swirled. On a stone podium that should have been holding up the tablets Moses brought down from Mount Sinai, a directory displayed twenty business names in white plastic letters, including "Red Rose Raw," on the top floor. I took the elevator. I guessed they put the building up in hopes of filling every office and that the growth of downtown hadn't reached quite so far south. I entered unnoticed onto a bustle of activity two stories high.

The ceiling was over twenty feet up. A rectangular window on the far wall started six feet from the floor and soared to the ceiling, spreading the entire width of the room and opening on to a stretch of greenery and houses south of Austin, reaching toward San Antonio. Sunlight shone on two levels of activity: work areas on the floor were separated only by blond wood desks and file cabinets, created with the assumption that everyone was too motivated by his work to need walls as blinders. Wrought-iron staircases rose to a second level of work areas on steel scaffold. Everyone could see what everyone else was doing, to the right, left, below or above.

While I was taking this in, a young black woman walked up and asked, in an English accent, "C'n I help you?" She was wearing gray nylon warm-up pants and a tight black T-shirt with a low neckline displaying an expanse of bosom proportional to the size of the room. She followed her question with a playful smile that brought up her high cheekbones, with her upper teeth gently pressed against her lower lip. The smile was almost enough to distract me from the rest of her, but not quite.

"Can . . . you tell me who's in charge?"

"I am." She seemed glad to give the answer.

"Really?"

"Is that so surprising?"

I noticed that there was no reception desk. They weren't accustomed to walk-ins, whatever they did. Then I tried looking at her professionally. I said, "I believe you *could* be in charge. But you're not."

She smiled again, cheekbones and teeth. "No I'm not."

"What do you do here?"

"We're a video production company."

"Did you employ a woman named Faith Copeland?"

"Faith! Are you a fan?" She seemed particularly excited to meet a fan of Faith's, and I suddenly didn't want to take a chance at disappointing her.

"I guess."

"What's your name, dahling?"

I said, "Dan."

"I'm June. Follow me, Dan," she said with enough allure that, subconsciously, I wondered if she were leading me off to her bedroom.

Her hair was twisted back in braids. The T-shirt pulled tight against her back, which narrowed from her shoulders to her waist, and her nylon pants rustled as she led me off to the left and into an outer office bigger than the whole Homicide squad room. The secretary's desk was empty, and June tapped on the inner office door of carved oak and opened it onto a darkened room. The only light came from the screen of a video monitor against the side wall. A man hunched over the screen, paused it and looked up. The image landed on one woman rapturously burying her face between the thighs of another woman and froze them in time.

"Knock, knock," June said. I put the guy at something over six feet, though it was hard to tell with him sitting. He had slicked-back hair and a pug nose. "This is Becket, my associate," she told me. "Becket, meet Dan. He's with the police."

Lessons to remember: If something seems too good to be true, it is. And if you think you're putting one over on someone, odds are they're putting one over on you.

Becket switched on a lamp that shone near me if not quite in my eyes. "What can we do for you, Officer?"

"You can get that fuckin' light out of my eyes." He did. I found the light switches by the door and flipped them on. It was his turn to squint.

Becket swiveled his huge leather chair toward me and sat back. Sitting up, he was the size of a semi, large enough that the chair looked small. He could call himself a businessman, but the cut of his silver hair and black satin shirt gave him away as a pimp. June leaned on a second table on the wall opposite Becket's great oaken desk. Her smile had gone.

"Faith Copeland," I said. "I want to know what she did for you. I have a guess. I want to know when."

Becket said, "We're legal here." I didn't comment. In big cities organized crime always got its hand into anything illegal. The mob controlled whorehouses, narcotics, everything. Porn was legal, but the mob didn't know that, so they muscled in on the pornographers, too. In Austin organized crime didn't even exist the way it did in the big cities. Most of what we had involved men with crooked side businesses, bar owners and jewelers fronting for narcotics operations and fencing stolen goods. But then, we used to say we didn't have street gangs.

Becket smelled like a big city. If the porn itself wasn't illegal, something else was.

June said, "We can sue you for persecuting us."

"Please, please," he said, waving a large, hairy hand. "We're all friends here. Isn't that right, Officer?" I sensed the threat, but I didn't answer. "Junie, fish out her stuff for the nice man." June stepped out. "Faith," he said, "great girl. Talented. Came to us looking for work. Not like we went after her."

"Interesting accent. Where you from?"

"Guess."

"I say you're an Irishman from New York."

"Not bad."

I went on. "I say you're fronting for the mob." His eyes bulged. "You have goons on call, but you don't keep them here because you want this to look like a real business, like an ad agency or a magazine. And the mob is branching into a new market, growing Austin. And while we're at it, put your hands where I can see them."

He laughed, but he kept his hands in the vicinity of his lap, under the desk. I drew my .38 fast and walked to him, yanking the top drawer. Cigarettes, pens, some change. He laughed loud. Then something like a cinder block hit the side of my head. I wobbled and fell backward, sitting on the video editor.

"Oh, jeez," he said. "Accidental head butt. Shouldn't rush up on a guy like that. You okay?" He'd knocked my temple with the hard part of his forehead. I could arrest him but it wouldn't stick. He was reminding me of my limitations. I thought of shooting him, but I was afraid he wouldn't bleed.

June came in with a few videotapes.

He said, "Get him a chair. Siddown, dickhead. Pull a gun on me!" My head throbbed. I fell into a chair and June handed me three videos. He said, "I have *ten* men on call, and they're not goons, they're lawyers." Another valuable lesson I wished I remembered earlier: Not everyone is afraid of a gun. And those that aren't don't give a rat's ass about a badge. As my vision cleared, I saw that the packaging was first rate: their photos and graphics were probably as much of concern as the product itself, since each video box was the video's own advertisement.

All the tapes were variations on a theme: Faith in Catholic school plaids, kneeling between two priests. Faith in a classroom with a lunchbox on her desk, being taken to task by a teacher. Faith in a locker room with two other cheerleaders.

All star vehicles for Faith. All using her real name.

June said, "There's so little sexual freedom in the world. Like free-speech areas. You have a spot on campus where there's free speech allowed for an hour a day. One location, one hour of free speech. Free-sex areas become the realm of entrepreneurs. So for a price—"

Becket broke in. "A reasonable price."

June said, "You can have a certain amount of sexual freedom."

My head throbbed. Becket said, "Think about it. You pay a girl to suck your cock. That's against the law. But you pay a girl to suck your cock in front of a camera, that's just commerce. Your laws, asshole. I didn't make them up."

June plucked Faith's file from a drawer. Faith made these three videos, all in the last eight months at fifteen hundred apiece, which seemed a little chintzy and I said so. They paid her for the last two at once, two months before.

"Why didn't she make more of them?" I asked.

They looked at each other. June looked down. "I don't think she liked it."

The last item in the file was a photocopy of her DPS ID, with the fake birth date. I fished the real one out of my pocket and handed it to Becket. He compared the ID to the photo, then leaned back. "We had no way of knowing this." He handed the documents to June.

She looked them over, then said, "What do you want?"

I held up the videos. "Who orders these?"

"Everyone. Stores. Mail order."

"I want to know who bought all three Faith videos. Names and addresses."

Becket said, "You can't do that. That's private." He looked to June, but she shook her head. He shifted. "Give us a few hours."

I headed out, and June followed me to the door, opening it for me. By then a few people had looked up from their desks, all early twenties, well dressed and hip.

I said, "Listen, I'm not such a bad guy. Someone killed Faith Copeland and I'm trying to find out who."

Her eyes seemed to sparkle again, but not with warmth. "Bloody fascist! You threatened us. Now you're warming up? Ooh, I c'n hardly wait to fuck you."

20.
ⅢⅢⅢ

I pulled in to the municipal parking lot by APD and considered a new area of organized crime inching into Texas. Maybe.

I considered Faith Copeland at sixteen, breaking into the exciting, fast-paced world of adult video. Most adults don't understand money that well; it'd be even harder for a kid. Kids are desperate, maybe on the street, and somebody makes an offer. They discover their potential, as if no one ever did this before. A sixteen-year-old girl realizes she has built-in money.

In the squad room, I saw a message from Torbett. I went down to Internal Affairs and found him in his office. He let me in and closed the door.

I envied his promotion but not his job. People in Internal Affairs didn't make friends on the force, and, being black, he didn't have too many friends there to start with. Next to one of the assistant chiefs, Torbett was the department's highest-ranking African American. And the assistant chief was hired from outside so he'd never really been part of the department. He was also on the Fifth Floor, which made him untouchable.

Torbett was not untouchable. He looked like he'd aged ten years in the four since his back injury, and he'd never looked that happy to begin with. His face was tense and haggard, and his hair had gone an ever-lightening gray. He was also, in a way, one of the best friends I'd had in the department. I put aside that he didn't like me.

Torbett sat behind his desk. Neither of us ignored the authority that went with it. I didn't hold it against him.

"I need a favor," he began, and it wasn't his kind of opening. I nodded. He said, "You had a conversation with Sergeant Czerniak yesterday morning on the first floor by the elevator bank."

My jaw dropped so hard I could hear it. Torbett had been in Internal Affairs for two days, and already he had eyes and ears everywhere.

He said, "I need to know the specifics of that conversation."

By then I managed to close my mouth, swallow and find some words. "Why don't you just ask whoever was listening in?"

He rubbed his eyebrows. "No one was listening, Reles. Czerniak came in to tell me what you talked about. He was acting on your advice."

"Great."

"And when he came back for a formal statement, he got laryngitis."

"Someone got to him."

Torbett nodded his head down and didn't quite raise it. He was learning how to answer questions without answering them. "So I need you on record telling me what Czerniak told you."

"Why are you leaning on me? Why not Czerniak?"

"Czerniak will lie, and you won't."

"You'll get me killed."

He stood up tall. I knew it hurt. "I need you to step into the other room with me. And I need you under oath."

He opened the door. I jumped up and pushed it shut.

"What are you gonna get from this?" I was close enough to his face to whisper. "You know who runs the department. No one wants this shit on paper. Who do you think you work for?"

He breathed in deep through his nose. "God," he said. Then he opened the door. "Go inside."

In the interview room, there were two women, a reel-to-reel tape recorder, and a stenograph. We kicked around formalities until he got to the hot question.

"And what did Sergeant Czerniak say?"

"I don't recall."

Torbett said, "Try."

"You know," I said innocently, "it was the morning after the banquet, and I was so hungover, everything's a little hazy."

I promised Czerniak I would back him up. I wasn't going back on my promise, no matter what Czerniak did. And I wasn't going to get him killed.

Torbett said, "Did he tell you anything about another police officer?" I didn't answer.

Torbett tried again, louder. "Question: Did Sergeant Czerniak or did he not tell you anything about Lieutenant Clay?"

I said, "Clay? Terrific guy. I was at his daughter's confirmation."

I hated doing this to Torbett. But he was committed to his job, and I was protecting my neck. I couldn't violate the police code of silence or, worse, mention the Family, with tape rolling. Not if I wanted to live.

Torbett was fuming but he kept a tight lid on it. "Reles, I understand why you're doing this. But the less attention on this interview, the better." He upped his volume again. "I *will* arrest you if I have to, which will draw more attention to the interview and the information you may be protecting." I looked into his eyes. He was willing to hold my life over me. I had one less friend on the department.

He went on. "How far are you willing to go to cover up Clay's felony?"

I thought hard. Speak now and risk a face-off with the most corrupt circle of cops since Prohibition. Or stall and face the same interview later, with a bigger audience.

Finally I said, "Czerniak asked me about a hypothetical situation where an officer sees another officer consort with a felon."

Torbett said, "What do you mean, *consort?*"

21.
|||||

Mora made copies of Mrs. Ortiz's snapshot of Rolo, got some to the patrols heading out on the evening shift, made it back to the squad room, flipped through her phone numbers and dialed.

"*Vivian Ruggleman.*"

Still in her small office, answering her own phone. The fate of that rare breed, the honest lawyer.

Mora said, "Chase any good ambulances lately?"

Vivian's laugh barreled out, warmth from way back. They'd been in criminal justice classes at UT together, two tough broads in a boys' club.

Mora said, "I have a hot client for you."

"*Don't tease me.*"

"Arrested in the Salina Street incident, wrongly. They set the bail at fifty thousand. She couldn't raise it, and she's sitting in jail till the trial. They gave her an attorney and he's not worth a shit."

"*Sabotage?*"

Mora said, "I think they're stalling. They're trying to turn around the department's reputation before the trial."

"*My dance card's a little full,*" Vivian said. Mora could tell she was probably reading two files and talking on the other phone at the same time. And she couldn't blame the woman for not being up to the challenge.

"Prioritize it and you'll be a civil rights hero."

Viv said, "*If they're setting her up to stay in jail, how am I supposed to get her out?*"

Mora thought it over, considered an impossible goal. "The department has all the paperwork: arrest reports, medical examinations, testimonies, enough conflicting details to prove the patrols were lying. Everybody knows this because Internal Affairs interviewed everybody. They're sitting on it."

"*Then how do I get it?*"

Mora braced herself. "I'll get it."

⁙

On the way into Internal Affairs, Mora bumped into Reles and two stenographers. She nodded at him and kept going. It would have been better not to be seen there at all. But Reles was sweet on her. He wouldn't be a problem, unless that sweetness turned sour all of a sudden, the way those things always did. As if she didn't already have her hands full.

The secretary's desk was empty, the secretary tossed out or reassigned with the shakeup that put Torbett in charge of a division he'd never worked in. Mora knocked on his door and introduced herself. Please be seated. Torbett looked beat.

She said, "I have a question about the Salina Street incident."

"I haven't been over the files yet."

"A woman, Carla Ortiz. You IA guys been interviewing people since the day of the incident, and she's still in jail on bogus charges with a court-appointed lawyer who can't help her or doesn't care. Her son ran away from a foster home. What I need you to do is release the relevant files to Mrs. Ortiz's new attorney and get the charges against her dropped."

"I'll look into it."

She said, "She was throwing a fucking kids' party. She's been in jail for *two months*."

Torbett said, "I'll look into it," with only a little more irritation. She'd faced worse.

"I have a theory," she said. "Mrs. Ortiz is an embarrassment to the department. The Fifth Floor is leaning on you to sit on the Salina Street files until the smoke blows over. You could release her today if you want to, but instead you're going keep her in jail, to protect the department's reputation."

In Torbett's silence it occurred to her what a risk she'd taken, by mouthing off to the head of IA.

But the pained look on Torbett's face was giving way to a very subtle smile. Not a leer. It was a soft glimmer, mostly in his eyes. It looked something like respect.

He said, "You find the boy. I'll take care of Mrs. Ortiz."

"When?"

He said, "Do you trust me?"

She said, "No."

He smiled again as he shuffled through some files on his desk. "Good."

Mora drove into El Barrio and tried the neighbors and friends Mrs. Ortiz had told her about. She greeted them in Spanish and told them Rolo was missing. They seemed to recoil from her. She tried to impress on them that he wasn't in trouble, that he was missing and his mother was worried. They hadn't seen him. Yes, they would call if they did.

When she was done with those, she knocked on doors all up and down the block.

"No, I didn't know her. Try across the street."

"No, I haven't seen him."

Finally she gave up on the street and headed off to the home of Rolo's uncle.

In situations like this, a child was always sent to the home of the nearest relative. Mora wondered why Rolo hadn't been sent to stay with his uncle. Until she got to the door.

A rotting wooden house stood near East Seventh, the screen door off the hinges and laid out on the overgrown grass. Mora knocked, and the door opened suddenly, revealing a darkened living room. Two couches, a man sprawled on each. Beer cans. Clouds of marijuana smoke. A tall, handsome, muscular Latino in tight jeans and a sleeveless undershirt, wavy hair and a mustache, cannabis-red eyes, glared at her. She disarmed him with her warmest smile.

"Are you Rolo's uncle?"

He answered in English. "Your Spanish stinks."

She forced a giggle. Girl shit. "I know."

He looked into the house and stepped out into the daylight, closing the door behind him. "You with Social Services?"

She nodded halfway.

"What did he do?"

"He was in a foster home, and he ran away. We thought he might come here."

"No place for a kid."

She didn't argue. "Visit your sister lately?"

He winked. "I try to stay away from jail. How do you like that? I'm the bad one, and she's in jail." He laughed. Mora tried to join him.

She asked, "You know where Rolo might have gone?"

"He's a man. He can take care of himself."

Mora let go of her smile. "Sure," she said, "what could happen to a thirteen-year-old boy alone on the street?"

Mora realized what she'd said. Now she had to find Rolo, fast. Not just before he got killed but before he got absorbed into the fabric of the street. And that could happen in a night. One long, bad night.

"Don't worry about him," Uncle Stud said. "He'll be fine."

And with that he tested the waters by putting his hand on her shoulder. She grabbed it with both her hands and twisted it hard toward his forearm, pinching the nerve as the man's knees buckled.

"Ah! What are you doing?"

She growled. "Did I *say* you could touch me?!"

22.
|||||

Back in the squad room, I called the Department of Public Safety to see how the DNA tests were coming, looked over my notes on Faith—interviews, connections, ideas—and realized I was stuck. I'd been on Family Violence for five years, comparing he saids and she saids. Now I was wondering if I still had it to be a real detective. I called a few of Faith's phone numbers again with the added insight that she was running around appearing in porn movies and paying her own bills, all at the age of sixteen. I had a notion of asking more questions of her stage mother, but I figured, considering her drinking habits, I'd have to get her earlier in the day. It was nearly 5:00 P.M. Mora stuck her head in the office door, spotted me, looked to see if anyone was paying attention and motioned me to follow her.

In the hall she handed me a splotchy copy of a photo, a boy with curly black hair and dark eyes.

"Rolando Ortiz," she said. She gave me his sad story, ending with, "Help me find him?"

Mora needed an extra hand and Marks sure wasn't giving it to her. On the personal front, I'd guessed by now that even if Mora were single, I still wouldn't float her boat. I also guessed that if I weren't saddled with Jessica, every other woman in the world wouldn't look so good to me. I'd been single for long periods without being on the prowl all the time, like I was now. Life with Jessica made me desperate.

And since my work on Faith's case was in about the same shape as my personal life, I figured I could spare a few hours away from showing Faith's snapshot around, and instead show the boy's. It was simple work and would ward off my feeling stupid. I took the photos and headed out.

I started at the day-labor market, the corner of Seventh Street at

I-35. No one blinked at the sight of a cop asking around about a missing kid. The streets were full of missing kids and their ghosts. Just west of the interstate around Sixth Street were the low-end labor markets, temp agencies for the homeless. Also low-end lawyers and bail bondsmen. A club I would come back to in the evening had been called Planetarium and later Sanitarium and finally, acknowledging that its clientele consisted largely of underage kids, Curfew. I hit the head shops on Sixth Street, video-game parlors, anyplace a kid might wander into. By sunset I figured I'd go home and relax, when I remembered that Jessica would be there. Instead I radioed Dispatch. I left them a detailed message to relay to Mora, where I'd been with Rolo's picture and who I'd seen. They gave me a message from the video producers.

I pulled over to a pay phone, dialed their number and asked for June, the British woman with the good visuals.

"The third vid just came out, and we got advance orders. She's popular because she was a TV star. How the mighty hath fallen and all that. Anyway, I have a hundred names, people who bought all three of her videos."

I said, "How many in Texas?"

"Twenty, maybe."

"How many in central Texas?"

"None." She offered to send the list to HQ. *"Something else. People think she did the vids because she wanted to be famous again."* Silence.

I said, "What do you think?"

She said, *"I think she needed the money. And she needed it fast."*

I thought about that as I headed over to the Drag, the strip of stores and restaurants running along the western barrier of the university. I questioned the storekeepers about Rolo. On the open mall, I talked to the sellers of painted T-shirts and handmade jewelry. A dreadlocked white kid with a flute and a cat shook his head and asked me for money. There were other runaways who someone might have been looking for, if anyone wanted to find them.

"Seen this kid?"

"No."

"He's thirteen. He's out on his own."

A dark-haired white girl in baggy army fatigues tattered at the cuffs looked again at the photo and said, "He'll get by."

"What does that mean?"

She shrugged. "He's cute."

I'd spent eighteen years working on the streets, but I wasn't part of the streets. It took me a minute to get that she meant Rolo was cute enough to sell his body. I looked at her and her white friends, other minors living by their wits. They looked like runaway middle-class kids, living this life as a semester project. I was pretty sure at least some of them were doing it for the adventure; others were getting away from parents who were no better than the johns they'd meet on the street. Faith Copeland started out as a middle-class kid, too. As much as street life meant grubbing for change or stealing, it also meant getting picked up, which opened the door to getting beaten, killed or infected with AIDS. And then why they'd hit the streets in the first place—adventure or escape—wouldn't matter.

The woman at the video company said Faith needed money fast. I had to find out why.

23.
||||||

When I got home, Jessica greeted me with, "I've been home alone all day!" like it was my fault.

Get a job, I thought, and you won't be home all day. I was too tired to coddle her.

"What's this?" she said, with the same accusing tone.

It was a photograph, square with a white border. Printed in the border was the indicator "AUG 63."

"I found it behind the drawers of the dresser."

"Were you cleaning?" I said absently.

"What does that mean?"

"When people find things behind the dresser, it usually means they were cleaning."

She stormed out of the room and I watched myself stand in place. Normally I would chase her, fighting down my rising bile and saying, "Sweetie, baby, it's okay. . . ." I was going through a shift and it was happening on its own.

The photo showed, in 1960s lurid color, a thirtyish man holding a five-year-old girl. The man had just begun to lose his hair. He wore a white tennis shirt and green pants. The girl, who shared about half his facial features, wore a red patterned sunsuit, her brown hair in a short Dutch-boy haircut, courtesy of Mama. Her eyes were deep blue but with a subtle Asian turn at the corners.

It didn't take much to figure that the daughter in the picture was Rachel.

Rachel had lived with me in that house for over two years. So when she packed and left suddenly, it wasn't a surprise that she would leave some things behind. The most obvious were a few of her spring jackets and a formal dress I'd never given her an occasion to wear. I parted with these as soon as I could, reminding myself at the end of a very brief mourning period that she hadn't died but ditched me. The jackets and dresses went to Goodwill. The abandoned panties and hose and one satin teddy went, with a little more effort, to the trash.

But the photo was a rarity. I had very few photos of her. We'd never taken any. And I wasn't letting go of this one. I slipped it into my billfold.

I pulled some hot dogs, whole wheat bread and a beer from the fridge. I boiled three hot dogs, wrapped them in the bread and laid my notes on the table. Jessica stood in the kitchen archway.

"What about me?"

I talked as I chewed. "There's more in the fridge."

"I don't eat hot dogs."

"Then get a job and buy your own food."

Boom.

She said, "You hate me."

I dropped the food. "What are you gonna do? Not fuck me? Be less fun? *Why don't you leave?*"

She whimpered to the sky. "I can't *afford* to!"

"That's it? That's the only reason?"

"Yes!"

I said, "So if you had money, you'd leave me."

"Yes!"

"So you're not here because you like me. You're here because you're broke."

"Yes!" she cried.

I got up and wrote her a check for a thousand dollars. She stared at it for a count of three. Then she went into the bedroom and made a phone call. Half an hour later, a tricolored VW Bug with battered fenders pulled up in front of the house. Jessica brought out her cocktail dresses on hangers and drove away with them. I watched her drive off, feeling a surprising jolt. There was nothing good left about having her in my life, no loss in seeing her leave. But a breakup is a breakup and draws attention to itself.

I drank the cold hot dogs down with the warm beer as I went over Faith's case.

Child star but no childhood. Washed out at ten. Struggled. Back to Texas. Emancipated at sixteen from her alcoholic stage mother. Porn. She hated it. People bought the stuff, though she was no great beauty. Get to see Baby Faith naked, compromised, degraded. Enjoy the downfall of a star.

Among those fans maybe a stalker. Why not? Only eight years since the peak of her stardom. Maybe he waited. Maybe.

Raped, bath, possibly intended to destroy evidence. No prints.

The autopsy: An overdose. A broken thumb. Why?

June at Red Rose Raw said Faith needed money, fast.

My father was a muscleman for the mob back in Elmira, New York, after they'd finished with him as a boxer. He hated the work and hated himself for doing it. But cracking thumbs was a cliché, almost a joke, so much that most people didn't believe it really happened. Until they missed a payment.

Loan sharks in sweet little Austin? Why not? We had porn producers. We were growing.

Maybe Faith borrowed the money in a pinch and built up a debt. She did the videos to pay it off. Maybe the money went straight to the loan shark and it still wasn't enough.

I picked up the phone and called HQ, had them hook me up with Vice on the odds someone would still be around. It rang five times.

"*Vice, Edwards.*"

"This is Reles from Homicide. I wonder if you can tip me about loan sharks operating in town."

"*Oh, uh, hey there, Reles. Been hearin' lots about you. Big cheers on the transfer.*"

He was playing with me. I said, "Thanks."

"*Yeah, uh, don't know what to tell you about the sharks. Maybe we got 'em. Say, why don't you give us a call on Monday and we'll get it all straightened out.*"

I thanked him and hung up. I tried Organized Crime and got the same response. I'd spoken to Internal Affairs three hours before, reluctantly, and now I was a leper.

The phone rang again before it got cold.

"Reles? This is Kelly from Public Information."

Kelly was the one who stalled dropping the bomb of Faith's rape/murder on the press. I asked what was up.

"The story leaked," he said. *"I'm playing it down. But figure something on the news tonight."*

A big news story put me at a disadvantage. I had to move fast if I wanted to stay a jump ahead of the press. I'd have to find the loan shark, if there was one, on my own. Even in booming Austin, the underground was still small enough for people to know what other people were up to. But I'd shown my face in enough dives and back alleys over my nearly two decades as a cop that people knew who I was. Some had known me for years. There were whores and junkies I'd watched grow up.

My supply of allies was limited. I couldn't send Jake out, or Torbett. I called HQ for Mora and didn't find her. I had Dispatch try her at home and in her car. We figured she was out canvassing for her kid. I could grab a patrol with the Street Response Unit and send him out in plainclothes. But to do that I'd have to get permission from his superiors, and my name wasn't worth much at the department. I had to send someone else, but who?

I was washing down the last of the hot dogs with the last of the beer when the name came to me.

24.
︙

Rolo Ortiz wiped his sleeve across his nose as the sky darkened and he headed past a shopping center and a tire store.

It was warm out, even hot. But it had been misting all last night and he couldn't shake the chill from his bones. The jacket the Leitches gave him wasn't much more than a shirt. His mother would have run him a hot bath and made soup.

He ran when he left the house, ran hard as he could. "Pull, Ortiz, pull!" his gym teacher yelled during sprints. He thought about Joyce, dancing around. Then on the floor and vomiting blood. Pull, Ortiz. He imagined Mr. Leitch running after him. The man would catch him and kill him. His heart pumped in his throat. And he kept running even though he was sure there was no one behind him.

When he finally stopped running, he was wheezing. He couldn't get air. His legs hurt. He saw a school, stopped at the playground and took off his shoes, the Sunday shoes he'd been wearing when his mother was arrested. Blisters formed on his big toes and his heels. His white shirt sweated through, and he was feeling the cold. He didn't know where he was. His mother was in jail. He couldn't go to the police—they'd lock him up, too. Joyce was dead and it was his fault. He sat on the swing and cried.

His mother always told him stories about his father, an orphan at the same age, how he worked the fishing boats. How he took care of his own little sister.

Rolo looked around at the monkey bars and the slide. It was where children played. He wiped his face. He didn't belong here. He was a man.

He walked farther along the dark, unfamiliar road, fighting back tears. He ducked into the grass when a car passed. Where was he? He knew that the Leitches lived north. Which way was he going?

Rolo realized the police would be quicker to spot him on a main road. So he started on the side streets, zigzagging blindly into dead ends, backing up and trying again. It was the only way to get home without being seen. But at every turn he got more confused. At dawn he passed a bakery as a tall, skinny lady loaded sacks of bread into a truck. She sat at the wheel and caught his eye. He didn't say anything. She got out of the truck, opened the back, took out a bread two feet long, handed it to him, got in again and drove away. There was a sign pointing to Pflugerville. He'd been walking the wrong way.

By day it would be easier to blend in with the crowds, though people stared, a boy walking around alone in messed-up Sunday clothes, no book bag, in the middle of the day. A man asked him what he was doing out of school. He looked for sweaters on clotheslines, jackets that people had thrown away, and didn't find any. And he was still nowhere near home.

He felt hungry again. He looked at the shops and tried to see if there was a way he could steal something. But he kept thinking they'd call the police and he'd go to jail, too. At a gas station, he went to use the bathroom. His socks were soaked with blood. He washed his feet one by one in the sink, wrapped them in paper towels and pulled the socks on over the towels.

Things started to look familiar.

He had to get home. He could break in to his house when it got dark. They'd taken his key, but it was his house. He could eat and watch TV and sleep in his own bed and pray for his mother. Then what? He couldn't get a job. He couldn't go to school. They'd send him back to the Leitches or, worse, jail. Could he even chance going home?

He saw an old lady carrying two bags of groceries in her arms. She looked tired.

"Can I help you, lady?"

She smiled, then looked him up and down and her smile went away. She was wearing a raincoat even though it was sunny and warm. And carrying her stuff in paper bags. She raised her chin and said, "Yes, thank you," then handed him one of the bags.

"I can take both," he said. "I'm strong."

"I'm sure you are. This way," as she veered off onto a smaller street. He followed.

They turned up the path of her house, a little house like his, with no car in the driveway. She reached for her key and smiled at him. He wondered if she wanted to do stuff with him. Maybe she'd give him money. Inside, there were two dollars on the end table by the door and a stack of newspapers.

She pointed him into the kitchen and followed. "Just put it on the table. Aren't you the perfect gentleman?" They put the bags down. She stood between him and the door.

"Would you like something to eat? A banana?"

He was so hungry his stomach burned. But for some reason he shook his head. His hands started to shake.

"Are you sure?" she asked.

He saw her smile, saw the food around them and the clean house.

And without knowing why he shoved her down. Just for no reason he could think of, pushed her and watched her fall on the floor on her back.

She was screaming on the floor as he grabbed the two dollars from the end table and ran out of the house.

25.
||||||

Mora backtracked over the areas Reles covered, with no result. She circled the boy's school. She questioned teachers and classmates. She threatened the Leitches with charges of criminal neglect. She talked to neighbors and friends and the only relative in town. As evening set in, she hoped Rolo would turn up downtown, the center of gravity for the homeless and drifting. And she looked at the photo enough to memorize it.

Curly black hair, round dimpled cheeks, beaming dark eyes. Thirteen. A cutie. In three years he'd grow a foot taller. He'd be the tallest, darkest, handsomest boy in his class. If he lived.

Mora was in trouble. She was getting sucked in, sentiment-wise. Rolo was a kid on the street, another one in a town full of them. She shouldn't get drawn in. They'd say that was why women shouldn't be detectives. They don't have the balls.

But just to make sure, she alerted the patrols to keep an eye on Rolo's mother's house in case he turned up. It was the least she could do.

26.
|||||||

As I pulled up in front of Czerniak's house, he was crossing the lawn by the light of the porch lamp, keys in hand, and heading for his car. He'd dressed like he was delivering a dishwasher. I wasn't sure, but he looked like he was limping.

He saw me pull up and he froze. I got out to greet him, staking ground on his lawn.

"Got a date?" I asked.

"I'm married."

"Touching. You set me up."

He looked around like he wanted to run. There was no place to go where I wouldn't catch him. "You set *me* up," he said, a counter-attack. "You told me to go to Torbett. I never shoulda listened."

"What'd they do, Czerniak? Threaten you? Bribe you?" I could tell there was something wrong with his face, but it was too dark to tell what it was. "They fuck you up?"

He couldn't quite look me in the eye when he said, "You . . . you get off my lawn." He looked up and down the block. He was afraid to be seen with me.

Something fell into place. "I've been thinking about this," I said. "Torbett asked me all about you. Then I walked out of IA. There was no one in the hall when I left." That wasn't true. Mora saw me come out, but I wasn't going to tell him that. "And in a few hours, I can't walk past the elevators without getting dirty looks. I'm like the plague. Maybe the steno girls gossiped, but I don't think so. And I know Torbett didn't tell anyone I was there."

His breathing sped up. "I didn't say nothin'!"

That was it. "You . . . you told your boss. You had to throw the heat on someone, so you blamed me."

He bolted for the house, and I doubled his speed, tackling him to the grass. That was especially stupid, because he rolled over on top of me, knocking my wind out and threatening to flatten my rib cage. He tried to get me with his elbow. I freed my right arm and punched him with all my might in the groin. He howled, and the front door opened, little Mrs. Czerniak standing framed in domestic light. I rolled him off me and climbed to my feet, struggling for breath.

"Tell her," I said.

He winced. "It's fine, honey," he said. "Go inside."

She didn't like it but she closed the door.

I said, "I need you for something."

He stopped panting long enough to say, "Whut?!"

"You crossed your CO. Your days on Organized Crime are numbered. You're only alive because you gave them me." He didn't argue. "Do me a favor and I'll get you back on Homicide."

He thought about it for five heavy breaths. "How?"

"Jake Lund is my buddy. He's in with the Fifth Floor. He can do it."

He sat on his lawn, weighing options. It wouldn't help him to be associated with me. But he'd crossed the Family. He needed an ally.

27.
‖‖‖‖‖

On a humble twenty acres now sandwiched between the Barton Creek Country Club and the Lost Creek Country Club, stood the stately mansion of the Addisons, ruled over with an iron fist (Paul thought but never dared say) by the stately Suzanne Addison Wade.

As a swish waiter replaced his drink, Paul Wade tugged at his cummerbund and turned to survey the room. Central in the construction of the three-story palace, the second-floor ballroom was built to host debuts and cotillions of generations back. Its ceiling reached to the top of the house's third story, thirty feet up, with a skylight in the roof, a twenty-by-ten-foot rectangle over the center of the dance floor, to allow a view of the stars, a sense of the limitless potential of the children of the ruling class. Carved mahogany columns rose from floor to ceiling, crossing the railing that framed the third-floor balcony, its outer walls pasted with leather-bound books of earlier generations, designed so couples could retreat to the corners of the library to pitch woo or, more likely, plan the joining of family fortunes, then look down on the waltzers below. Four bartenders and twenty cater waiters kept the food and liquor moving. Tonight no one danced. That would be fun.

Two hundred of the most influential men in Texas and their wives (and Suzanne, arguably the most influential woman, with her dutiful husband, Paul), downed drinks and canapés and chatted busily. Present: Nearly the entire membership of AARO, the Austin Area Something Something, an affiliation of presidents and CEOs, leaders of organizations public and private—three local universities and their business schools, four local colleges (but not the community college), IBM, Dell, Motorola, 3M, Texas Instruments, all the major banks, a hundred law firms, fifty brokers, twenty prominent judges, senators and representatives both state and national, the entire board of the

Chamber of Commerce, energy companies including Austin Power and Light, Shell, Exxon, BP, Arbusto, Halliburton and Enron. And all the major developers, led by Lockheed, Freeport McMoRan and Orion. They'd gathered in Austin for a conference this weekend—Easter weekend, to Suzanne's chagrin—planning to set the tone for the new governor's tenure and for the future of the party, though they claimed no political affiliation. They were meeting on the holiday in hopes of avoiding attention and, more important, press, but they hadn't managed to escape Suzanne's radar. She considered them the secular core of the party and, as such, her misguided, if not deadly, opponents. She invited them all and they all showed.

The only absence was the governor himself. He wanted to come, but she insisted the gathering was too small and insignificant and an appearance would cheapen his act. Paul thought she didn't want his smirking presence to rob her of the spotlight.

Suzanne was born with the connections to be a kingmaker and the governor knew it. She had regular contact with him and with every other Texan worthy of note. She made deals that were none of Paul's business.

A cluster of tuxedos near him babbled about pardons and paroles. One of them, apparently, sat on the board. The two others were oilmen Paul knew from the old days.

"The bill would make parole hearings public," the board man said. "That includes all discussion. We're against it, of course. The governor agrees. We think it would make the hearings too emotional."

Paul, emboldened by his fresh bourbon, turned and joined the trio. "On the other hand," Paul said, "you couldn't settle anything in secret. People would know how you make your decisions, and why."

An awkward silence fell, followed by one of the oilmen saying, "What's your angle, Paul? Planning on going to prison anytime soon?"

The two oilmen laughed boisterously. The Pardons and Paroles man watched Paul.

"No," Paul said to the oilmen. "You know I'm not in the business anymore."

Another burst of laughter, and the three shifted away from him.

Paul spotted Suzanne across the floor. She had swept back into the room, probably after terrorizing the caterer. She wore a crimson garment that struck Paul as a hybrid dress and poncho. Strategic, of course. A formal occasion would have most everyone else in some conservative combination of black and white. And she'd adorned her neck with a display of Victorian diamonds.

He tuned in to the men talking behind him. Something about "can't get the bill through with that commie LG running the debate. . . ." and then, something about "who's gonna run the state?"

The response came back, "Forget about who runs the state. This is about who runs the governor."

"Look at that," a woman said under her breath. There was no one near her except Paul. The woman, petite and unimposing, wore a plain dress in a few shades of black. It rounded at her neck, showing off a simple silver pendant. Her chestnut hair wrapped neatly around her slender face, and she wore no make-up. Paul put her at early to mid-forties. She was looking at Suzanne, saying, "Can you believe her?"

"I try," he said.

The woman said, "One minute she's all smiles at Bill Oliver," the head of AARO, "the next she's stabbing someone in the back."

Paul tried to hide his delight. He knew that Suzanne made enemies. None had confided in him before.

She said, "I'm sorry. I shouldn't go on like that."

Paul said, "I like when people say what they think. I don't hear it much." She blushed. "Can I get you a drink?" he asked. She showed him her full glass but smiled. Then the woman looked to see if anyone was listening and leaned toward him. He could smell her understated perfume.

"She hates that things have to pass in votes. You can tell. She's already talking about the governor's reelection. But she thinks elections are just a nuisance."

"You may be right," Paul said. But there was a contradiction in Suzanne, something this wonderful, unaffected woman didn't see.

The other side of Suzanne was a petulant little girl. Because when Suzanne Addison Wade wasn't manipulating gubernatorial elections, making and breaking careers, bestriding the narrow world like a colossus, she was lost in frustration, ready to explode each time she didn't get her way. So when she wasn't being a god, she was being a child. An angry, ruthless, superhumanly powerful child.

Just then Paul realized he was talking to the woman who Suzanne had beaten in the fight for state party chairmanship. He felt himself grow lighter.

"You're active in the party yourself," he said.

"And in the church. And you don't see me talking about Jesus at the conventions. Wrapping herself in the Bible like that. You'd think He endorsed her."

Paul looked at her tiny hands on her drink, barely touched, and noticed the absence of a wedding ring. He gauged the chances of proposing before introducing himself.

She said, "Excuse me, I'm Kathy, Kathy Holtz," and put out her hand.

He held the hand in his, a small embrace, before saying, "I'm Paul."

"Paul," she said, trying the name out. Then something caught her eye, and he followed her trail of vision. It was Suzanne, waving and beckoning Paul to come to her.

He could feel the regret in his eyes as he said, "It was a pleasure meeting you, Kathy. I hope I see you again soon."

"What does she want with *you?*" said Kathy.

Paul said, "Damned if I know."

When he reached Suzanne, she made a show of taking his arm, then babbled with the wives as if he weren't there. He caught Kathy's eye across the room as she figured him out. He felt he'd betrayed her.

Suzanne turned to her mousey little secretary. "Remind me to tell the governor's office what a wonderful job that Kathy Holtz is doing."

Paul's heart sank as he realized his conversation with Kathy Holtz might have ended the lovely woman's career. "That's not necessary, Suzanne," he said.

"Of course it is."

One of the women said, "Is that . . . ?" She didn't finish the question.

The ladies turned to spot Suzanne's protégé, chatting with another cluster like their own, wealthy dowagers with gigolo money. He towered over them, broad and solid like a tree trunk, Roman nose, hair to his shoulders, emanating charisma and virility. He'd been with them for months. He was large and powerful and had come from nowhere. His purpose was unclear. But he was the only servant or staff member living in the house. And he knew more about Suzanne's business than Paul did.

"And what does he *do* for you?" a bluehair said to Suzanne, eyeing Paul with amusement the same way the oilmen had eyed him, a failure in the shadow of his wife, a cuckolded fool.

"Oh, he does everything. Fixes things before they're broken. He lives with us, one of the family."

"Isn't Paul good around the house?" They all giggled.

Suzanne said, "Paul?" as if the idea of Paul's usefulness had gone out with the Lindy Hop. "No. Paul can't do anything!"

Much laughter. Paul glued the smile to his face but felt it pinching.

Suzanne went on, breaking away from Paul and heading toward the larger young man, begging the question of what, indeed, the young man spent his time doing for Suzanne. "I don't know what I'd do without him," Suzanne declared. "Where would I be without Judah!"

28.
||||||

I waited with Jake Lund and a tech whose name I'd missed, parked at the dark end of Sixth Street near the overpass in a white commercial van with a couple of antennas that were supposed to be inconspicuous: anyone who saw us would have figured we were monitoring transmissions between China and Mars. I sat in the driver's seat wearing headphones and turning periodically to see what was going on behind me, while Jake and his buddy tinkered with the dials and tapes. Jake's face widened with the frenzy of a kid playing a video game as he tried to pick up static-filled, barely intelligible transmissions from my low-functioning agent, Sergeant Jeff Czerniak. Czerniak walked like he was avoiding unnecessary movement, and I'd noticed his eyebrows were mostly gone but I opted not to ask why. Because an earphone would have been more conspicuous than the wires and transmitter under his shirt and jacket, we could hear him but he couldn't hear us. This gave him a certain authority.

Jake managed to get a short list from Vice of bars with "heavy criminal activity" of a nonspecific variety. He made the point that loan sharks, like any predators, are most likely to hang out in places of shame. An accountant won't call the cops if he gets robbed in a whorehouse. So Czerniak headed off in his delivery uniform on a short tour of Austin's darker establishments, with us tagging along well behind.

After I'd talked to IA, my reputation in the department was such that there was no getting cooperation from Communications. But Jake was a loyal pal, and highly placed enough to take out the van and the tech that went with it.

It was a mild Thursday night, temperature in the sixties and clear, and the downtown foot traffic was brisk. Czerniak headed east.

Among the darkened buildings beyond the interstate, he walked into a particularly uninviting bar, the first on the list. Through the static we heard faint music and chatter as he ordered a gin and tonic. The glass landed on the bar before him. He tried twice to engage the bartender in conversation and failed. When he stepped outside, he said, *"Hookers,"* and kept walking.

This was his pattern for the next three bars working east, now on Seventh Street, which is busier than Sixth that far east. Here he stood out because of his size and color. He'd had a stiff drink in each bar, though, so by the time he got three blocks into East Austin, he was conspicuously toasted. One more dumb white guy, looking for a hot night on the east side.

I drove slowly, keeping as much distance as I could without falling out of the short range of the transmitter, and parked in the shadows just beyond the lot of a cocktail lounge as he walked in. Cool jazz on a jukebox and chatter and laughs and a slight hush as he entered and made his way to the bar. A few moments passed before I heard, *"What can I get you, my man?"*

"A gin and five grand."

The bartender laughed. *"One gin comin' up."* Then, later, *"What do you need five grand for?"*

"I'm six months behind on child support. My wife's gonna throw me in jail. So I took what I had, like eight hundred, and I got into this card game. You wouldn't believe it. Two pair, full house. I'm way ahead,

throw back a few drinks, before I know it I'm four grand in the hole and
they knocked my tooth out—look at this."

"Shit!"

"So I gotta come up with five grand if I wanna keep my kneecaps."

There was a silence, and the bartender ended it, saying, *"Damn,"*
and finally, *"Good luck."*

Five minutes passed, and the bartender came back. *"My man, I*
got a name for you, just a name and a place to ask for him."

Jake said, "Goddamn, he's good."

I didn't hear anything, then a rustle of paper and Czerniak leaving the bar. I saw him stagger out the front entrance. Without looking
toward the van, he showed a slip of white paper and said, *"Cost twenty*
bucks. Call me a cab, we're going to Eric's Billiards."

29.
||||||

Judah cruised up Bee Caves Road with the windows down and the
cool night air blowing through. It was nice. But it wasn't home.

He never felt at home anywhere, the way he had in the Gulf. He
was part of something, an invasion, a cause. What was more, he could
kill with impunity.

He had excelled in basic training. The first at assembly. The
strongest, fastest and cleanest. The soldier closest to God. Basic is designed to strip men of their individuality. Judah never had any individuality to begin with. He was glad to be in the machine.

But the war ended fast, and they sent him home. They offered
him a promotion if he would reenlist. But he couldn't just stay in the
army and sit around waiting for the next war.

Back to Texas with his transferable skills: munitions. He was a
trained killer. There was probably a great job for him with the

government, but all the agencies bounced him after the interview. An FBI recruiter smiled and told him he was *too* dedicated.

He headed north on MoPac and flipped on the radio. Kids' music.

He'd made a few false starts, finding a proper mission. But now he was established with Suzanne. His usefulness was that he could do anything—and he *would* do anything—with both religious and military efficiency. He had a purpose: supporting her and her work. He was making himself invaluable to her, attaching himself to her. And to her estate.

Music gave over to the news. *"Police report no progress in the murder of Faith Copeland. . . ."*

Faith Copeland. He'd heard the name before. Where?

He rolled off the exit at Fifth Street and headed east toward downtown.

Tonight all he needed was a plan to make the lieutenant governor more pliable.

Threats? Too easy to trace. Blackmail? Judah would have to find something on the LG, if there was something to find. That could take months. Unless . . .

He crossed Congress Avenue and headed into the thick of Fifth Street, the quiet shadow of hopping Sixth Street. Darkened stores. A few bars and clubs. Some restaurants. Yuppies, preppies. They made him seethe.

And as he got closer to the interstate, he noticed, in twos and threes, young people, teenage boys and girls. In tatters. Black eye makeup. Shredded baggy pants. Thin. Homeless. Desperate.

And he got an idea.

30.
|||||

Mora made her way into the dark, winding caverns of the club Curfew. She'd shown Rolo's photo at the door and been paid for it with a couple of professional shrugs. She promised she wouldn't bust them if they let her move around freely and didn't point her out. Twenty years older than the typical club kid, she circulated in the flashing lights and the pounding beat—an explosion of bright colors and hair gel—blinking and trying to focus. The dreamlike atmosphere lifted the restrictions of consciousness, financial prudence and sexual restraint. A thin boy and girl of about sixteen clinched on a zebra-striped sofa. Glassy-eyed white kids dressed like ghetto blacks exchanged money.

She showed Rolo's picture. Some of the kids looked at the snapshot, then her, and tried to determine the relationship between the two. No question: On the police force, she looked like a Latina and a woman. Here she read cop.

She'd put out a BOLO, Be On the Look Out for Rolando Ortiz, photo and description. Talked to a few conscientious patrols. Sent the photo to the TV stations. No guarantee they'd show it. And each minute he was on the street decreased the chances of his being found. She should have passed the case off to Missing Persons by now and got on with her own business. She shouldn't be forming a connection to a victim, or whatever he was.

By now he was like a brother to her. The little brother she'd dreamed of but never had. Fool, she thought. Idiot! She almost slapped her forehead. She shouldn't have let herself form a connection. Now it was too late.

Three club kids, two boys and a girl, hung on to a king-size promoter in his thirties, black leather jacket and sunglasses. They spotted her. She made a beeline for them and tried a new tack, yelling above the pounding speakers:

"Have you seen my son?"

31.
‖‖‖‖‖

We'd picked up Czerniak a block from the last bar and dropped him two blocks from Eric's Billiards on Airport Boulevard, making sure no one saw us. On the way Czerniak flipped through my notes and my stack of Rolo Ortiz snapshots.

"Who's this?" he asked.

"Missing kid." I gave him the specs.

"Mind if I look for him?"

"Knock yourself out," I said.

The parking lot by the billiard parlor outsized the typical lot at an eastside dive by five times, the pool-hall equivalent of a supermarket. Pink neon lights arced in deco curves. I watched through the glass walls as Czerniak made his tenuous drunken steps through the door, between the tables and over to the bar, and ordered another scotch. I would have suggested coffee.

The drink served, he said, *"Are you Carlo?"*

Silence. Then, *"Who are you?"*

Czerniak said, *"A guy at this club on East Seventh told me to talk to Carlo."* He told the five-grand story again.

Jake said, "It sounds less true than before."

The tech said, "Maybe he's the kind of guy who always needs a new story."

Jake said, "Must be rough on his wife."

In the shadows I thought I saw the bartender walk away, and a few minutes later a bulky white guy in a biker jacket sidled up next to Czerniak. *"Let's get a smoke,"* he said.

They hit the front door, and I slid down in my seat. I watched them live but heard them on the radio.

The biker guy said, *"You need five K."*

"Who told you that?" Czerniak asked.

"What?"

"No, I don't need five K," he said. *"I'm gonna give you five K."*

Jake said, "What?!"

The drinks were catching up with Czerniak, and he'd gone off script.

The loan shark, his sideburns cut in muttonchops, said, *"Why?"*

"A girl here in town. Used to be on TV. Her name is Faith Copeland. Heard of her?" He didn't answer. Czerniak went on. *"You deliver her to me, you get five grand."*

If Czerniak weren't so drunk, he might have known not to risk this. He might have asked me first about ad-libbing; and I might have told him that it was a toss-up whether anyone on the street, or everyone who watched TV, would know by now that Faith was walking with the angels.

"Why would I know her?" the shark asked.

"Maybe you don't."

Long silence. *"Let's say I don't know her, but suppose I know who does. What do I get?"*

"Work it out with him. You can split a five thousand-dollar finder's fee. But I don't pay anything till I get her."

"What do you want with her?"

Czerniak leaned toward him. *"What do you think?"*

The man disappeared to make some calls. In ten minutes they were in a cab headed west on Fifty-first Street, with Czerniak sweating in his shorts, unless he was too drunk to know the stakes.

"Cagey," Jake said.

"What is?"

"Stringing out Czerniak. You wouldn't get me out there."

Jake was right. I only thought about using Czerniak to solve a problem. I never considered that I might get him killed, just what I promised not to do.

We followed the cab at a generous distance, praying that the news of Faith's death hadn't reached the loan sharks yet and that Czerniak wasn't about to become a statistic.

The cab turned up the gravel alley behind Avenue B, and I parked on the street so they wouldn't see or hear us drive onto the gravel. I stepped out and peeked up the alley. The cab had dropped them and left, but I could see the biker with the muttonchops, Czerniak and a third man, a white guy in a baseball jacket and slacks, clean-shaven, dark hair, no distinguishing marks of any kind. He was the most typical guy I'd ever seen. He spooked me.

If anything was going to go wrong, it would happen at the moment Czerniak was supposed to hand over the money.

I stuck my head back into the van. "I'm not hearing anything," Jake said.

His buddy spun knobs. "He's gone."

"Okay," I said, checking my weapon. "Get ready."

"For what?" Jake asked.

"To move on them."

Jake's buddy looked like someone had pointed a shotgun at him. Jake grinned, pointing to him. "He's not a cop."

"Shit. All right, you are."

"Yeah, but—"

"You have a weapon?"

"Yeah, I have a—"

"Is it loaded?"

He puffed air out of his mouth like he was insulted by the question and took a small automatic from a waist holster. He was required to carry a gun on duty, and it passed the minimum qualification. "Of course it's loaded!" He checked the magazine.

"All right, fuck it. Just . . . just be ready."

By this time Czerniak's transmitter was completely dead and I had to go by what I saw. I left Jake in the van and slipped down the alley in the shadows. The three men talked. Then they headed single file toward where the wooden steps would lead up to Faith's home, Czerniak first, followed by Biker Guy and Baseball Jacket. I slipped up to the alley side of the building, drew my .38, steadied and swung around the corner.

Baseball Jacket was holding the barrel of an automatic against my skull.

32.
||||||

It was dark out, maybe past eight when Rolo finally saw the sign that said Salina Street. His feet throbbed and his legs were sore and his stomach groaned from hunger. His house was dark. He could see something posted on the little window in the front door but he was afraid to walk up and read it, for fear his neighbors would see him and call the cops. He ran to the back yard, found a big rock, wrapped it in his jacket and smashed his bedroom window. Then he reached in and flipped the lock, opened the window, laid his jacket over the ledge and climbed in.

He stepped over the broken glass and tried to flip on the light, but they'd cut off the electricity. He found the kitchen and tried to flip on the stove, but the gas was off, too. The water still ran. By light from outside the kitchen window, he found a candle and lit it, then pulled the shade. He looked in the fridge. Everything inside stank enough to make his eyes burn. He opened a can of peas and ate them cold. There was Cream of Wheat, but he couldn't boil it. Mold grew all over the bread.

The house was still set up for the Valentine's party, bridge table against the kitchen table with a paper tablecloth over them, chairs on both sides. Someone, maybe the other ladies at the party, had cleaned up and put what was left of the cake in the fridge, where it turned from pink to green. Rolo's mother's room stood as she left it, bedspread in place, Jesus on the wall, everything embroidered and nice. He heard a car outside and peeked through the curtains. It was a police car. His heart jumped. Hold still, they'll see the curtains move. Don't even breathe. The car slowed down in front of his house, then kept going. They were watching the house. He took the candle to his room and knelt next to the bed.

"Hail Mary, full of grace . . ." Something stopped him. This was the time to ask for help. Say something. Jesus, help me. He couldn't. It was all too hopeless. He felt the tears well up inside, and he began to cry, a gut-wrenching sob that shook him to his heels. He worried people would hear him, but there was no stopping. He'd never been so alone.

It could have been half an hour. When the crying finally stopped, he went to the bathroom, wiped his nose and showered. He clipped his finger- and toenails. His feet weren't so bad. It was the toes, mostly, and the heel. He wrapped his feet in clean gauze and put on clean socks. He brushed his teeth.

His father was an orphan, on the street. He had to be smart. Smart and tough. Be a man.

Rolo put on clean underwear and jeans and a polo shirt and his spring jacket, blue and padded but not too warm. He put on his good sneakers. He put two pairs of clean socks and underwear in the pockets, along with his toothbrush and toothpaste and a jackknife he wasn't supposed to have. He went through the house and found all the money he could. It amounted to twelve singles and about five dollars in change. He put the money in his wallet, took the last soda from the fridge, warm, and put it in his side pocket. And he thought about his father at the same age. He looked through the house again and climbed out his bedroom window.

He wanted to stay, at least for a night's sleep. He was tired, so tired that he was twitching. But the police had been by, and they'd be back. It wasn't his house anymore.

33.
‖‖‖‖‖

I stood on the gravel with the loan shark's automatic cooling my forehead. Both my hands gripped my .38, which was pointed in the direction of a neighbor's bedroom window.

Baseball Jacket held me at bay. Biker Guy, behind him, had Czerniak similarly compromised.

"Easy," I said. "Easy."

There are times when showing your badge solves your problem. And there are times when it will get you perforated. I looked into Baseball Jacket's cool blue eyes. He could hold a gun steady. He had no qualms about using it. I felt a rumbling sensation.

"Who sent you?" he said.

Never trust a guy not to shoot you. Even if you give him what he wants. Even if he's better off not shooting you. Sometimes he has the chance to kill someone and it's just too tempting to walk away.

The rumbling got stronger. There was no right answer to his question. Whatever hope I had dropped out of my shoes when I saw Czerniak's face wide with horror.

That's when it happened.

Suddenly the ground hummed. I saw a flash of white and heard a loud *cra-a-a-ckkk* as a shot fired and the staircase collapsed, Baseball

Jacket falling forward on me so that I managed to twist his arm backward and drop my weight on him, his face landing in the gravel and skidding before I saw what was happening.

Jake had raced around the block and up the alley from the other end, barreling into the wooden staircase and toppling it. Biker Guy fired blind. Czerniak threw his bulk onto Biker Guy and tackled him to the van's roof, then kneed him in the balls, took his gun and shoved him off the van. Biker landed hard on the gravel.

In the interrogation room at HQ, I had tapes rolling as I questioned the second loan shark, Baseball Jacket, now identified as Roger Barry. His face badly scraped and his hands bloody from the fall, Barry had refused medical attention and was shifting gears because I'd told him Faith was dead.

"You set me up," he said in low, even tones, his regular features twisted into a cruel smile. I was still buzzing from being held at gunpoint and from the moment of frenzied terror that followed. Barry was cuffed and cool as ice, and I couldn't help but think he had an advantage. I could guess what kind of effect his demeanor would have on a lonely sixteen-year-old girl.

He looked through the glass walls of the interrogation room at the uniforms standing guard and the tech operating the video camera. "He assaulted me. He's not allowed to do that."

"Did you kill her?"

"Kill who?" he sneered.

"How did you know her?"

"I didn't."

I'd seen this before, but not often. He was a sociopath. He could kill someone in one room and then pass a lie detector test in the next, swearing innocence. Because a lie detector works on anxiety, and you only have anxiety if you have trouble lying. Or if you have a conscience.

"Try again." I'd already questioned Biker Guy, and I was sure it was Barry who knew where Faith lived.

He looked around the room, considered various options and said, "Lawyer."

"In a minute."

He shook his head, quietly satisfied.

I stood. "Okay." I slapped the door and shouted to the uniforms. "Book him for homicide."

"Okay, I knew her."

"Did you lend her money?" Long pause. I said, "Fuck it. Kill the tape." The light on the video camera went off. "Tell you the truth, I don't even give a shit. You lent her money, you put the squeeze on her, you broke her thumb. She was sixteen. If you didn't kill her, you'll do." The uniform outside made to unlock the door.

He said, "Yes."

"Tape on. Yes what?"

"I lent her money. Two thousand."

"Percentage?"

"No, just a favor."

I stood again.

He said, "Five."

"Five percent?" He nodded. "Compounded how often?" No answer. I said, "Daily?"

He nodded.

"How much was she into you for?"

"Maybe ten thousand. I want my lawyer."

"Just a second. So that's why you broke her thumb."

Pause. Nod.

"When?"

"Last month."

"And she made movies. She must have given you some big payments." No answer. "When's the last time you saw her?"

"Two weeks."

"How much did she pay you?"

He thought a moment. "Two thousand."

It made sense. She'd been paid three thousand for the last two videos. She kept a little to live on. She hated doing them. She needed to do more.

"I blame the parents," he said.

"Yeah?"

"She was in trouble. She needed help. Where were the parents? Bad parenting, that's what this comes down to."

I told him I'd keep it in mind. "Anything else?"

He thought for a moment. "She asked how she was supposed to get the money. I told her to get a job." He smiled. "She didn't know what a job was."

By 11:00 P.M. or so, I had the two loan sharks moved to Central Booking. They were, technically, suspects, though if they'd known that Faith was murdered, they wouldn't have been so casual about stopping by her apartment. Still, Barry had the opportunity to kill her. He had hurt her, and there was nothing to say he couldn't lose his temper and kill her. He sure didn't have a conscience to stop him. I ordered DNA tests on both of them. I sent Czerniak home to his wife with a promise of favors and a pat on the back for his courage.

Faith Copeland grew up onstage, in talent shows and pageants, graduated to Hollywood as a little girl, peaked at seven or eight, floundered for years and came home to Texas. She moved out on her own at sixteen, distanced enough from both parents not to ask them for money, even in the face of a loan shark, three porn videos and an arrest for burglary. Barry was right. It didn't speak well for them as parents.

The squad room was abandoned at that hour but for a package on my desk, a mailed videotape from Faith's agent, one he forgot to give me when we met. I unwrapped it and popped it into the VCR and rummaged through the other desks for something to eat or drink. The coffeemaker was off, but there was some cold coffee in it and I poured myself a Styrofoam cup full, with nondairy creamer made of roughly the same ingredients as the plastic container it came in. I was taking my first sip when Mora walked in, dropped a small aluminum-foil-wrapped package on my desk and sat down in front of the TV, unwrapping a sandwich that looked to be made on an onion bagel. My snack proved to be a chicken fajita, white man's Mexican food.

The credits introduced Faith at age eight, cute and pretty at the same time, a combination she didn't maintain through puberty. Bouncy music, a prime-time show for kids. Faith turning palms up to the camera giving an "oops!" look, pompous adults furiously impotent.

We watched the first ten minutes, fast-forwarded into the next episode and watched a little of that. The setup featured her as the precocious live-in niece of two incompatible brothers, a womanizer and a schoolteacher. The show oozed incest dynamic and pedophilia, Little Faith perpetually manipulating and flirting with her stud uncle, himself a beefed-up ex–child star, while the prissy schoolteacher uncle clucked disapproval.

"What's up with *your* kid?" I asked between bites of chicken and swigs of cold coffee.

"Nothing," she said. "I can't find him. I put out reports. I sent it out on the wire. I'm getting heat from Marks. I can't stay on it. He's a missing kid. I'll turn it over to Missing Persons in the morning and sign off, go on to the next thing."

That hung in the air. She didn't want to sign off. She wanted to save the kid, an impossible goal. They discourage idealism in cops. People who join the force hoping to do good are the first to get burned out, jaded and in trouble. Mora seemed like she'd learned to negotiate that. But the kid got stuck in her head.

She looked in my open desk drawers and started rummaging though the tapes, then pulled out the more recent ones, the adult tapes. I saw her flip through the covers. "Look familiar?" she asked.

I said, "I've never seen the films." If she asked, I was ready to say I'd never seen pornography before and that I didn't exactly know what it was.

"Look," she said, holding up the tape box. I saw it. The outfits, the situations with men standing over her in her school clothes or while she sat at a desk with her eyes at zipper level.

I said, "They're all ripping off the TV show."

"One way of looking at it." She munched on the bagel. "Or the show was a setup. Raunchy, soft-core porn, like they just never got around to taking their clothes off."

I looked at the TV screen. I'd just missed a gag. There was a moment between Faith and the uncle, bare-chested and in a towel, while Faith smiled at him knowingly. The laugh track was going nuts.

Mora popped out the video of the TV show and popped in one of the pornos.

I said, "Are you sure you want to . . . ?"

She was sure. She fast-forwarded through the credits, which consisted of Faith being caught in various compromising positions, while the camera zoomed in on her "oops!" face. If I hadn't been looking for it, I wouldn't have noticed that her right thumb was already broken.

The film started on her walking down a school hallway in a Catholic school uniform and opening her locker.

"She's acting like a little girl," Mora said.

"That's what they pay her for." My heart was starting to jump at the impending scenes and the fact that I was watching them with Mora. "Hey, why aren't you with your . . . um, friend tonight?"

She glared at me. "Why aren't you at home?"

I thought, Because I'd rather be here watching porn with you, that's why. She popped out the video and plugged in Faith's audition tape again, the monologue. "Watch this," she said. At the end of the monologue, Faith looked at the camera and sort of giggled and did a joking curtsy at the same time. Mora said, "Little-kid shit. Like a little girl flirting."

"Little girls don't flirt."

"Little girls flirt like crazy. The problem comes when grown-ups take them up on it." She took another bite of bagel.

I watched the screen.

Mora was coughing and looking for something to drink. With nothing else, I handed her my coffee. She swigged and said something in Spanish close to "fucking onions."

I said, in my textbook Spanish, *"You got something against my people's food?"*

Her face lit up. I thought she liked it that I understood her well enough to respond. She kept testing me. *"Your people make me thirsty."*

"Give us a chance," I said. *"We'll make you tired."*

I didn't know where the comment came from, raunchy and convoluted, and we both gaped at it.

34.
||||||

It was closing on midnight when Cate Mora and I left the squad room and took off in our separate directions. There was someplace she needed to go. I headed north on the upper level of I-35, windows open, cool breeze whistling through my Caprice, thinking about her.

Mora was one of a small but growing class of female detectives. I considered that, like Torbett, she had to be smarter and better than most to gain that rank against prejudices of race and, in her case, gender. And she had a nonspecific romantic attachment that I sensed, or hoped, wasn't doing her any good.

I slowed down to forty, causing what struck me as a heavy flow of cars for a weeknight, to beep and pass me. The town's traffic had increased over the years. I was stalling, putting off my arrival at a house that had seemed less like home with each day of Jessica's residence there. I wasn't looking forward to seeing what her absence did.

I peeled off at Thirty-eighth Street.

I'd had plenty of sexless stretches over the years before Rachel and I hooked up and in the four years after she left. My libido seemed to be settling down with time, and I could roll with the losses, the things I managed to do without: love, friendship, laughter. I lived a simple life. Work, go home, work, go home.

But Jessica made it hurt. Jessica moved in and stayed and filled the place once occupied by someone I'd loved, who I figured loved me. Jessica showed me how lonely and miserable I was. That she was gone should have been a relief. But it just showed me how empty my life had become.

I saw the house on my left and kept going.

Soon I was cutting across Thirty-eighth past Duval and my old neighborhood and turning right on Guadalupe, by the state hospital. I followed Guadalupe north, past Forty-fifth Street, where it became narrow, past the intramural fields and the Department of Public Safety, with the shame creeping up on me and the sense that someone must be watching, some deity, some authority, some camera, as I was pulled between the wise decision to turn around and go home before I landed myself on the front page of the *Statesman* and the burning need for both sex and love. But I knew it wasn't love. I didn't care.

Whatever it was, I sure wasn't getting it at home. I hadn't had it at home for years. Four years.

And I pulled up in front of Vita's house.

|||||||||||||||||||

Inside her apartment Cate Mora checked the locks, checked the windows, looked in the closet and under the bed. Only then did she put her gun and holster on the nightstand and go to pour herself a drink.

In the living room, she slouched on a low chair, feet up on the coffee table, sipped scotch and closed her eyes. She was saving the good scotch for a special occasion. The last such event was making sergeant. By the look of things, there wouldn't be another promotion for a long time. Affirmative action meant moving women and minorities into middle management, making them office managers and heads of information technology and sergeants. The whole business confused her mother. Her father, who had wanted a son anyway, would have been proud.

With one reservation.

Mora checked the clock.

She'd always kept her love life a secret, a series of secrets. Both parents would have disapproved. And she started with two strikes at work, Latin and female. She couldn't take a third.

The doorbell rang, more or less on schedule. She took another sip to brace herself. What she didn't do was jump up and brush her teeth. What she didn't do was check herself in the mirror. She'd be herself.

And if you don't like that, she thought, you can go home to your family.

|||||||||||||||||||

Vita opened the door a few inches. She wore an oversize T-shirt and no makeup. The living room, I noticed this time, could have been anybody's. There was nothing erotic about the matching couch and chairs or the light blue carpet or the TV or the pictures on the wall. She'd bought everything new, that much was clear. And she bought it with the idea of having a regular home, not of moving her business to the suburbs.

She didn't say anything, so I said, "It's late, I know."

She sniffed and turned to the side. Then she said, "I'm not really in the business anymore."

I stepped back from the door. She looked scared, checking over my shoulder to see if the neighbors were spying on her. I realized we must have made a sight in the darkness, silhouetted in the light of her doorway. Lonely cop asks retired hooker for comfort.

She said, "No, wait. It's just . . . For the money you could have the prettiest woman in town."

"You're the prettiest."

She rolled her eyes. "Come on," she said.

I thought about the money, how fast I'd go through my savings at that rate and what else I could get for it.

"Look," I said. "You've known me since the old days. I know you don't love me."

"I don't hate you," she said.

I thought about it. "Long time since a woman's told me that."

|||||||||||||||||||

Rolo followed Third Street to I-35 and walked underneath. Homeless people lay on the sloped concrete under the overpass. He walked up the frontage to Fourth Street, then over the creek and up Sabine, when he realized he didn't have anyplace to go. At Fifth Street he saw some dark buildings. One looked like it was a bar, maybe, but there were only two cars outside. He sat on its porch and popped open his soda.

He was sipping the warm Coke when another kid, maybe fifteen or sixteen, walked up to him and said, "Hey."

"Hey."

"What are you doing here?"

Rolo braced himself for a fight. "Nothing."

The kid sat next to him. He was wearing Levi's and a jean jacket. He had bad breath and rotten teeth and pimples, but he didn't seem drunk or crazy. He put out his hand. "I'm Vic."

Rolo shook. "Rolo."

"What kind of name is that?" Rolo shrugged. Vic said, "Wanna get high?"

Rolo thought about his mother and every warning she ever gave him. Strangers, drugs, cars. He'd paid attention and never wavered.

And look what happened. His mother was in jail. Joyce died, and he ran away from a foster home. The police were looking for him. And now he couldn't go home. Did he wanna get high?

"Sure."

They were behind the building finishing off Vic's joint and Rolo's soda. Rolo's fingers buzzed, and something vibrated from his throat down to his stomach and back, and everything kept stopping and jumping ahead in time, in little flashes like a strobe light. The Coke was gone and he was thirsty when Vic said, "You wanna go inside?"

"I guess."

They went in the back door, and Vic said, "I'll get us a drink," and Rolo was lost in the lights and the flashing. Music blasted from somewhere. People were shooting pool, and he couldn't find anyplace to sit. Someone said, "First time?" and he didn't want them to think he hadn't been high before, so he said, "No," and they were asking him how old he was and where he went to school, and Rolo was so thirsty his mouth was like paste when Vic finally came back with a drink, and he swigged and swished it around in his mouth and felt better. And then someone came in from the front and said, "What are you trying to do, get me arrested?" and Rolo worried about the drugs, and they were out on the street again.

He wasn't sure how far they walked or for how long. Vic stopped to talk to someone, and at first Rolo was sad that the boy was ditching him, and then he worried it was a cop, and he ran on ahead and came to a bodega, and Rolo thought how lucky it was that he had money. He went to the penny candy and grabbed two of everything. Then he thought he'd have to save some money, it would have to last, so he put back everything but two packets of Smarties. He bought two things of beef jerky and quart of juice and a fruit pie, paid with all his change and sat outside eating the jerky and the pie and drinking the juice and feeling fine, and this car pulled up and this man came over and looked at him and asked if he loved Jesus and Rolo said he did and the man said he knew a safe place where Christian kids could go when they were in trouble but it was too far to walk to. Then the man asked if Rolo wanted fifty dollars and he said yes and the man got back in his car and opened the other door for Rolo to get in and Rolo's chest was buzzing and the world was flickering forward and back in time and the car door was open and it seemed like a very bad idea but his feet moved like they were someone else's and he got in the car anyway.

||||||||||||||||||

I threw my jacket and shirt over a chair in Vita's bedroom and kicked off my shoes and pulled off my slacks and wrapped my arms around Vita in her T-shirt. She'd softened and widened over the years, but she felt fine. She waited for me to finish the embrace, then pulled the T-shirt over her head and lay down. I climbed into bed and curled up to her, wrapping my arms around her and pulling her close. Finally she said, "Don't you want to fuck?"

"Um, sure."

"Well?"

"I just . . . I don't know."

She waited. "You don't want to."

"No, I do, I just wanna . . . lay here for a while."

She sighed, and I realized she didn't get it. Why would two people just want to lie in bed together?

||||||||||||||||||

Rolo's throat felt funny, rippling up from his stomach like he was going to vomit, but he didn't feel nauseated. A picture of Jesus dangled from the rearview mirror. His mother would like it. But it felt so strange, to be alone in the world, to meet people and do drugs and get into cars. Like he was watching someone else's life on TV.

"Where do you live?" the man asked.

"No place," Rolo said. "Where are we going?"

"Someplace wonderful. Do you go to church?"

"Sundays and during the week, too, except I was in a foster home. That was weird. But I ran away."

"I'm going to help you."

It sounded weird, so Rolo ignored it. "What do you want me to do for fifty dollars?" he asked. Somehow he knew the answer. Not exactly, but he knew it was too horrible to think about. Maybe the man would give him something to drink first or more pot so he wouldn't have to think about it.

The man asked, "What's your name, son?"

He said, "Rolo. Rolando." The man nodded. The car turned off Sixth Street onto MoPac Expressway.

The man said, "Nice to meet you, Rolo. I'm Judah."

||||||||||||||||||

I was on top of Vita, rising and falling at regular mechanical rhythms when I slowed down and realized that I didn't care if I finished or not. I withdrew from her and rolled over onto my side, facing the wall.

"Is something wrong?" she asked.

"No."

What was I supposed to say? *I'm here because I'm lonely and I want to curl up to your ample bosom and pretend you like me.*

Another silence, and I felt her roll away also, facing the opposite wall. We lay back to back, not touching.

The dresser mirror tilted forward, so we could watch ourselves. I saw myself: a single man, with a rented house, a car that belonged to the department and a job that could kill me, lying in bed trying to have a warm conversation with a rented friend.

Finally she said, "So how's work?"

I turned and smiled at her. "Thanks for asking."

|||||||||||||||||||

"Every day souls are lost, misplaced or tossed to the winds. Children sell their bodies in the streets. What if you could pluck one lost soul, save him, use him to help others . . . ?"

Rolo didn't understand what the man was saying. As the trees swooshed past, he felt something change. Before, he was buzzing and everything felt fine. Now he felt scared. Something terrible was about to happen. It bubbled in his stomach and up his throat. Bats were going to fly out of the back seat, or they were going to ride over a cliff. He said, "I want to get out now."

"We're almost there."

"I don't want the money. Let me out here, please."

The man, Judah, took an exit and made a few turns, and then they were driving on gravel near the train tracks with nothing on both sides but trees. Rolo could see only by moonlight. Judah stopped the car and stepped out, then walked around and opened Rolo's door. "Get out," he said.

Rolo was afraid to stand. His legs were still buzzing and half asleep. He climbed up out of the car. It was the first time he realized just how big the man was, huge and broad like a truck. He felt himself start to cry in pulses.

"Please, mister." Rolo could feel tears and snot running down his face. He shook too hard to wipe them away.

The man leaned over, put his mouth so close to Rolo's ear that Rolo could feel the mist of his breath in the cool night. "Get on your knees."

Rolo ran. He knew it was too late, but he ran on the white gravel. Pull, Ortiz, pull! The man was behind him, a step away. Rolo pulled with all his might, but the man grabbed him by the shoulders and yanked him back so he fell on the stones. "Please! Please!" The man was above him, grabbing at him. Rolo struggled and kicked, inched away and felt himself pulled back.

The man said, "Get . . . on . . . your . . . *knees!*"

Rolo choked out a sob as he got up on his knees in the sharp gravel. "Please, mister," he cried softly. "Please."

The big man blocked out the light of the moon and breathed again into Rolo's ear. "Now pray."

ⅢⅢⅢⅢⅢⅢⅢⅢ

I lay in Vita's bed listening to her breathe. It was an intimacy, what struck me as the kind of thing you should do with someone you loved. And while paying for sex humiliated me, paying for love, or its illusion, was worse. A sucker's game. I should leave. Lots of bad stories start with someone falling asleep where he shouldn't. Instead I laid my head on the pillow, figuring I'd just close my eyes, just for a moment.

‖‖‖‖‖‖‖‖‖‖‖‖‖

"Our Father," Rolo said. "Our Father who art in heaven," and the man was behind him, "hallowed be thy na—"

And it was just then that Rolo felt something coil around his neck and pull tight.

The man said, "Don't think of death as the end. It's the beginning."

Rolo tried to get his fingers under the cord, but it was digging into his skin. He flailed and kicked, choked for air, but he couldn't get any, thinking, Help, help, as his vision turned dark.

Part Two

||||||||||||||||||||||||||||||||||||||||||||||||||||

GOOD FRIDAY

It was 1991, four years back, and I was living on Thirty-eighth Street with Rachel, and we were in love. But I kept coming home late and jumping up to leave every time the phone rang. This made her nervous. And one day I came home and she wasn't there, only signs of a struggle and blood on the floor and queasy terror in my gut. She's been kidnapped. I have to find her. And I get where she is, where she's trapped, and I'll do anything, die to get her out and think I got away easy. And he's got her in this basement and God knows what he's doing to her and I pull open the door and he smiles and stabs me in the leg and I fire wildly and graze Rachel and she screams and she's gone and I kick my legs and wake up.

I pulled on my pants and found Vita in her kitchen having coffee. "Sleep okay?" she asked, but she didn't mean it.

"About last night . . ."

"Don't worry."

I said, "I want to explain."

"You're paying. You don't have to explain."

I put money on the table and left, swearing up and down that I'd never be back.

It was way too late to go home and change, so I arrived at HQ, close to nine-thirty without a shower or a shave, dressed in yesterday's clothes and looking like a cop who just spent the night with a hooker. As I crossed over from the parking lot to HQ, I saw two black sedans parked in the zero-tolerance no-parking zone in front of the entrance area. Two TV vans stood sentry with cameras, satellite dishes and all. A small crowd gathered, employees and a few passersby who saw the tumult. Four feds in stock black suits and shades escorted Lieutenant Harland Clay, Jeff Czerniak's hard-partying CO, toward the first sedan. Clay wasn't cuffed, which meant he was being brought in for "questioning." But I guessed from his posture that he was facing hard time in federal prison. A wrong step in any direction would be interpreted as a confession, and he might not live to tell the tale. With his longish, slicked hair and his drooping mustache, he looked more like a street hood than any other cop I knew. He'd have been great undercover if only he could remember he was a cop.

I wondered who had alerted the TV stations. I saw a few of Clay's compatriots, men from Organized Crime and Narcotics, looking at him and each other, wondering which of them was next or what a high-level bust like this would mean to all of us. It was the kind of event that forced a shake-up, and no one could guarantee where they'd be when it settled.

I wondered what the Family would have to say.

Clay had reached the curb and was about to step into the car when he spotted me. "You!" he yelled, and I hoped he was looking at someone else. "You set me up!"

The cameras and crowd swayed to find me. A denial on my part would have been sure proof of guilt. The Family would be watching.

A fed said, "Let's go." Clay stepped down into the car, the fed placing one hand on his head to keep him from bumping it, and he pulled his feet in. Then he gave me a look that couldn't be missed or misinterpreted. *You.*

Whether he got five months or five years, he'd be after me when he got out. If the Family didn't get me first. I went inside, barreling through a sea of unfriendly faces and muttered threats, and headed to Internal Affairs.

I'd just reached the outer door of IA when it opened. Torbett saw me, pulled me in and dragged me back to his office. As he went back to shut the outer and inner doors, I figured this was where he was going to tell me how he'd made a federal case, literally, of my second-hand testimony about Czerniak and about Clay with the dealer and the whores. While he was at it, he could tell me what I should do now that half the force would be gunning for me over a testimony I didn't want to give about something I didn't see.

The downside of a shake-up is that people are scared, of losing their sweet assignments, of getting fired, of prosecution. And when they get scared, they get desperate. So a police department becomes a place where twelve hundred trained killers don't know who to trust.

Torbett took his seat, shifted, chose his words. I could see how the new gig was weighing on him.

"I have word," he said, "that you spent last night at the home of a known prostitute, Vita Carballo."

I blinked. The cleverest comeback I could manage was, "What?"

"If it's not true . . ."

I hadn't been out of Vita's bed for an hour. If Torbett got the message a little earlier, he could have found me snoozing between Vita's sheets. I tried to think who would have a bead on my movements or be motivated to watch me. Clay. Clay and his friends.

"Indulge me," I said to Torbett. "Who spotted me?"

"I can't tell you that."

"Someone told Clay about my statement." I knew it was Czerniak and not Torbett, but I didn't let on.

Torbett straightened his back, pain visible in his face. "We have other evidence on Clay. He's not going to prison on your testimony."

"But you're protecting them and you're not protecting me."

He said, "I don't leak information."

"Well, fuck it. Send me up for consorting with prostitutes. We all have something tucked away we wouldn't want people knowing about."

Torbett looked to see if I was blackmailing him, and I could have backed off but I didn't have a chance. Torbett had made a mistake years earlier, an illegal seizure that compromised a big case, and he'd confided it in me. With the odds against Torbett out of the gate for being black, it would have been a career-breaking blunder if anyone found out.

"I'm trying to help you, Reles."

"Help me into a fuckin' box!"

Torbett sat straighter, the muscles in his face tightening. I guessed he was having a back spasm.

I could have said, *Of course I'd never rat you out.* But that would have made it worse.

He said, "Did you or did you not spend last night in the home of a prostitute?"

I snarled, "I don't recall."

In the lobby crowds of patrols and civilians buzzed around the circular reception desk, making me wonder if our security was tight enough. I got dirty looks from young patrols I'd never met. Some dumb kid from Criminal Investigation, in his first jacket and tie, got in front of me and said, "Why don't you die?" Another suit pulled him away. The kid learned devotion before he learned subtlety. The idea is to stab a guy when he's not looking.

I was twenty feet down the hall when Czerniak appeared, grabbed me by the arm and said, "I gotta talk to you."

Two detectives I knew by face, nodding acquaintances, passed us and didn't nod. The signs could be that subtle.

He said, "You talked to IA. Now we're both screwed."

I yanked my arm free. "Fuck you, Czerniak. You dragged me into this. And then you tried to back out." I tried to get past him. He was fixed in front of me, like a roadblock. A stupid, doomed roadblock.

A few steps past him, the elevator opened and one of the Homicide guys, Fuentes, came out. He took a step toward us, saw me and headed the other way. People were afraid to be seen near us.

"Who's following me?" I said. No answer. "Suits me fine," I said, and walked around him.

"Wait a minute, wait a minute," he said, and shifted positions. "I got a trail on your kid." He handed me the photo of Rolo Ortiz.

"When?"

"Last night," he said. "I was too wired to go home." He began his story.

Last night after I dropped him off, Czerniak, armed with Rolo's snapshot, a canine sense of smell and no human intelligence to keep him out of trouble, sniffed around some more in the haunts of his greatest comfort: the sleaziest bars and porn parlors. Something about Czerniak didn't read "cop"—he read "whoremonger" or maybe "pedophile." So people who saw him running the streets, flashing a photo of a boy he claimed was his nephew, wouldn't worry he was a vice detective after them. They'd frame him as a perv on the make. Sure, they'd tell him where they'd seen the kid. For all they knew, the kid needed the business.

Czerniak kept asking questions until he hit pay dirt. Rolo had appeared in a hustler bar at Fifth and Sabine around midnight. The bartender bounced him for fear of the law—Rolo looked like a boy, not even a teenager—and there the trail went cold. Except that a guy followed Rolo out.

"Did you get a description?"

Here he got excited. "Sure I did. A heavy guy, like me, about six feet. Fifty or so. With one eye straight ahead and the other heading for Houston. And a scar on his right cheek."

I said, "Great. A fat, wall-eyed scarface. Was he twirling his mustache?"

Czerniak lost his smile. "What do you mean?"

"Did you pay for that tip?"

He bowed his head. I could hear hope drain out.

"Listen," I said. "Who told you that?"

"Some kid," he said. "A hustler. Maybe fifteen or sixteen. White. Skinny. Pimples. Greasy hair. Levi's jacket and jeans."

"You get a name?" He shook his head. "Never mind," I said. "You did great."

"What now?" Czerniak asked, looking up and down the hall, his voice broken to a desperate hiss.

The last time I gave Czerniak advice it worked out badly, but I couldn't blame him. I said, "Now we try not to get killed."

I headed up to Homicide and passed Mora in the hall. She was striding with purpose but with her head down, which you seldom see cops do because they're always trying to look everywhere. "Mora," I said. "Mora!" She stopped and turned. "What's up with Rolo?"

She blinked, distracted, and pulled notes from the pockets of her

APD windbreaker. "A woman . . . saw him yesterday, on . . . Springdale, wearing a white shirt and brown pants. They looked dirty, she said, and she was sure he'd slept in them. He had a cold. She let him carry her groceries home, and she was about to offer him dinner. He pushed her down and grabbed two dollars from the table and ran."

"Christ," I said.

I gave her Czerniak's tip, along with the description of the wall-eyed, scarfaced boy chaser and the kid hustler. She looked upward like someone calculating, *click click click,* and then walked off.

Just outside the squad room, I realized I could hear the men talking inside, and I stopped and pretended I was reading an announcement on the wall, something posted about people taking off today for Good Friday.

"I *like* 'em dark," one of the squad said, the short one, I thought. LaMorte. "And mean."

"Shee-it," Highfill twanged. "She don't stay in that kind of shape just to get pounded by some fat white man."

"Says you." They were talking about Mora.

A third, Halvorsen, chimed in with his Chicago pinch. "Forget it, the two of ya. She's got something going on. And you're not her type."

A moment and they both said, "No. Naw!"

"In the suburbs," Halvorsen said. "In Pflugerville. And married."

I walked into the squad room, head held high, nodded at the men on the squad with no noticeable response. They all turned back to their work. I pulled my chair out from my desk to check for booby traps. For good measure I opened the drawers one by one with my face to the side. All clear.

The desk faced the wall, which wasn't the strategic position I would have hoped for. I added up the entire department, about twelve hundred enemies and potential enemies, broken up by a few allies and a few hundred who just wouldn't be seen with me. Torbett had it worse. He was black and the head of Internal Affairs. At least I wasn't Torbett.

I found an interoffice envelope on the desk addressed to me from Senior Patrol Officer Scotto, who was with me when I scoped Faith's apartment. The envelope held Faith's phone records. I looked them over and checked the reverse directory for addresses. The dates, I noticed, charted her phone conversations for the two weeks before her death, except for the last two days. A note from Scotto apologized and promised the rest ASAP. Some of the numbers overlapped with those I'd found on scraps—her mother, her agent and her pals. I called DPS and asked if they had any DNA results on Faith Copeland's perpetrator. My clothes were beginning to crawl, and my stubble was growing in dark. I spotted some pink message slips on the floor and fished them up.

There were three from Jessica, no time written on them. And one from Marks, my new CO. It read "Copeland progress?" I phoned him across the hall and hung up on his voice mail.

What I had on Faith was a thumb broken by a loan shark, the loan shark in custody but not a likely bet for the murder. Also, a fake ID and some porn videos. The killer needs a motive and an opportunity. She lived alone on a dark alley, so anyone had the opportunity. Motive? She seemed like meat for a crazy stalker. But that could be anybody.

I announced, "Anyone know who took this message for me from Marks?" No answers. "Anybody know where he is?" Again no answer. I stood up and boomed, "DOES ANYBODY KNOW WHERE MARKS IS?"

They all spun. Highfill, the one with the hound-dog look, said, "Shit!"

Halvorsen's Chicago pinch made him sound like a cabdriver. "What's yer *prablem?*"

I stepped toward him and said, "I wanna know where Marks is. *You* got a fuckin' problem?"

I could see him tally the situation, as he weighed my size and potential strength against the advantages of his height and agility and figured a painful draw. "He ain't here."

"I got that. Where is he?"

LaMorte said, "He's gone. Out of town for the day. He'll be back Monday."

I spat out a thank you and left the office to chase down the last of Faith Copeland's friends. My name was mud in the department and shit on the squad. I had to make something happen with the case. I had to get out from under Marks. And I had to do something big that would make me look good in the department, make me untouchable, too important to kill.

And I had to do it fast.

36.
||||||

Mora headed down to Records and spent the next two hours sifting though mug shots. She looked at a thousand known and suspected pedophiles, harmless-looking old men with grandfatherly smiles and snide twenty-somethings, male and female. She looked at hustlers and johns. She looked in a section cross-filed for facial scars, wrote down the numbers and then sorted through the books, seeking out the scarred faces one at a time—knife scars, missing lips from chewing-tobacco cancer and in one case the distinctive results of a house fire— and she came up empty. No surprise, but it was two hours she had to spend.

Around noon she headed to the area that lived in the shade of the interstate and parked at Fifth and Sabine, just a few blocks south of HQ. The front door of the bar was bolted, but she saw light through a hazy window and she headed around back, where a beefy white man of fifty or so was tossing cardboard boxes of beer bottles into a Dumpster. After the beer was done, he set in on the whiskey bottles, throwing them in one by one, with force and a grunt. She walked close enough that he stopped on the windup.

"Yeah?"

She showed him Rolo's picture. "Have you seen this boy?"

He said, "No," and quickly dumped the rest of the bottles.

"Are you sure? Take a closer look."

He moved his face closer to the photo but didn't take his eyes off her. "I ain't seen him."

He dumped the boxes and went in the back door. She followed him past the pool table and some darkened neons, up a narrow unlit hall stinking of liquor, urine and cigarettes, past a men's room and into the front room: a bar, stools, tables, ledges and corners to sit or perch on.

"How about a man, maybe fifty or so, husky build, with a scar and a wandering eye?"

He pointed a thumb over his shoulder and busied himself with the beer taps. A cartoon portrait hung over the bar, painted in bright colors on a circle of wood. A heavyset pirate with a scar down one cheek and eyes pointing in different directions. A parrot on his shoulder had a similar affliction. Mora sighed.

"How about I come back here and raid the place for prostitution?"

He stopped. "Lady, look at this place. I'm just trying to stay alive."

She held up the photo. "So's he."

The bartender looked close and nodded. "Last night. Around

midnight. He sneaked in. I bounced him out. I didn't let him in, and I didn't serve him. That's the God's-honest truth."

"How about a hustler, a teenager with bad teeth?"

"They all have bad teeth."

"Skinny, with greasy hair and pimples. Levi's jacket and jeans." She saw it register on his face, but he didn't say anything. She headed for the door. "I'll come back later. When you have a crowd."

"No, wait." She turned. "His name is Vic."

"Where do I find him?"

"In the daytime?" He shook his head. "Good luck."

Mora hit the phones and asked where the nearest soup kitchen was. She found it, Ebenezer Baptist Church, just east of the interstate. Among the drunks and the junkies and the just plain out-of-works was a teenage boy with bad skin and bad teeth, his denim jacket hanging on his skeletal frame. Many of the customers looked clean and well kept, broke but not homeless, but Vic stayed to himself along the sidelines, at the end of a long table with chairs along one side facing the stage. He was picking at a soggy piece of meat loaf with a plastic fork while a Latino of about thirty preached Jesus to the crowd through a microphone, alternating in English and Spanish. Nothing for nothing.

"Remember, my friends, Jesus wants you to be joyous. Jesus wants you to be free. Jesus wants you to be taken care of. Remember how He said to His disciples, 'Your Father knows what you need.'"

Mora walked to the boy's table and pulled up a chair opposite him. She sat and smiled as he looked up from the meat loaf. She asked, "How'd you like to make ten bucks?"

The boy's blank expression turned into a leer as he surveyed her up and down for, she guessed, attractiveness and potential bankroll.

"Forty," he said with a display of rotten, partially blackened teeth. Speed.

"How'd you come up with that figure?"

"Pretty lady. Other factors." South Texas accent, maybe Galveston. Came to the big city to be free.

The preacher boomed into the mike, *"No matter how little you have at any moment, God can and will multiply it in your life if you will let Him."*

Mora said, "Let's get out of here. I'll buy you a decent meal."

They found a fast-food Tex-Mex place with neons, and he ordered a fish taco, the heaviest thing he could hold down, he said. Also the most expensive. He seemed to have trouble putting the food into his mouth. She waited a while and said, "I'm looking for a boy named Rolo."

That stopped him. He set his taco down. "You ain't gonna give me forty bucks."

"Help me find my boy and I'll give you something better."

He leered again, flashing his discolored smile in misunderstanding. Underweight and pockmarked, with rotting teeth, bad breath and a distinctive body odor, the boy seemed to have an inflated notion of his attractiveness. She let it slide.

"Some big dude asked me about him. Friend of yours?"

Mora nodded.

The boy said, "Met him last night in front of Junior's on Fifth. Midnight, maybe. We went out back, smoked a—" He stopped himself.

She said, "It's okay."

He said, "We got high. I got him in the back door and went to get drinks. Then he was gone."

"Do you know where he went?"

"No. How about twenty bucks?"

"You're sure you don't know where he went?"

He rethought it, then said, "They chased us both out. We were gonna go get some candy, and we headed up Red River looking for a Stop'N Go or something, and I saw this guy come out of a bar and look at us, so I went to talk to him, and when I turned back, the kid was gone. I woulda looked out for him."

"Of course you would."

He pushed the food away. "I can't eat. You ruined my appetite."

"I won't give you cash," she said. "I can get you into a program. Clean you up, put you in foster care."

He gave her a drowsy smile. He was wide awake from the speed, she was sure, but too weary for someone of so few years. "Lady," he said, "that's how I got here."

37.
||||||

Over lunch I hit a market research company where Faith once worked for about forty minutes, two weeks earlier, trying to get people to take telephone surveys. She got frustrated and walked out, then called back to ask for her pay. I talked to her acting teacher, an older woman with a bad face lift and a complexion like Saran Wrap. Faith had certain "gifts," not least her ability to scrape up a hundred a month to sit in acting classes in a rented dance studio downtown and screech out scenes by New York's hippest playwrights of 1974. I found a boy she did a scene with, a romantic bit about two junkies holed up in a tenement. He was working at the community college bookstore. No, he didn't know she was sixteen, but he wasn't surprised—she was really immature. She tried to make out with him, but he wasn't into it.

Back at HQ, I checked all of them for priors and involvement in other cases, came up blank and figured it was time to go home for a shave and shower and change of clothes. I was in the parking lot starting the car when I heard someone pound twice on my trunk. It was Mora.

"Kill the engine!" she yelled.

I got out, and she pointed to the exhaust pipe. Someone had stuffed a rock into it.

"I saw you get in and I heard the engine start, but I didn't see smoke."

"Good catch," I said. I pried the rock out, round like a potato and carefully chosen.

"Follow me," she said.

As I trailed her inside HQ, I noticed she had two more videotapes with her but I didn't feel like asking. Instead I said, "You sure you want to be seen with me?"

She dismissed the question with noise from her throat.

When we got to the squad room, I saw that LaMorte and Highfill were still there. I lobbed the rock against the metal side of LaMorte's desk. It crashed like thunder. They both jumped and recoiled.

"What the fuck!"

I said, "Any of you guys lose that?"

I scored two dirty looks but no guilty twitches.

Mora ignored the exchange and popped a tape in. She said, "I tracked Rolo from the bar to a convenience store and got this." A black-and-white security tape showed a curly-haired boy in a spring jacket and jeans walk up to a magazine stand, peek at a *Playboy,* turn to the candy bins and grab two of almost everything, then put most of it back. Mora popped the first tape out and put in the second.

This was hazier, a shot of the front of the store from a camera over the entrance. "The outside camera is hidden," she said. "You could look for it and not see it." She fast-forwarded through cars pulling up and leaving. Finally a light-colored car pulled up in the darkness. A large man got out, features blurry, and walked out of the frame. In a few minutes he came back and got back into the car. And Rolo got in on the passenger side.

"Parents are worried about their kids sneaking into bars," she said. "But the chickenhawks are cruising the convenience stores and pinball palaces."

"License plate?" I asked, squinting.

Mora said, "Texas, that's all I can tell, and a station wagon, an old one, maybe early seventies. Silver, gray or light blue. Ford Gran Torino. I know the contours. My dad had one."

"Maybe we should talk to your dad."

She said, "Come to DPS with me."

I looked around at the room and nodded her outside. In the hall I checked up and down and said, "Listen, I'm dead-ending on Faith Copeland. I can't take time out."

"Best thing in the world," she said. "Work on something else. Two of us together, we'll be out of there in ten minutes."

"No," I snapped in a harsh whisper. "I'm serious." I didn't want to give that much away but I didn't have anyone else to tell. "I have to show something, and I'm stuck."

She said, "Help me with this. I'll help you with Faith."

I'd heard promises like that before but never from a female detective so I went along with it.

We headed up to DPS in her battered white Honda Civic and sifted through records of station wagons. The Ford Torino wagon had been made with significant variations from '68 to '76. It was supposed to be a family vehicle with a sporty feel and a roof rack. We narrowed it down to four possibilities, two in Austin, then we headed out to check them in the thickening afternoon traffic. Driving around, I thought about the rock in my exhaust pipe and who might have planted it.

"Thanks for looking out for me," I said, "back at HQ, with the rock."

Instead of answering, she said, "Word is out you spent last night with a hooker."

I took the hit and bounced back with, "Word is out you have a married lover." Long silence.

Then she said, "I'm just saying what I heard."

"She's an old friend."

"You don't have to apologize to me," she said, but it felt like I did. We drove a while longer and she said, "I make my dumb decisions around my bed. I use up all my genius for work."

I considered my chances of being her next dumb decision.

The first Torino, a faded blue, was sitting in front of the house it was registered at, with the front end smashed in and the dents rusted. Negative. The second, similarly, was rusted in spots where the one in the tape hadn't been and looked generally more beat up. At least in the fuzziness of the tape, our Torino was like new.

The afternoon breezed by and I was sorry it was over, wondering if we should be heading out of town after those last two Torinos, maybe make a weekend out of it, when we got a call on the car radio.

"Homicide 6."

She grabbed the mike. "This is Mora, go ahead."

"You wanna see this."

38.
|||||||

The setting sun shone gold on a white-graveled stretch of train tracks running parallel to MoPac Expressway along the western border of town, just north of Anderson Lane, between rows of trees. The gravel wound back through heavy shrubbery to the dead end of a very nice street, providing a path for the local kids to explore. One such kid had chanced upon Rolo's wallet.

The boy, Jimmy Pomeleo, swore he hadn't taken money from the wallet. It was a black vinyl wallet holding seven singles, Rolo's school ID (Kealing Magnet Junior High) and, in the change pocket, one latex condom. A good boy, Jimmy showed his mother the wallet and she called the police.

Mora, two patrols and I fanned out over the graveled area, stooped like rice farmers, and sniffed for details. We wandered in straight lines, circles, squares. Finally one of the patrols hollered. What he'd discovered was a length of wire, coiled at the ends. Flies buzzed around it. The center of the wire was deep red: blood. Nearly fresh blood. I turned to see the last of the hope drain from Mora's face.

"He's dead," she said.

I said, "Someone's dead."

If it was Rolo who got garroted, we could set the death sometime after midnight. We had a guess about the car that brought him here. The gravel negated the chance of tire tracks or shoeprints. But DPS would be able to do something with the wire and the wallet, maybe. We waited for them to show, and sat around while they combed the area for traces. Then we followed them to their lab for no real reason.

It wasn't until we got back outside in the dark of evening and dropped into Mora's car that I got a good look at her. Her thick black hair, usually bound in a clip, had fallen loose around her shoulders. Her mouth hung open and she stared somewhere around the dash-board. For the first time in our short acquaintance, she looked wiped out, like the air had been drawn out of her. I wondered if she'd have it in her to start the car. I didn't want to be in it when she was driving.

"Listen," I said. "We have two leads on Torinos. We can check them out now, call the local cops."

She took a minute to answer: "I wanted to prevent a murder, not solve one."

"Maybe we still can," I said, desperately. She looked at me. We both knew better. "Okay," I said, "we'll shift gears. We go after the killer, right now."

Another minute, and finally she said, "I'd rather go after the bottle of Chivas in my kitchen. Interested?"

Something told me to say no. Instead I asked if she would let me drive us back to HQ.

"I'm okay," she said. "I'll drive."

I watched her hand as she turned the ignition.

39.
∣∣∣∣∣∣

I figured it was a courtesy to me that Mora drove us through the middle of town rather than shooting down the interstate. The sky was black and her mood was dangerous, and she cruised down Lamar Boulevard past the state hospital and Pease Park, cutting left on Seventh Street. She stopped at two red lights and ignored a third. We made it alive to the municipal courts and Central Booking. With no sign of slowing down, she rolled toward the red light that was supposed to protect us from the frontage-road traffic. "Stop here," I said. I looked to the left for approaching cars, and then behind her I spotted a familiar face walking out of Central Booking. It was Roger Barry, the loan shark I'd busted last night, who confessed to breaking Faith's thumb as part of his collections policy. He looked spiffy in his baseball jacket, breathing in the night air. His face bore scratches where I'd landed it in Faith's driveway last night, but he wore them well.

"Son of a bitch," I muttered.

"What?" She turned to see where I was looking.

"That's Barry, the guy who broke Faith's thumb. Hit the horn."

I stepped out of the car, and she tapped the horn twice. I stood on the far side and waved Barry over. He'd feel safer with a car between us.

He walked toward us, coolness in his moves. He saw Mora at the wheel and put on his game-show smile. "Evening," he said.

"Out on bail?"

"The judge took a look at my injuries and dismissed the charges." He must have seen the expression on my face because he went on, gloating. "It's your own fault," he said with a sparkle in his eye. "You didn't say I resisted arrest. Wait, what is it you guys say? You *feared* for your life." He showed me his shiny white teeth.

"Anybody take a sample from you?" I asked. "Blood, cheek cells . . ."

"No. Why?"

I shook my head.

"Let me know if you need anything," he said, stepping back from the car. Then he eyed Mora and winked.

I got back in the car, muttering something about the impurity of his relationship with his mother, as he walked along Seventh Street, cautiously crossing the frontage road, into East Austin.

The light turned red, and we sat in silence and watched Barry disappear into the darkness, looking for the next desperate gambler or runaway to rope in. The light turned green, and Mora didn't move the car. But where she'd been wearing a look of despair, now she wore one of focused rage, even a slight cruel smile, as she stared at a fixed point in the darkness ahead. Finally I said, "Listen, I'm parked across the street. Maybe I should drive you home." She held up a hand, and I waited as the light turned red and then green again, and she rolled slowly down Seventh Street under the interstate at fifteen miles an hour.

We traveled four blocks that way before we spotted Barry on the

left walking along a crumbled curb and the chain link fence of a ceme-
tery. She slowed to a near stop, then said, "Hold on," and gunned the
engine, steering across the oncoming lane, bouncing up the busted
curb and missing Barry by inches as he threw himself backward out of
her path. Barry took a few steps back, eyes wide, then turned and ran.
Mora popped out of the car and followed, and before I got moving,
she pounced and took him down on the sidewalk.

When I caught up, Barry was kissing the pavement and Mora had
twisted one hand behind his back, but she wasn't trying to cuff him.

"Why'd you run?" she said.

"You almost hit me!"

"You tried to run from the police. Suspicious behavior. Probable
cause."

I stood over them. "Mora," I warned.

Mora said, "My friend wants to know about Faith Copeland.
What was she to you?"

"Nothing. I told him. She borrowed money."

"You fuck her?"

"No," Barry said.

"Never?" Mora asked.

"Never."

"You know anyone who did?" She twisted his arm harder.

"No. Shit!" He turned back and saw me. "Tell her. I told him all
this. She was in trouble, she borrowed money."

Mora said, "And you busted her thumb."

He said, "I popped it out. A doctor could have popped it right
back in."

Mora said, "She couldn't afford a doctor!" Then she looked up at
me. "Hold him."

I sat on his back and held his arms down.

"What's the matter with her?" he said, and tried to get to his feet.

"You know. Dames. You better hold still."

He stopped shuffling and lay still with his arms splayed, palms flat on the concrete.

I couldn't figure what Mora was up to. But she'd looked desolate ten minutes before, and now she was on fire. It seemed like a positive change.

Barry said, "I didn't kill her."

"I'll give you the benefit of the doubt."

"You want to blame someone, blame her parents."

"Yeah, yeah, bad parenting."

Mora appeared in front of me, palming a grenade-size chunk of loosened sidewalk. "Hey, Barry!" she shouted.

Barry saw her. "No. No!"

I said, "Don't."

And as she raised the concrete above her head and brought it down hard in the direction of Barry's thumb, she cried out the street cop's defense: "I feared for my *life!*"

40.
||||||

"What difference does it make if a few souls get to heaven earlier?" Judah said. "The point is they got to heaven."

Suzanne pulled her shoulders up, cuddling into herself in her fox coat. She leaned her head back and looked at the spectacle of stars in the clear night sky. "You inspire me," she said.

He thought for sure she'd say something about what he'd done for her. But she didn't know exactly what it was. That was the rule. He went on. "Do they think Jesus complained about being crucified? And that saved us all." The history of man had shown nothing but war and plagues, God's attempt to bring more people to Him. That was why Judah didn't worry about war and plagues. He was sure he was on the right track. Certain.

"That's what I keep telling them," Suzanne said. "But they won't *listen.*"

They sat on the hood of Judah's station wagon, in a clearing in the middle of Suzanne's family estate. She'd told him that AARO, the Austin Area Reclamation Organization, was having a conference in town, making their own plans for the future of the governor and of the party. And she wasn't invited, and he couldn't get her to think about anything else.

"They think I'm the enemy," she said. "I'm not the enemy."

He turned to her, her dark hair set against her fair skin. She saw him and blushed at his attention. Under the stars, with her broad smile and small eyes, she looked mature and young at the same time. He leaned forward to kiss her.

She laid a palm on his chest. "Oh, Judah, no."

Judah scowled.

"Don't be angry," she said. "We have to be good."

He realized he could take her by force, her small, weak body against his. She'd be glad in the long run. It wouldn't be her fault. He said, "I've made sacrifices. I'm fixing things for you. For us."

She pouted. "I can't leave Paul. It would ruin me."

They sat in the silence under the stars. Finally he said, "He can't love you like I can."

She smiled sweetly, placed a hand on his cheek. "Oh, sweetie."

"You talk about real religious freedom, a Christian nation. But you're married to a man you don't love."

"That's my cross to bear," she said.

"It's dishonest. When God comes, He'll find you in a dishonest marriage."

She ran her fingers through his long hair. "Do it for me, Judah. Do it now."

He looked over to see if she was serious.

He said, "You're holding on to earthly things."

She said, "Please."

Judah stepped down from the car and looked around. All clear. He slipped a hand into his coat pocket and pulled out the pineapple-sectioned grenade. For show he turned to Suzanne as he pulled the pin with his teeth and spat it out. Then he counted. "One." She yelped. "Two." She squealed and kicked her feet. He reeled back and flung the grenade high and far.

41.
|||||

Mora drove me to her condo complex south of the river, parked and led me inside. Everything about the apartment looked very new and orderly, like it was the model home they showed prospective tenants. A ground-floor one-bedroom, wall-to-wall carpet, matching couch and chairs, dining table, oversize living room window looking out onto a stretch of greenery behind the complex. Nothing to indicate who lived there. What's more, it lacked the feminine touch.

On the flip side, she'd just battered a loan shark, knocked his thumb loose with a chunk of concrete. All I could figure was she thought Rolo was dead and she couldn't do anything about that. But Faith was dead, too. Mora wanted revenge on someone, and Barry was right there. The logic was convoluted and felonious, but it wasn't about logic. She needed something, and he got in her way. It didn't make her much better than a thousand other street-level criminals, operating on rage and misplaced vengeance.

When she told me to get back in the car, I figured it was easier not to argue. Barry could go straight to the station and file a report, which would go to Torbett, who wouldn't ignore it. Barry could go to the hospital and tell them what happened, and they'd have to file a report. Or, more likely, he'd say he slipped and settle his business himself when Mora wasn't looking. She had a new enemy and so did I. He could join the club.

I dropped into a low chair with scratchy wool upholstery. I still wore yesterday's clothes and yesterday's beard. My feet itched from dirty socks. If I'd eaten anything since the morning, it hadn't taken root. I sure hadn't brushed my teeth. I was no closer to finding out who killed Faith Copeland than I was two days before. I needed a shower, a shave, clean clothes, a steak dinner and a good night's sleep. Instead of all that, Mora handed me a heavy cut-glass tumbler with four ounces of twelve-year-old scotch over two ice cubes. Four ounces times twelve years divided by two ice cubes. I poured the iced scotch into my mouth, swished it around like mouthwash and swallowed.

It landed with a splash. The nerve endings in my scalp tingled and relaxed. Mora sipped in front of the window and paced the carpet. I stared out at the bushes.

"You should close the drapes," I said. From the shrubbery we'd look like a fishbowl. Security issue.

"I don't walk around naked," she answered, and if I looked disappointed, she didn't comment on it. She had some papers on the table, and she was looking at a calendar mounted on the wall over them. "Hey, isn't this Passover? What kind of Jew are you?"

I said, "Isn't this Good Friday? You should be off somewhere eating fish."

She dropped her jacket by the door. She was wearing a shoulder holster over a blue tennis shirt and slacks pinched at the waist and pulling at the hips.

"Do you believe that fuck?" she said. "Released for a black eye and some scrapes. Heading into El Barrio to do his thing."

"Technically speaking," I said, stretching my legs out, "breaking his thumb was a felony."

"Who's he gonna tell?" she asked. "Bam! I feared for my life! Hah!" She threw back half a glass of scotch and poured herself another, glugged it down like cold water on a hot day.

We didn't talk for a while. I thought about Barry, a sociopathic loan shark with a new vendetta. Then I noticed that the scotch went down even smoother on the second sip. The third went down so easily that I downed it and reached it out for a refill.

I was feeling the drinks when she asked, "Where do you think he is?" She was staring out the window. "The kid, I mean."

"Rolo?" She nodded. I took another healthy swig "I don't know. A sewer pipe somewhere?" The liquor doused my diplomacy. She looked at me like I'd put him there.

"He was just a kid."

"So was Faith," I said. I drained my glass. "I should go."

"You just got here," she said, and she refilled my glass to the respectable halfway mark and drifted toward the window. "I ain't drinkin' alone. You got a date?"

I said, "No, but—"

"You're supposed to be home."

I hadn't been home since the morning before, and no one was waiting there for me. But Mora's attitude was starting to piss me off.

"How about you?" I said. "You got a date?"

She eyed me hard from her station by the window, like she was figuring something out. "What's the story, Reles? You got that big-titted bimbo and you can't stand to go home to her. I saw her at the banquet. Something." She cocked her head at a different angle, like she was adjusting her reception. "No, you're not like those other guys. If they had what you have, they'd think they were lucky."

"All right, that's enough," I said. "They'll miss you in Pflugerville."

"I got it," she said. "Broken heart. The one that got away."

I took up my drink and swished half of it around in my mouth. It was tasting more like the wood it was aged in than I'd noticed. I swallowed it and stood, a little shaky on my pins. Quick drinks on an empty stomach. "Thanks for the drink. Let's do this next time you lose a kid."

"You were in love. It was real. But she bailed. Maybe for someone with money. Maybe she couldn't take the lifestyle, the midnight calls. She ran off with some doctor. So now you only chase bimbos—"

I reached the door and struggled with the dead bolt as she walked closer to me, like she couldn't call me an asshole from across the room. I said, "It's great knowing I have a friend on the squad."

The meanness went out of her voice as she continued, now maybe six feet from me. "You only chase bimbos because anything else would be an insult to her memory. And you don't want to do that," she said, and her eyes lowered. She wasn't talking to me anymore. She was a few inches away. "Because you miss her so bad. You miss the comfort of being with someone you loved, who loved you back. Knew who you were and loved you anyway."

There was a tear in her eye when she looked up, and I don't know if it was because we were lonely or angry or drunk, but before I knew it we'd bridged the space between us and she pressed against me, and we locked in a twelve-year-old-scotch-flavored kiss.

42.
||||||

Paul Wade turned one of the heavy wooden chairs to the stone fireplace in the back room, sat and watched the fire rise high, its warmth a few feet away, almost toasting the skin on his face. Sweat rolled down his cheeks. He thought about his days as a prosperous oilman, before they wiped him out. He thought about the honest jobs he had as a college student and as a kid, making deliveries, hauling things—hard, honest work that gave him self-respect, a trait he couldn't claim today and wouldn't recognize if he felt it.

He looked at the iron tools by the fireplace. What were they for? The iron broom and dustpan made sense. The poker made sense. The second poker with a hook at the end like an arrowhead, what was that? As if he would poke it though a wall and pull the plaster out. Who needed a dozen tools to tend a fire? It looked like a medieval torture kit.

Suzanne had no respect for real work, had never done any and didn't know what it was. Everyone she knew was in oil or in politics, and they all had to navigate around Suzanne. As far as their treatment of Paul, some were polite. Most made no effort to hide their contempt. Paul the failure. Paul, Suzanne's devoted wife. They laughed in his face.

The fire crackled.

Suzanne involved herself in something, always. He grew used to not knowing what it was. But now there was Judah, and Judah knew what Paul didn't. Why?

And why were there always questions like this? Why did the staff know more about Suzanne than he did? Why did half of Texas?

And where was Suzanne right now?

┊┊┊┊┊┊┊┊┊┊┊┊┊┊

Vita Carballo lay on her sofa in a soft, white terry cloth robe, sipping a tasteful cabernet sauvignon, watching the late news and thinking.

Thirty-nine. Homeowner. Money in the bank. Retired. Well, *semi*retired.

She'd worked it better and more carefully than anyone she knew. No drugs. Freelance protectors to keep the pimps away. Humble living, cautious saving. Americans in their sixties had done worse.

What's more, she'd escaped the business before the lines in her face appeared and deepened, before her tits sagged flat, before she lost her dignity. Disease-free and financially secure. Not that the neighborhood was anything special, but still.

So now what?

Friends weren't so easy to come by. Other call girls got tangled up with drugs or pimps. The girls had a short life span, sometimes less than a year before they disappeared. What would she do? Go to school? Get a diploma, maybe go to college? Become a social worker. The idea came out of the blue. Work with hookers and help get them off the street. Or at least show them how to keep from getting killed.

There was some film footage on the news, something about some kid star. Vita took another sip, almost giggling at the idea of her as a social worker. It seemed crazy. And possible.

There was a knock at the door.

Who the fuck could that be? she wondered, looking at the door and making no effort to get up. She had three or four occasionals, but they always called first.

He knocked again.

Reles.

He knocked again, with urgency.

No dice. No. You can have my body. But don't fuck with my mind. She tried to focus on the TV.

But she noticed some rustling under the door. Peeking underneath, attempting to crawl onto the carpet, was some greenery. She put down the wineglass and walked over, plucking out hundred-dollar bills, four of them.

Four hundred dollars, tax free, for some conversation and maybe a fuck. Why not? Come on in, Reles, she thought as she unlocked the dead bolt and reached for the knob. You can't hurt me.

ⅲⅲⅲⅲⅲⅲⅲⅲⅲⅲ

Without breaking the seal of her lips to mine, Mora unbuckled her shoulder holster and yanked off my jacket and shirt. I hesitated a moment, and she pulled off her own shirt over her head. After the jacket and holster and button-down shirt, the business of a lacy white bra confused me, but she didn't keep it long, snapping it off to reveal the contours of her smooth, tan skin and high, dark breasts. I pulled her against me, and she jumped up, legs around my waist, and kissed me hard. I blinked and noticed that the window was still uncovered, and I carried her away from it into the bedroom. Our eyes met for a moment, only long enough to remind us why we were doing this, not because we liked each other but because we were sad and lonely. Because we were in love, but not with each other. Because love was hopeless.

And with that in mind, we fell onto the bed.

ⅲⅲⅲⅲⅲⅲⅲⅲⅲⅲ

"Can I help you, sir?"

"I can do it." Lieutenant Governor Win Muller climbed out of the limo in the dark by his house and propped himself upright.

"I'll help you inside."

"I'm fine," Win said, pushing against the car to gain momentum. He wavered on his feet, listed east and west and then settled upright. "There. Pick me up at nine tomorrow. I'm going home for the holiday."

"It'll be the weekend driver, sir."

"Then make it ten."

The house was too large for Win alone. His wife and children would move down in June. Bringing them here in the middle of the school year was pointless.

He placed his feet carefully, one before the other, and made it up the walk without incident. Found the key, found the lock with the key and made it inside.

Surely he could find the bathroom.

It was the privilege of an accomplished man to have a few drinks now and then. Established in the legal field, rising in politics. Protecting the poor and the something. That was democracy, he thought, running one hand along the corridor wall in the dark. Not just the rule of the majority. But a system to protect the minority as well. There was a door. He opened it and stepped in. He couldn't find the light. In the shadows he could make out the porcelain sink, the crossed hot and cold knobs. Somewhere in the room, there had to be a toilet.

When he was done, he managed to flush and head farther down the hall, following the wall with his hand until he got to his bedroom. He could just make out the great bed in front of him, the spruce headboard almost visible against the wall. He dropped his clothes where he stood.

The room smelled foul. Something wrong with the plumbing? He'd call in the morning. He walked in tiny steps until his knees hit the bed. Then he let himself fall forward on the soft mattress and sink in.

Something rolled on top of him. Something large, soft. Cold. A moaning sound surged from his throat, like he'd woken with a rat on his chest. But bigger than a rat. He tangled in the sheets, saying, "Help, help," though the sound didn't carry, and if it had, there was no one to answer. He tried to pull away, but it followed. He groaned, a desperate "uhhhhhhh!" His hand fell on something soft, wet. A face. Teeth. He tumbled off the edge of the bed, his legs entwined in the sheet, and hit the carpet hard, scrambling for the light.

And there on the bed, with a blood-tinged face, a red line of blood around his neck and curly black hair, was a boy: naked, cold and dead.

I woke up like a chunk of pavement crashing down on a loan shark's hand, my breath tasting of missed toothbrushings and twelve-year-old scotch and the intimate places of another police detective. It was still pitch-black out, the only light coming from the living room. Red digits on the alarm clock told me it was 4:02 A.M. The bed was mine alone. I pulled on my shorts and found Mora wearing a man's office shirt loosely buttoned, sitting stooped over a table full of papers and notes under a hanging lamp. I stood at her side. Smooth, dark legs stretched out in front of her. I felt dazed from the scotch and she couldn't have been in better shape than I was.

She must have heard me moving around, but she didn't comment. I reached over to touch her shoulder. Just before I made contact, her hand grabbed mine, squeezed it and let it go.

"I got some work to do," she said with just a little warmth.

I tried to focus on the table, on some note about what she had on

Rolo Ortiz and the station wagon that had picked him up. "Can I help?"

She sat up straight and turned to me, sucking in air like she was about to say something, then holding it. At last she said, "I'm okay."

Back in the bedroom, I got dressed and holstered my weapon. I headed out, passing her at the table. I said, "I'll call you later."

She didn't raise her head. "I . . . have something going on now, Reles." Then she looked at me, dark brown eyes set in dark skin, thick black hair hanging just to her shoulders. She added, "And, you know, we work together."

I noticed that the curtains on the living room window were still wide open as I walked through the door and headed out into the dark. I'd barely heard the door click behind me when I realized I didn't have my car.

There's a kind of disorientation that goes with being awake between the hours of, say, 2:00 A.M. and 6:00 A.M., when no one with any sense would be up. You're so tired you can barely see, trying to make sure you don't wander blindly into traffic. You've been woken from the deepest sleep, or maybe you're coming from a rendezvous that will land in your biography on the list of your worst decisions, alongside the time you knew you were too drunk to drive but drove anyway and the punch you should have seen coming but didn't. You need to shave and shower and brush the grit and paste off your teeth and tongue. You need steak, eggs, coffee and clean sheets. You need to go home, where you haven't been for two days, and you need someone to notice that you were gone.

At Riverside Drive, I saw a gas station with a pay phone, and I pulled some loose papers out of my pockets, items from Faith's wallet: pawn tickets and her mother's phone number and the business card from a cabdriver who hadn't picked up his phone when I called earlier. I fished out some change and dialed.

"Manny's Cab."

"I'm at Riverside and Faro. Can you pick me up?"

"Gimme ten," he said, and hung up.

Twenty minutes later he appeared from the west in a red sedan, his company name and phone number hand-painted on the side in yellow. I'd probably seen the car before and never registered it. I waved from the sidewalk, and he turned into the gas station, circling me like he was casing my potential for danger before he stopped. He was an older black man, the skin on his neck sagging with time. He wore black-framed glasses that had never been chic and a snap-brim cap. He looked me over with my two-day beard as I climbed into the cab.

"Where to, boss?" he rumbled, though I could hear the suspicion in his voice.

I said, "Go north on Pleasant Valley."

He chuckled through his nose, "Hm, hm, hm," and put the car in gear. I saw him scoping me in the rearview mirror to see if I was going to have trouble raising the fare.

Riverside runs east-west, just south of the river and the down-town area. But downtown was growing, so the area south of the river became more developed each day, with more office parks and chain restaurants and condos. As we drove west on Riverside toward the center of town, I could see the city lights. He turned north on Pleasant Valley Road, and I said, "You mostly work nights?"

"Mostly," he said. We drove past the fire department and a soft-ball field where the river narrowed, and crossed over to the north.

"Turn left on Seventh," I said, then added, "I used to drive a cab."

"Is that so?"

It wasn't. My greatest connection to cabs was the one my mother climbed into when I was ten, the last time I saw her.

"Yeah," I said. "I drove nights. Radio-dispatched. But you don't have that."

"No, I stay busy though. I pass around my card and get lots of re-peats. And I stay at the airport a lot. And the hotels."

"Pull over here." We'd reached the chain link fence and the stretch of broken curb where Mora had made herself memorable to Roger Barry. I climbed out, saying, "Stay here," before he could protest, and found the exact spot where Mora dropped the stone. The chunk of broken concrete was where she had left it. There was a blood spot on it the size of a quarter. I had no kit, so I took the stone back into Manny's back seat with me. "Let's go."

We rode in silence. He pulled up to a red light. In the parking lot of a doughnut shop, two patrol cars were parked close, facing opposite directions so it looked like they were mating. The driver chuckled through his nose again. "Hm, hm, hm."

"What?"

He said, in a down-home accent, "My little ol' policemens are eatin' doughnuts."

I glanced over the seat to see if he had a log next to him, listing his pickups and drop-offs. "You don't keep a log like the company driv-ers do."

He looked into the rearview mirror again, then pulled into the lot by the cops and parked. His eyes bored into me from the mirror. "Why don't you tell me what you want and if I can't help you, maybe these gennelmen will."

I showed him my badge and Faith's photograph and asked if he knew her. I slid as far to the right of the cab as I could so I could watch his profile as he talked. He pursed his lips and said, "Tuesday evening."

"Just this Tuesday?"

"That's when I give her my card."

"So you never drove her before?" He shook his head. "How did she get your number?"

"She flag me down. Early, five, five-thirty P.M. She was comin' from some party, maybe a club, on South Congress. Near the Continental."

"You think she was coming from the Continental?"

"Don't know. Was pretty early. I took her home. Place up in Hyde Park, back of Avenue B. I can show it to you."

"That's okay. Anything else?"

"She was crying like. But she tipped good."

I had him drop me off at Magnolia Café, where I feasted on coffee, eggs and bacon until I felt sober. It was still dark before six when I phoned for a regular cab and waited on the bench outside the restaurant until the cab got me and dropped me and my rock at the municipal lot by APD, where I found my car, dropped the rock in an envelope, and headed home up I-35, traffic brisk for a predawn Saturday. I realized with dread that I hadn't taken Jessica's key. She could have pissed off her friends by now and come back. Maybe she'd greet me at the door with a drawing, or maybe she'd decide that the planets had converged and it was the right time in the dwindling millennium for us to have sex.

Then I remembered I'd spent the last two nights chasing other women. One was a prostitute and the other only wanted me because she was drunk and traumatized. None of this added up to my being a lady-killer.

I was still considering all this when I pulled up in front of my house and saw that the glass in the front door was broken. I drew my .38 and opened the door. A brick and a puddle of shattered glass bejeweled the front carpet. And walking in from the kitchen in a heavy, dark raincoat, smoking a cigarette, was my true love, Rachel.

44.
||||||

Mora put on her sweats and ran laps around the condo park until she was sure she'd sweated out the liquor. Back at home she took aspirin for the pounding in her head. Then she showered and ate some eggs and dressed. Five hours' sleep was enough for anybody.

She scoured the notes as much as her hazy head would allow. Rolo got into the Torino wagon with the man at the convenience store. Maybe they did their business and the man dropped him off. Maybe someone else picked him up and brought him to the railroad tracks and strangled him. But she'd find the man in the Torino first.

She had two cars from DPS in Texas that shone as possibilities. The first resided in Lubbock. She called the police there, identified herself and gave them the details. A few minutes later, they called back, said the car had been impounded for traffic violations and sold at an auction for parts, with no plates. No, they didn't have the buyer information. They'd look for it and get back to her. Right.

Mora asked, "Maybe they're driving around with stolen plates."

"You have the plate numbers?"

She didn't, and that ended the call. The other car was in Mexia, wherever the hell that was. She made calls and learned that yes, thank you, Mexia did have its own police department. She found it on the map, ninety miles straight up I-35 to Waco, then maybe forty miles east on Highway 84.

Meanwhile Reles had been in her apartment. Reles was all right. A kindred spirit. And single. But she'd gotten angry and drunk and fucked a cop, one on her own squad. Bad business. And she wasn't even that drunk. Just a dumb, impulsive move.

She could go and track the killer. But she had to see Mrs. Ortiz. There was no getting around it.

And she *had* to stop going to bed with cops.

45.
||||||

When I saw Rachel standing in the house where we once lived together, I wondered if I was dreaming. She'd become part of my past, not my present. I almost wondered who the woman was in front of me, less real than the Rachel of four years earlier, who would be forever perfect and forever thirty-two. This Rachel was four years older. She still had the rich blue eyes of a model with an Asian grandmother. She'd cut her hair shorter so it cleared her shoulders. Her high, wide-set cheekbones seemed to sag under the weight of pale, puffy cheeks and heavy makeup. She was standing among the furniture she had bought six years earlier. She'd put on some weight. It wasn't so much that she looked older, older than her years. She just looked sick.

I'd imagined reunions between Rachel and me, maybe a few thousand of them. In all of them, we were both young and in shape and happy and she'd left for no reason and everything was fine now that she was back. None of them had me sporting a two-day beard and the clothes I'd put on forty-eight hours before. None of them had both of us looking like hell. I knew from the look in her eyes that she felt humiliated. Before, she was always the most beautiful woman everywhere she went. Now she looked like every other woman in the world, maybe worse. And she must have known from my eyes that I was embarrassed too, not just for the beard and bad breath but for my life, for not having changed anything about the house since she left, for not having changed myself. I was more of the same.

In the imagined reunions, I would explain why I had been such a lousy boyfriend, how I got caught up in the frenzy of my job, how I would quit immediately and we would spend the rest of our lives together. And she would understand and forgive and we would start over.

And as I stood in the open doorway with my keys in my hand, Rachel across the room from me, I said, "Hey."

Rachel said, "Hey." Then, looking at the brick and the broken glass, she added, "It was like that when I got here. That's how I got in. I called the glass people."

I thought of a few questions. Are you hungry? Did you just fly in? Where ya been? Why did you leave me? I knew the answer to the last one, and I couldn't decide between the others. Instead I held my palms up and looked dumb. The universal question. Any answer she had would help.

Rachel said, "We should talk."

I turned and saw two patrols standing just outside the front door: a tall, ruddy one and a short, fat, dark one, maybe Indian or Pakistani, who noticed the broken glass but didn't comment on it. They looked like a French version of Laurel and Hardy. "Sergeant Reles?" the tall one said. I nodded. "You'll have to come with us."

The patrols—summoned here from their separate duties—refused to tell me where we were going, even when I asked if it was something to do with Faith or with Rolo Ortiz. The short one stammered when he spoke, and both looked shaky about giving orders to a higher-ranking officer. I leveraged their insecurity to score ten minutes to shower and shave and to get the privilege of following them in my own car. Rachel offered to wait until the people showed up to fix the glass. She wouldn't tell me where she was staying but promised to call.

I got in my car and followed the fat cop, while the tall one drove behind me to make sure I didn't run for the border. We drove west on Thirty-eighth Street in linear formation, made a right on Duval through Hyde Park, my old neighborhood. I took a census of my world: Jessica. Vita. Mora. Rachel. My love life had reached an all-time peak, at least in complexity. And I was in police custody.

We made a left on Fifty-first, and something felt suspicious. I'd taken that run lately, been in that area. Short Fat turned right on Guadalupe Street, the narrow street and its procession of houses bearing no resemblance to the broad, busy stretch of the same street that ran along the university twenty-five blocks south. It cut across Koenig Lane and the Department of Public Safety complex and led to the humble houses to the north, including the one, just two blocks north of DPS on Hammack Drive, where we turned in, where I had spent two evenings in the last four.

But when we pulled over on the left side of the street, across from the house I'd become familiar with, we weren't alone. We shared the area with a fire truck, an ambulance, another patrol car, two unmarked cop cars and the wagon from the Travis County Medical Examiner.

46.
⸿⸿⸿⸿⸿

Vita Carballo lay faceup on a sky blue carpet, leaking blood from the right side of her skull into her black hair, which was splayed out around her. Her burning green eyes had frozen wide open, right pupil expanded. Both corneas looked cloudy. Blood caked on her right cheek. They'd found her facedown and turned her over. She wore a white terry cloth bathrobe and nothing else. This, I was told, had made the initial once-over easier: they had no trouble looking for other injuries. There were none. The Homicide detective on call, Fuentes, had the decency to close her robe after the inspection, the type of courtesy not normally granted to women of her profession. I got down on one knee and touched her cool cheek. Vita. Life.

When I looked up, I noticed that I was being watched by the three patrols, along with Fuentes, Torbett and Dr. Margaret Hay, who had finished her preliminary inspection and was headed back to the office.

To cover my sentiment, I said, "She's cool. How long has she been here?"

Hay said, "Body temperature eighty-four degrees. Milky corneas. Rigor advanced but not complete. More than eight hours. Less than twelve."

Between 8:00 P.M. and midnight. Fuentes kept wiping the sweat off his upper lip, though it wasn't warm in the house. He operated in the shadow of James Torbett, whose presence on the scene hadn't been explained. Torbett, Fuentes and I stood close. I said, "What do you have?"

Fuentes furrowed his brow at me and turned to Torbett. Torbett said, "You're not on this case, Reles."

I said, "Then why am I here?"

Fuentes didn't quite manage to look me in the eye when he asked, "Where were you last night?"

I looked at each of them, then said, "Are you fucking kidding me?"

Fuentes said, "We know you were here Thursday night."

"How do you know that?" No answer, but I didn't expect one.

"Where were you last night, Reles?" Torbett's voice sounded weighed down with fatigue when he repeated Fuentes's question. It was one of his old tricks and I'd seen it before.

"I was home."

Fuentes said, "We know you weren't home." They'd probably swung by.

"Then I was out." I'd seen how the word of my night with Vita traveled through the ranks and how I was paying for it. I couldn't tell them I spent the night with Mora and wait to see what that cost Mora.

Torbett said, "When were you last in this house?"

I thought about it. "Yesterday morning. Around nine."

Fuentes said, "You'd spent the night?"

I said, "Yes. Cause of death?"

Torbett: "Bludgeon. Something round-tipped, like a ball-peen hammer."

I looked into the dent in her skull. Amid the hair and blood, her skull had been smashed in. Brain oozed out. A perfect cast of the weapon would be impossible.

Fuentes: "Did she have a pimp?"

"I don't think so."

Fuentes: "Why not?"

I thought about it. Police protection? She'd had some protection from my old partner. I couldn't imagine her getting out from under a pimp enough to buy her own house. She never would have asked for my help. I said, "I don't know."

Torbett: "How often did you see her?"

"Once before that, on Tuesday night."

Fuentes: "We found some wasted condoms in her garbage. Think we'll find your prints on one?"

I ignored the question, which was harder than you'd think. "Signs of rape?"

Torbett: "No. And no sign of forced entry on the door. Maybe a customer. Maybe a trusted customer."

Fuentes: "Tuesday was your first time?"

I almost smiled at how easily he would have been fooled. I was pretty sure anyone who could connect me to Vita in the past was dead. But I didn't want to chance getting caught lying. I said, "I've known her for a long time. On and off."

"How long?" Torbett asked.

I saw her dead on the rug and wondered what I could have done to prevent that. "Fourteen years."

I could have pointed out that we only had sex once before, making me an occasional purchaser rather than a regular whoremonger. Suddenly I didn't care what it cost me. I wasn't ashamed to be associated with her. And whether it was exactly true or not, I said, "She was a friend."

47.

By the time we finished talking, Hay's people had loaded Vita into a body bag and into their wagon. The fire engine and ambulance headed off. The three patrols stuck around to fill out reports. I suggested Fuentes start with her phone records. He sputtered, "You're not on this *case*, Reles. You're a *suspect!*"

I got in my car, Torbett and Fuentes got into theirs, and we all headed out in different directions. I made a big loop and came right back and looked at the house. A small, light green home, the sum of a lifetime. She'd worked and stayed alive longer than most of the women in her trade. She didn't have a pimp or a monkey on her back. She accomplished more than most women in any field had. And she was dead.

Yellow crime-scene tape sealed the front door, and only one patrol guarded the scene, sitting in his car. I waved at him, peeled the tape off the door and went in.

Blood stained the rug where she'd fallen. I wondered if she had next of kin or a friend to see to her burial. I opened some cabinets in the living room, dark wood veneer. One had a few bottles in it, not the well-stocked bar she kept back when she worked and lived in a tiny apartment and had to have drinks on hand for clients. Another held a turntable and her record collection. Frank Sinatra, Tony Bennett. Tunes for young lovers. Background music for dates. Dave Brubeck. Thelonius Monk. That spelled more than background. An interest in jazz. I never thought of her having interests.

I went into her bedroom. Her dresser held every conceivable garment: Panties made of silk, lace and licorice. Corsets of nylon and leather. Handcuffs with pink fuzz, whips, vibrators. An entire drawer with sections, probably intended for jewelry, now holding every type of condom in every color and size. Also dental dams, rubber gloves, finger cots and the limited-supply female condom. Other drawers: dildos and steel marbles and contraptions whose use I couldn't guess. And dust. None of this stuff, save for a few of the condoms, was getting any use. The elastic in the garments had stiffened, leftovers from a former career.

If there was a personal phone book, Fuentes had taken it, along with her wallet, checkbook and anything that would help track contacts. Good for him. I couldn't find any photographs, though she must have had a family, at least once. But then, there was a reason she'd become a hooker.

The closest thing to a personal effect I came across was her electric bill, and I found myself falling back on her bed to read it as if it were a letter: 6510 Hammack Drive. Eva Carballo.

Eva. Evita. Vita. I never thought about it before. I'd known her since my early days as a detective and I didn't know her real name. We weren't romantic. But after a certain number of years in the same place, the people who still know you and don't hate you, those are your friends.

Vita's green eyes stared at me.

My brain spun. Think, Reles. It's Saturday morning and you're in Austin. Why? Because when you were ten your mother ran off and when you were fifteen your father ran from the mob and landed here with you in tow. And you stayed. Why? No place else to go.

Vita's dead. One of a slim and thinning group of people who didn't hate you. You're not on the case, not officially. You're a suspect, facing possible arrest or indictment for murder. The force hates you for talking to IA. Mora's a stranger. Torbett's a company man. Rachel's back. She wants something. What? She said she'd find you.

Faith Copeland is dead. That's your case. Let Vita alone.

It's Saturday morning. Faith's family will be having a funeral. You should go.

I headed outside and resealed the front door with the yellow tape, then waved again at the patrol as I crossed the lawn. He waved back, this time with suspicion. He'd report that I went back in the house. So what? In my car I fished out the address the second Mrs. Copeland gave me on Thursday, the Hite-Wallis Funeral Home on Lamar. I had a dark blue necktie rolled up in my glove compartment for just such events. I smoothed it out the best I could and put it on. Along with the shirt and jacket, I'd probably be the classiest of Faith's friends. Maybe they'd think I was an agent. I dropped off the bloody chunk of broken curb at DPS, stained with the loan shark's DNA ("We'll do what we can"), and headed to the funeral home.

Redbrick building, six limos, three cabs. Inside, a black sign with white movable letters and an arrow: COPELAND MEMORIAL, BAY CHAPEL.

I recognized the first Mrs. Copeland, Faith's mother, by her waxed blond curls and floral-print showgirl dress, holding court among Faith's wide-eyed classmates, all swearing undying love for their fallen comrade and asking Mrs. C questions about her own career and agents she might know. I took the liberty of interrupting.

"Mrs. Copeland?" I made my way between the fans and stood close to her. "I'm Dan Reles. We met at your house."

Her jaw dropped slightly—we'd met in two of her blackouts—and she put her arms around my neck. If I hadn't turned to the right, she would have planted her tongue in my mouth, such is my appeal for women when they're blind drunk or in shock.

"God love you, baby," she murmured into my neck.

I said, "I'm sorry for your loss," or something like that.

She said, "She was *my* baby," putting the accent on "my" like someone would question it.

I asked, "When did you talk to her last?"

"She was a swell little gal. A real trouper. I'm thinking of opening a school."

The actors, four girls and three boys, all about college age, wondered if they should beat a quick retreat before things got embarrassing or stick around and see what she might do for their careers. She'd done such great things for Faith's.

Mrs. Copeland said, "Do you believe this dump?"

I saw a few adults about Faith's parents' age, men in suits and women in prim dresses. The church folks. Drifting back, my eye landed on a young woman in her mid-twenties, the oldest of the young actors. She had long, wavy dark hair, very light skin with a few too many layers of makeup, and dark eyes. She wore a black dress, something she saved for auditions. Young, pretty, overdone. But for an actress she looked sane. I walked over.

"Friend of Faith's?" I asked.

"Not really. You?"

"Friend of the family."

"They said she was murdered."

"That's what I heard. But no one knows who saw her last."

"She had class with us on Tuesday."

"When?"

"Tuesday afternoon. It broke up at five, and someone said we should go out for drinks, but only a few of us are of age. So Brian— that's him"—she pointed out a thin boy with baggy clothes and a prominent jaw—"said we should get beer and come up to his place." Then she asked, "Who *are* you?"

I told her. She nodded and considered the weight of what she was saying, but she didn't stop.

"Brian shares a house with two other boys off South Congress. There were maybe twelve of us. Faith was the youngest."

"You knew she was sixteen?" I asked.

"We all knew. But she was famous, so people sucked up to her. Anyway, people sort of spread out over the house. A couple of the girls were jealous of her because she already had a TV show."

"Were *you?*"

She rolled her eyes.

I said, "Did you know she made porn films?"

Something shifted in her eyes. She looked over at the three boys, who were talking and laughing.

"No," she said. "But I bet *they* did. They were always making cracks behind her back. And the girls, the jealous ones, were talking about her having no talent. It was true, though. She was terrible."

"And that's the conversation Faith walked in on?" I asked.

She nodded. Then she said, "I'll show you something." I followed her a few steps down the hall. There was a small room with padded benches around its perimeter. Faith's father sat opposite the entrance in a rumpled tan suit, necktie loosely fastened. He perched on the edge of a bench with his knees spread and his loafers planted on the floor. His wife and another woman flanked him, both in their church dresses. They tried to comfort him but it was no use. His mouth spread in a painful grimace and he kept collapsing downward in sobs, as if a mallet were hitting him over the head four times, then giving him a chance to breathe. Tears poured down his cheeks.

I wondered who would cry like that for Vita.

Then the young woman led me back to the crowd, some of them filing into the chapel. Mrs. Copeland was surrounded again by a cluster of young actors. Her eyes rolled up the way people's do when they're traveling into a glorious past. And she was singing some bouncy song and delicately laying out the dance steps that went with it.

The young woman next to me said, "Tell me who loved Faith. And who loved showbiz."

48.
||||||

West of the National Guard division at Camp Mabry, high on Mount Bonnell overlooking the river as it curved north, sat the stately home of Judge Earl Munson and, near it, the battered white Honda Civic of Sergeant Cate Mora. Mora's lawyer friend Vivian Ruggleman was on Mrs. Ortiz's case. She said the first lawyer filed suit for wrongful arrest. The suit got thrown out. The bail never got lowered. It came down to the judge.

Mora braced herself, walked up the front path and knocked. The door opened on a small, white-haired woman in her sixties. "Yes?" she said with apprehension.

Mora put on her military voice. "I'm Sergeant Mora with APD. Sorry to disturb you. May I speak with the judge?"

The woman closed the door. In five minutes it opened again. Judge Munson stood about six feet, reddish hair turning gray, slicked straight back from a puffed red face with broken blood vessels in the nose and cheeks. He wore loose gray slacks and a red-striped, long-sleeved shirt, straining under the pressure of a huge gut. It crossed Mora's mind that he'd be more comfortable in a white sheet. He didn't speak.

"Sir, I need to speak to you about Carla Ortiz." Not a nod. She went on. "She was arrested at Salina Street—"

"I know who she is."

Mora said, "Then you know she's still in jail. I have some papers here." She showed him the arrest report but he didn't open the screen door to take it. "The arrest report indicating that the officer who suppressed Mrs. Ortiz's alleged violence, the one responsible for her bruises, was Carlos Piñero—"

"Yes?" the judge boomed.

Mora kept going. "I have the duty roster for that day. Officer Piñero was out sick. The arrest report was falsified. The case is full of holes like this. I think the best thing to do is drop the charges quietly and hope she doesn't sue the city."

"You can leave your papers at my office on Monday," he said, and began to swing the door shut.

"There's something else, sir," Mora said. "I know you're a law-and-order man and a law-and-order candidate"—she noticed him lift a bushy eyebrow—"but Mrs. Ortiz's son, Rolando, was remanded to the custody of a foster home while she was in jail. He ran away. We found his wallet yesterday by the tracks, along with a bloody piece of piano wire. Do you think I can release her before I have to tell her that?"

He stared hard at her, then opened the storm door long enough to take the papers. "I'll look these over." He started to close the door again.

Mora said, "Just one last thing, sir. Back at HQ, people are afraid of how this whole Salina Street thing makes us look. She never should have been arrested. But now I think people are afraid to release her, afraid it might look like we're admitting we screwed up. When the business of the boy's wallet hits the papers, probably tomorrow, we're going to look even worse. I bet you won't even want to be associated with us. Or with keeping Mrs. Ortiz in jail."

Without taking his eyes off her, he closed the door.

Mora slipped back into her car. She'd done what she could to get Mrs. Ortiz released. Now she just had to find Rolo.

Wherever he was.

49.
||||||

A twenty-five-foot-long pewter fork stood on end outside the restaurant, piercing a sculpted artichoke two feet in diameter. Though they replaced the food product every few months, the utensil remained, allowing advertisers to mark the location of the Hyde Park Bar and Grill "at the fork in the road." Cute.

After I left Faith's funeral, Dispatch radioed me, *"Homicide 8,"* and I jolted because I figured they were calling me in to arrest me for beaning Vita. Instead they had a message from Rachel to meet her at that restaurant if I could and no callback number. Inside the entrance, at the height of the Saturday brunch bustle, Rachel waited in the middle of a crowd, still in her dark brown raincoat. At five foot eight, she stood taller than many women, but I noticed the low shoes that went with the dark coat in what looked like an attempt to blend in with the woodwork. She told the hostess our party was complete. The hostess responded with a shrug. There were too many people around for us to start playing catch-up or lie about how good the other one looked, so we squirmed in silence.

I thought about Vita staring up from the carpet, blood in her hair. Her eyes saying, *Look what you did to me.*

They finally got us to a table. Rachel ordered the *migas,* an interesting blend of eggs, peppers and whatever else is handy, and asked if she could substitute a baked potato for the home fries. The waiter, a musclebound dunce of about twenty-five, probably just Rachel's speed when she was his age, said, "No substitutions on the specials." He didn't smile and he didn't apologize.

Rachel smiled for him, attempting to soften the situation. "What if I pay an extra dollar."

He said, "No."

Rachel took the special as is, and I had the same just to get rid of him. The waiter left us alone.

Rachel broke the silence. "I saw you crossing the street. You limp."

"No, that's just . . . I favor my right leg."

"Oh," she said. "Favoritism."

In the silence she struggled for something else to say. I didn't help her any.

She said, "You look great."

I said, "So do you."

She shook her head. "It's hard now. You saw the waiter. I couldn't get a substitution by paying for it. Ten years ago he would have given me the meal for free."

She slouched in her seat like the weight of years was pulling her down. But it wasn't that many years. I knew women her age and older who looked great.

"There are things," she said, and stopped. "Things I need to tell you about."

I wasn't trying to make it easy for Rachel. She left me. She left me for being a lousy boyfriend, for jumping up and leaving at the ring of the phone, for putting my career before her. I deserved it. But she left me, took off like my mother. It was hard not to hold it against her.

She said, "I have this tape I listen to. Piano music. Keith Jarrett. I listen to it all the time. I don't really like it anymore. It makes me sad."

"Why do you keep listening to it?"

She looked away. "When I was a girl . . ." and petered off. Then: "Things were bad. My parents hated each other. It was a bad home. I wouldn't want that for any . . . for anybody."

I knew there were things about Rachel's past she hadn't told me. I'd pried before, and I wouldn't do it again. I noticed her hands shaking.

She turned to me. "I drink now. But it's okay."

Rachel spent her youth drunk and stoned. Her husband, my best friend Joey Velez, had sobered her up. She stayed that way the whole time I knew her, maybe ten years, including the two years we lived together. But the last time I saw her, she was drunk.

She said, "I live in L.A."

"I don't know why you're telling me this." Waiter boy clinked down our plates, nearly elbowing me in the mouth. I waited until he left, and then I said, "Any of this. Why are we here?"

She opened her pocketbook, a clasp number in a slightly duller brown than her raincoat. It was overflowing with junk— cigarette packs, matchbooks, used tissues. She used to be so organized.

She said, "I didn't come here alone. I brought someone with me."

Long about then I figured the icing on the cake would be a snapshot of Rachel with the new man in her life. Or maybe the new woman, the final insult: you turned me off of guys.

Finally she fished out a tattered envelope, and in it a three-by-five-inch department-store photo on a fake background of a setting sun. A small boy in a light blue shirt two sizes too big—charity clothes—and a striped tie. Brown hair and a low forehead like Rachel's, with Rachel's feline eyes looking sad, too sad for such a little kid. He even had Rachel's cheekbones.

But my nose.

"His name is Josh," she said. "He's three and a half."

50.
▏▏▏▏▏▏

Mora stood in the release area at Travis County Jail, looking through three sets of tempered-glass doors to the large, heavyset guard who escorted Mrs. Ortiz through the first door, which closed behind them with a loud clang and an audible automatic lock sliding into place, then the second door, then the door that let the little woman, in the bright blue dress she'd worn for the Valentine's party two months earlier, out into freedom. The judge had called. Smiling wide but with tears in her eyes, Mrs. Ortiz embraced Mora, called her *amiga* and *amor,* things you'd say to a beloved sister or daughter. Mora signed something for the guard and took Mrs. O's hand, walking the woman back into the sunlight for the first time. Mora wouldn't deny the woman her last moment of happiness. The small woman spread her arms wide, rosary still tangled between her tiny fingers, leaned back and breathed in the downtown smells of exhaust and hot tar that passed for clean air. Then Mrs. Ortiz turned to Mora with a smile and asked something as if there were no possibility but a good answer.

"Where is my son?"

51.
⫿⫿⫿⫿

I found my car near the restaurant and sat at the wheel, assessing.

I had a son. His name was Josh. He was three. We'd never met. He'd spent his life so far without a father.

Rachel was pregnant when she left me. Why didn't she tell me? Did it matter?

Meanwhile Vita Carballo, semiretired sex professional, was dead, still staring up at me from her living room carpet. I was a suspect. I couldn't give my whereabouts the night of her death because I couldn't tell anyone I'd been with Mora. But I sure didn't want to do time for killing Vita. I wanted to find out who did kill her. And I wanted to plant him in the ground.

I was meeting Rachel and Josh for dinner. I had Faith Copeland's killer to find. I thought about her funeral, her stage mother, her classmates who didn't give a shit about her. I thought of Faith lying about her age and going to acting class, living alone as an adult after she never had a chance to be a kid. I kept thinking of the loan shark who blamed her death on bad parenting. I thought about her father sobbing at the funeral, the way he'd sobbed days earlier when I told him about her death. I wondered what I would do if someone hurt my son. The idea made me crazy, more so than if someone wanted to hurt me.

And someone did.

52.

Russell Copeland sobbed as his wife led him in the door, sobbed as she sat him in his den and took off his jacket and tie and shoes, unbuttoned his suit pants and pulled them off his legs and laid a blanket over his lap. He cried as she poured him a brandy and tipped it into his mouth.

He'd laid his daughter in the ground. His only girl. Why?

She was out alone. She should have been with him. She should have been safe at home.

But she wasn't safe at home. Home wasn't safe.

It was his fault. She'd been alone because of him. She suffered because of him. He'd pay. He'd pay long and hard. He deserved it.

53.

I went by the home of Faith's mother and peeked into the front window. She was drinking in front of the TV again. I knocked.

I asked to take another look at Faith's scrapbook, which she produced proudly. The scrapbook had a story to tell if I was smart enough to hear it.

"That's Faithie at her first beauty contest," she said, pointing out a shot of a bald, sleeping baby with a bow taped to her head. Her father looking proud, happy. "Here she is with her first trophy." Faith at about four, peroxide hair, loads of lipstick and rouge. Mother aglow. Dad, I noticed, looking uneasy. "This is her at five as Miss Tennessee Valley. That's when we started traveling." Faith as a five-year-old whore, in a black sparkling gown, cut low to emphasize a future cleavage. My skin shifted. Mother in a shot from the same event, talking to an interviewer. Dad in a chair, courting a coronary. And around the same time, a shot of Faith from behind, white-blond hair falling over her shoulders, nude, coming from a dressing room wearing only a pair of red high heels. Tiny little girl's body with "adult" stamped on the hair and feet. People laughing, a little girl making a surprise display of self-confidence, or at least a lack of shame rare in adult culture. And the camera grabs good old Pop, seeing her emerge from the dressing room. In his wide eyes and gaping jaw, in his reddening complexion, a story: shock and surprise.

And, if I'm any judge of emotions, desire.

And a snapshot of Faith at the end of a long day, in her hooker outfit, sitting in her father's lap and leaning her head on his shoulder. Dad looking in the opposite direction, lips in a solid frown.

"Russ stopped traveling with us around then. He said she shouldn't do the shows, but we wouldn't stop. Showbiz was her life! He went all Jesus on me, but I didn't listen. Say, can I get you a cold one?"

I headed out and drove toward HQ in the afternoon haze.

I tried to put together the story. Russ Copeland squirmed at the sight of his daughter playing dress-up for adults. Maybe, just maybe, he turned a corner and discomfort got replaced by desire. Maybe he had a conscience, so he felt bad and worried and wanted to protect her from himself or from thousands of others just like him. He wanted her away from the stage. But Mom was a stage mom, and she wasn't having it. So he left, figuring the kid was safer with her drunk stage mother than with her horny dad. And he tied himself up with the church, married a grown woman who saw things the same way and led a normal life. But desire doesn't just disappear.

He was fine as long as he stayed the hell away from Faith. Meanwhile her mother led her through a world of people just like him, coaches and judges and casting directors, an elaborate system designed for the tasteful pimping of a child. At sixteen she was used up, alone and unemployed. And since she'd never had a childhood, she was at a disadvantage. So she lived like a grown-up. And when things went bad, she called her father. Just a guess: I was still waiting for the last of her phone records. She was humiliated at a party. She took some pills. She was stoned and maybe naked. She didn't know where she was.

He arrived, and he was weak. And he jumped on her. Maybe he was crying the whole time. So what. When it was over, he felt bad and tried to clean up his crime and put her in the bath. And that's how Faith Copeland became a statistic.

It was a neat idea but it needed proof.

I called Dispatch to ask if there was any word from DPS about Faith's DNA test or any matches between the perpetrator and the various suspects. There was no word, so instead of calling DPS, I headed over.

54.
⫿⫿⫿⫿⫿

Mora had four potential matches on the Torino wagon in Texas. Two eliminated. One, in Lubbock, possible but missing. The last in Mexia. She checked her road map. North on 35 to Waco and then east. Maybe 120 miles total, to Mexia. She rolled east on Sixth Street and onto I-35 north, picking up speed. She flipped on the flashing lights in case anyone was looking, and she floored it. The engine revved and jolted into gear, roaring under her. She could do it in two hours if she beat the traffic, even at the speed limit. She'd make it closer to an hour, while it was still light.

Mora lied to Mrs. Ortiz, lied like a coward and said Rolo was out of town with his foster parents, that she'd track them down and get him processed. It might take overnight.

Maybe by then they'd know for sure, whether Rolo was alive or dead. Certainty was worth something, wasn't it? She'd done the right thing.

Meanwhile Mrs. Ortiz would be cleaning her house and getting ready for the homecoming that seemed less and less likely to happen.

Mora would get the bastard who killed Rolo Ortiz. She couldn't get the bastards who put him on the street and set him up to die. She worked for them.

55.
||||||

I got to DPS and leaned on them about rushing the tests. Since it was Saturday and Ron Wachowski wasn't in, I threw his name around like he was my brother. A grunt showed me a sample DNA result, the rows of black rectangles that I was somehow supposed to read.

Maybe I was off base looking at people she knew. Maybe it was some crazy stalker who'd been watching her since she was a kid on TV. Maybe a porn fan who tracked her and found her. Maybe someone who just liked the alley and cruised it until he found ripe prey. Maybe not.

As I stepped through the lobby toward the exit, a familiar voice said, "I thought you people didn't work Saturdays."

I spun around. "Miles!"

Miles Niederwald had been my CO from the day I was mentored

onto Homicide until he left the force for the DA's office. He hoisted his two hundred or so pounds up from a chair, and they sloshed like bags of water. As he smiled and shook my hand, I noted the strips of white hair still plastered over the top of his head, the chunks of dandruff, the odor of slightly used liquor. "It's four in the afternoon," I said. "What are you doing vertical?"

"I go light on weekends. Lets me drink more at the office." We stepped out into the light and leaned on my car.

"How's this for a coincidence?" I said.

"It ain't a coincidence. Dispatch said you'd be here."

"You were looking for me?"

He squinted in the sunlight. "Know a guy named Fuentes?"

I thought about Vita again, on the carpet. "Why?"

"He's been callin' our office, trying to put together enough for an indictment. Vita Carballo. Murder one. You know her?"

"You could say that."

Miles said, "Six times out of ten, you go through a victim's things, you find a picture of the killer and the victim with their arms around each other."

"What's he got?"

"Possible DNA. No alibi. Witness who saw you there, but not that night."

I said, "Who's the witness?"

He shook his head.

I said, "You don't know, or you won't tell me?"

"Don't get so righteous, Jewboy. Anyone finds out I told you this, it's me in the cuffs. What the hell's going on?"

I told him. I told him about me telling IA about Clay, and Clay getting pulled in by the feds, and the rock in my exhaust pipe and the brick in my front window. I told him about Cate Mora and our moment at her apartment. I told him about Rachel and Josh. I told him about Faith Copeland and Vita Carballo, both dead and waiting for me to do something about it. I waited. He hissed out air like a balloon.

"Shhhooooooo-eee. Boy," he said, "you fucked up!"

I passed on the chance to remind him that he hadn't exactly retired with a gold watch but instead cleared out of his office in the middle of the night rather than face a disciplinary hearing.

He looked off over the parking lot. "Worry about the rock and the brick. You know who did it?"

"No. Anybody. Clay and his friends. The Family."

He looked at me hard. Then he leaned back against my car and pulled his chins in. He looked scared.

I said, "What do you know about them?"

He shifted around, breathing hard through his nose. "We never talked about them. I don't know how I even knew the name. I don't remember anyone sayin' it before. Yeah, I know about 'em."

He hushed up. He wasn't even in the department anymore. He'd known me for years, stuck his neck out for me when he'd have been better off keeping his mouth shut. But he was afraid to talk about the Family.

He said, "Ever hear of Jud Holland?"

"Maybe the name."

"You can't tell this to anyone. Anyone!"

I nodded.

He said, "He pulled down this big case, grand larceny, second degree. Stereos, sound systems. Half a million worth of stuff, all disappears from the evidence locker. He don't want to lose the conviction, he goes over the duty log, figures who was there, who was on duty, nails it down to three names. Someone, I ain't sayin' who, tells him to drop it. He goes ahead, reports it to his CO, to IA, to the chief."

He stopped. His face faded a shade or two lighter than its normal pasty white.

"His neighbors called it in. I was senior sergeant then. I got the call. Four shots. His wife, his two kids and him."

"What?"

"I never told nobody this. You can't tell nobody."

"Tell them what?"

He licked his lips. I could tell he needed a drink, even water. "The bodies. They were all shot from different places. Not one guy standing in the living room and shooting. If that happened, they would have run. I'm talking four people, in the main room, all shot at point-blank range. So either they stood there and waited their turn . . ."

"Or?"

"Figure three gunmen, maybe four. I didn't say anything. Shit, I knew the slugs wouldn't match each other."

"I don't get it."

"You're not supposed to!" he hissed. "For the papers it was murder/suicide. He went off the deep end, killed his loved ones, turned the gun on himself. But they wanted it to look suspicious. They wanted everyone to know." He leaned toward me and whispered, even though we had the parking lot to ourselves. "You can't cross them. They'll kill you. They'll kill your family and make you watch."

"Jesus."

"You got a family of your own now. Ain't but one thing to do. Be a man. Buckle under."

"It's too late," I said. "I talked already. I told them about Clay and Czerniak."

He leaned back. "Then hope to Christ they blame Czerniak."

56.
||||||

In the dimming afternoon light, Judah knocked on the double doors of Suzanne's bedroom. Paul Wade was somewhere, somewhere in the house. But they'd had separate rooms for years, since before Judah came around. And it was clear Paul had stopped bothering to attempt intrusion.

Judah heard her cough softly, the closest she'd get to granting permission, and he opened the doors and slipped inside. Suzanne curled up on the enormous four-poster bed. A dozen satin-cased pillows propped her up and surrounded her where she lay, waking from her afternoon nap in a fuzzy white robe, one arm lying over the top of a thin blanket. Hazy light sifted in through the white curtains.

"Suzanne?"

She didn't answer. He sat on the bed. She winced as the bed shifted and settled. He put his great hand to her forehead.

"Judah?" Her voice was small.

"I'm here."

"Did you take care of everything?"

He said, "It's been a big week."

"You're so good to me."

"I love you."

"Oh, Judah."

"Do you love me?"

No answer. Even at a low point, she wouldn't say it. "I can't," she said.

Judah said, "Your true marriage is to the one you truly love, who most loves you."

She didn't answer. Instead she said, "What about tomorrow? The AARO conference."

"I'm working on it. Kiss me."

She giggled. Then she slipped out of bed and went into the bathroom, locking the door.

Suddenly Judah felt fury rise in his chest. He'd invested before once, worked hard for someone and then got squeezed out. It wouldn't happen again.

She'd be his, fortune and all, and soon. Or she'd be no one's.

57.
ⅠⅠⅠⅠⅠⅠ

I cleaned up the last of the broken glass, scrubbed the kitchen and bathroom and vacuumed the rugs and shaved and showered again and put on clean jeans and sneakers and a T-shirt in hopes of making myself less scary to a kid who would be looking at a strange man twice his size. I tried not to think about the possible indictment for murder that was waiting for me or who really killed Vita Carballo or just what kind of father Russell Copeland was or whether the Family would let me live out the week.

When I was a little kid in Elmira, New York, I was my mother's constant companion. That my father went off to prison when I was eight, to sit two years for one of the mob bosses, went almost unnoticed. I was glad to have my mother to myself, and she seemed fine with his absence. But the day he came back, she packed a suitcase and left. My dad came home to me alone, a kid he didn't much know or like, who had stolen his woman away. And though we lived together, we remained strangers. I'd be a better father.

I walked the house a few times, peeked out the window, brushed my teeth, changed my shirt, looked out the window again and saw the rented white Plymouth Rachel pulled up in. She talked to Josh, whose dark head was facing her, away from the house. I stood inside and waited.

I opened the door. The sun was low in the west, and Rachel stood smiling in her dopey brown raincoat, holding the boy by the hand. He stood somewhere under three feet. He wore a plaid flannel jacket, big enough to make him look like he was wrapped in a blanket, and his dark pants were cuffed. Clothes that had been bought for someone else. He looked like the picture, with Rachel's dark blue eyes and low forehead and my nose before it matured: longer than most from top to tip but still turned up. It would grow. With luck it wouldn't get broken so much.

Rachel said, "Dan Reles. This is Josh Reles."

I put my hand out. "How's it going, sport?"

By way of response, he put his arm around his mother's waist and pulled himself behind her. His father's son.

In the dining area at Pandemonium Playland, away from the trampoline tent and the rope bridges and the room of saliva-coated plastic balls, I sat with my lost love and my son over a pepperoni pizza and some root beers. Josh opposite me, Rachel to his right.

Josh tickled a half-eaten slice of pizza. Tomato sauce circled his mouth and filled some of the many gaps between his tiny teeth. It amazed me to see that children's teeth were that small.

He whimpered, "But I don't *like* pepperoni."

Rachel looked tired. "You said you did."

"No, I like the *other* kind."

"I can take the pepperoni off."

He puffed air in little bursts out of his mouth. No crisis greater than the wrong pizza.

Rachel was beginning to shift around in her seat. I suspected that the root beer wasn't strong enough. She needed to finish the evening and get a drink.

"So, Josh," I said. "What do you . . . what do you like?"

He looked worried, like he was taking a quiz. "I don't know."

"Do you like to play ball?"

"No."

Rachel said, with a touch of impatience, "He likes to watch TV."

I said, "What's your favorite show?"

He shrugged. Rachel was shifting around. She took hold of her pocketbook and said, "We should go back to the hotel."

I said, "No, stay with me."

Josh gaped. Rachel said, "You don't have space."

"Plenty of space," I said. "Josh can take the extra room, you take my room, and I'll stay on the couch."

The house, technically, had two bedrooms, though one was mostly used for storage. Its furniture was limited to my weight bench and a rolled-up single futon. If not for the window, it would have qualified as a large closet.

For whatever reason, Rachel went along with my offer.

Rachel and Josh went to the motel to get their things, and I waited for them in front of the house. I still lived on the southern border of the public golf course, a fenceless patch of greenery with some holes. Along the western border still stood the house where Rachel lived when I met her, when she was another man's wife. Now she was in trouble, and I could help. The sky had cleared and stars shone over the park. A thought drifted into my head, a complete thought, as if someone whispered it to me: not a bad place to raise a kid.

If I could make it safe.

58.
‖‖‖‖‖

Russell Copeland sat in his study, on his itchy chair, under his itchy afghan, watching a rerun of Faith's show on the local station.

"Uncle Jack! You're not gonna lie to that lady, are you?"

The audience laughed, though Russell couldn't see why.

He'd asked Lucille not to put Faith on the stage, insisted, begged, threatened. It made him crazier every time he saw her get dressed up for one of those stupid pageants. The fights with Lucille got worse. They became enemies. He'd come home with stomach pains at the thought of seeing her. Finally they went to Hollywood, Lucille and Faith. And Russell came to Jesus.

But the pain didn't go away. And the other pain, the pull to be with Faith, got stronger each time he thought about her. Not his fault. Lucille dressed her up like a harlot. He tried not to think about it. Remarried after the divorce came through. Sent Faith letters and Christmas cards like a good father. But stayed away when she came home and gave her a cold shoulder for her own good.

And now she was dead, and it was his fault.

Maybe at the last minute he could pray, take it all back and ask for forgiveness. Maybe he should make sure he was praying at the moment of death. A straight ride to glory. He wanted to believe it. But he didn't deserve glory. He deserved hellfire.

He looked at the screen. Sweet Faith. Little Faith. My baby. Rest easy. Your pain is done.

Mine is just beginning.

59.
‖‖‖‖‖

Rachel pulled up behind my car in her generic white rental, climbed out and gently closed the door. Josh slept in the back seat.

"He cried," she said. "He cries a lot. Then he falls asleep."

"He's terrific," I said. "You've done a great job."

She didn't answer, and we leaned on the sidewalk side of my car, looking up. The pecan tree was starting to bud. Pecans pummeled the lawn each fall. I never figured out anything to do with them besides rake them up and bag them like leaves.

"I'll take the couch," she said.

"No, I will."

She quivered. "I can't . . . sleep . . . in that bed."

I hadn't forgotten—I just didn't make the connection—that she was abducted from that very bed years earlier, kidnapped and nearly killed. The feeling was still fresh in her mind.

Rachel glanced at Josh. "He's done with diapers except at night. There's an accident once in a while."

I nodded.

She said, "You want to know why I left."

"Just tell me why you didn't say you were pregnant."

Her nose and eyes had taken on a reddish cast, and I could guess she'd stopped for a drink. With Joshua in tow.

She lit a cigarette and said, "I didn't plan on keeping him. It wouldn't have been the first time. But the first in a while. I didn't think I could get pregnant. I'd had some . . . problems, before. And things were bad between us so I didn't tell you."

She pulled in smoke and looked at the sky.

"You wouldn't understand," she said, exhaling. "When you're drinking, you don't stick to things. You can decide to take a shower and not get to it for a week. I had to find a new place to live and find work. But I would take a drink to ease the shaking so I could go into an interview. And then I'd try not to take another but I'd take it anyway, sucking it in like air. And then I knew I had to make calls about an abortion, but I didn't know who to call and time was passing. I was starting to show. I called different states trying to find out who would take me four months along. And then it was six months. It was too late. I tried to stop drinking. I promised myself a blowout when he was born. But it was harder than before. I'd string a few days together and then lose control, and it would be worse."

Long silence. I said, "You never talked to me like this before." Wind behind us rattled the reeds in the golf course. I said, "I'd have helped. You could have come here."

"Drunk and pregnant. Drunk with a baby. I couldn't."

"Why didn't you call me?"

"I *couldn't*."

"Why didn't you call someone else?" I could hear the mounting anger in my voice.

She screamed, "There *isn't* anyone else!"

Josh started crying. Rachel said, "Oh, God!" and stamped out her cigarette. She opened the car door and leaned the front seat forward. "Come on. Mommy can't lift you like this."

I tapped her shoulder. She moved over and let me reach in to pick up Josh. His eyes were closed, and he was crying, more or less, in his sleep, or he wouldn't have let me pick him up. His arms fell loosely around my shoulders when I moved him and then clamped on tight, and he fell asleep again. But he held on for dear life anyway.

I stood up and held him for a moment, looking at the sky over the golf course and feeling, for the first time, my son sleeping against my chest. She could be happy here, I thought. I'll *make* her happy. I turned to smile at Rachel and felt a warm, moist sensation as Josh wet his pants.

60.
‖‖‖‖‖

Russell Copeland slid the shower door open, rippled greenish glass that distorted the world, then closed the drain and ran hot water.

He stood before the medicine cabinet as the tub filled. Bowed his head. Then, with all his strength, he raised his face and looked into his eyes. Darkness. Shame. A man caught in a crime. He stripped off his shirt.

Gloria had stood so much. He should do this better, for her. Make it look like an accident. But he couldn't wait another minute.

Medicine cabinet: Iodine. Sleeping pills. Gauze tape. Razor blades.

He popped out a clean blade, peeled off a strip of gauze tape and wrapped it around one sharp edge, folded it over, wrapped it around again and laid the blade on the edge of the tub.

He turned off the water in the tub, slid the glass doors over to the side by the faucet and took off his pants. Steam rose from the water. He stepped in, wearing only his boxers and socks. The water scalded him. He squelched any sound. He'd have to get used to it.

He held both arms under the water, gritting his teeth. Then he took the blade and ran the edge gently along his wrist, a tiny scrape, mapping a path.

"Our Father, who art in heaven, nngh!" He cut into the vein. A dribbling noise sounded as the first drops of blood poured into the water. "Oh, God, it hurts!" he said, a tiny voice, like a girl. "Oh, God!" He realized what a rat he was for leaving this mess for Gloria to clean up. And he braced himself and cut again, thinking, Please, God, please, God. Send me to hell. But take Faith to heaven.

61.
⫿⫿⫿⫿⫿⫿

Exactly 47.2 miles east of Waco, on 5.2 square miles once under the authority of the heirs of Mexican general José Antonio Mexía, lived the 6,563 souls of the town of Mexia, Texas. The locals pronounced it "Ma-HAY-a" adding, "a great place to live, no matter how you say it." When Mora got to the police station, eight of the department's twenty-six employees were on duty, it being Saturday night, under the menacing mission statement "To maintain the social order in the City of Mexia." Of these eight, six were on patrol and two—one sworn, one administrative—were at the station. Both Caucasian, both disinclined to accept the intrusion of a Latin woman with a detective's badge from the city of Austin.

"People say Texas needs a state zoo," the uniformed officer joked with good nature. "Hell, just put bars around Austin."

Mora chuckled as loud as she could and wondered why she hadn't gone straight to the house of the Torino owner. But her badge counted for little outside Austin, and if she found legitimate evidence she didn't want it ruled out for an illegal search.

The officer on duty was named Walther, and Mora tried to impress upon him the situation. A boy was abducted and killed. He was picked up in a Torino wagon in great condition, vintage 1976 or earlier, with Texas plates. Four such vehicles in Texas, two ruled out. One missing. One here, registered to a Mrs. Violet Sayles of Mexia.

"Dee-ceased," Walther said.

"How long?"

"Six months?" he asked the secretary. "Maybe six months. Her daughter came from Abilene and saw to the funeral. She put the house on the market, I think."

"Do you know the cause of death?"

"Old age. Heart attack. Something like that."

"Was there an autopsy?"

"Was there an autopsy?" he mocked her. "She was an old lady. She died in her house. The coroner put it at heart attack, something like that! Damn!"

Mora knew that in some of the smaller counties, authorities awarded the job of coroner for reasons known only to them. Maybe the sheriff's cousin needed a job. More often than not, the sheriff's cousin wasn't a doctor.

She waited until Walther opted to radio the men on patrol and ask who wanted a date with "the pretty señorita from Austin" to go out to the old Sayles house. Someone named Russo was game, and with confusing directions Mora headed out to meet him, wondering how many Mexia residents could boast Italian descent.

Peeling off Miller Street on the northwest edge of town ran North Bonham Street, itself giving way to a tiny dirt road, or a long driveway, leading into the woods. And at the end of the driveway stood the house that had once belonged to Mr. and Mrs. Sayles. A small, simple structure painted red, it looked to Mora like the Christmas gathering place for a family of lesser means, humble and respectable. And dark.

The patrol she'd heard called Russo was a kid, a fat young rube with light hair. Mora saw by the badge on his shirt that his name was spelled Rousseau. With a little struggle, he resigned himself to the connection between a brown woman and a detective's badge. They both took flashlights from their cars, and Mora took a tire iron.

She pried open the front door. Its rotted edge broke off in splinters. She flashed the light around. Roaches scattered. She and Rousseau separated and scanned the house. Sad furniture in the living room, sagging cushions laden with doilies. Mora found a kitchen. Something crawled over her foot. She jumped and shuddered, shining the light. Mice. They scampered over the counter space. Cute magnets stuck to the cabinets, telling of trips to Florida. Contact paper. A quiet refrigerator, an eye-burning stench from within.

The family hadn't packed anything. They buried the old woman and, perhaps, called a real estate agent. In the master bedroom, Mora found Rousseau. He was standing at the dresser and shining his light over the family photos, children and grandchildren, mothers in high-necked dresses, ancestors posing stone-faced for nineteenth-century portraits, men in cowboy hats. Pioneers. She looked for something recent, maybe a current photo of a large young man. Rousseau moved from the dresser and made his way around the room. He found a door, a closet, and Mora turned when she heard it creak open, just as Rousseau shined his light in and said, "Uh-oh."

SUNDAY

*I was walking through my house, only it was bigger, old, with two sto-
ries and wooden floors and high ceilings and four bathrooms and secret passageways. And my family had lived there, parents and
grandparents, for generations, lived together and loved each other
and grew old and happy together. Josh is a baby, and I'm holding him,
and Rachel is with us, and we swing around in a circle. Josh is four, and
we're in the backyard, and I'm teaching him to throw a football. Josh
is seventeen and off at school, and Rachel and I sleep on a big bed, soft
and welcoming, and feel safe in each other's arms.*

And the phone rang and I opened my eyes and the clock read
3:40 A.M. I picked up. "Yeah."

"Sergeant Reles, this is Dispatch. You better get over to 4112
St. John's Avenue right now. And when you're done with that, they want
you on the Fifth Floor."

"Now?"

"Search me. That's what they told me to tell you."

"Who's 'they'?"

She said, *"Them,"* and hung up.

I pulled on my clothes, and as I left the house, I saw Rachel asleep on the sofa, her breath loud and regular. Josh slept in the extra room. She was a drunk, and he peed on my shirt, and as I closed the front door softly behind me, I noticed a strange, unfamiliar sensation beginning in my stomach, like the satisfaction after a rich meal, and radiating outward. I wondered if it was what people called being happy.

I blinked to focus my eyes, turned the ignition and headed north on I-35, which still hummed from the last of the evening's revelers. I peeled off at St. John's. Standard gathering: two patrols, a car from DPS and an ME van.

A glassy-eyed patrolman named Vetter greeted me at the curb and told me that, nearly as he could figure, Mr. Copeland locked himself in the bathroom around ten. Since his daughter's death, the second Mrs. Copeland, Gloria, had been giving him a wide berth and letting him do what he wanted without bothering him. So she didn't notice until she had to use the bathroom a little after eleven. She knocked and he didn't answer, and she started to panic and called 911, and by the time Vetter got there and kicked the bathroom door in, it was way too late.

Mrs. Copeland got hysterical and screamed for an ambulance like they were going to bring him back. Vetter called the ambulance for her, and they treated her for shock and carted her off to Brackenridge. Vetter and another patrol radioed Dispatch, and Dispatch called the next Homicide detective on call, Highfill, and he showed up and realized Copeland was part of an active case and left. And by then it was past 3:00 A.M., when they called me.

When I entered the house, the patrols and the ME's people were standing around the living room like chess pieces. In the bathroom I scoped Russ Copeland lying in a bath of cool red water. His face shone pale, his head leaning sideways over the edge of the tub, jaw gaping, eyes to the heavens. Deep gashes laid open the flesh of his floating left forearm, exposing ruptured veins and arteries. Some of the blood had coagulated, and it looked like dark red worms. His right arm, short and pudgy with a small, pale hand, hung over the edge of the tub, palm up. The bloody razor blade lay on the tile. The DPS officer followed me into the bathroom and closed what was left of the door.

There are two kinds of suicide attempts. The minor ones are the ones that shouldn't work—the girl whose boyfriend left her, the guy who can't get a job. They take a few sleeping pills and call someone to come save them. If they really die, it's by accident. This is called a suicidal gesture. A "real attempt" is more dedicated. Someone who'll do anything to die. Russ Copeland wanted to die.

The DPS guy opened a file and handed me some paper. "The DNA tests on Faith Copeland and her perpetrator. Director Wachowski said you needed 'em."

I realized I was looking again at rows and rows of black rectangles. And a set of graphs, two with matching peaks and valleys. "They match!" I said. It would mean Faith was raped by a relative, possibly her father.

"No," he said, "Those are both Faith Copeland." And he handed me another sheet. "These are her attacker."

Different graphs, different peaks and valleys. I said, "Any chance this guy was a relative?"

"None," he said.

Russ Copeland's troubled eyes looked up at me.

Okay, Copeland, I thought. You didn't rape your daughter. You're not the worst father in the world. That's the most eulogy you'll get out of me.

I stepped out of the bathroom, out of the house, and looked at the stars.

Copeland was the odds-on favorite for his daughter's sad death. Now he was off the hook, as well as out of the picture.

But if Russ Copeland didn't kill Faith, who did?

It was nearly 5:00 A.M. when I pulled in to the municipal lot and fished out my rumpled necktie. Someone on the Fifth Floor needed to see me, someone who would be there in the wee hours of Sunday morning. But who slept on the Fifth Floor besides Jake Lund? Or was this something to do with Vita? And considering the climate at APD, was I about to find myself in an interview, an interrogation, or a cell?

63.
||||||

Cate Mora headed south on I-35 toward Austin, among the newspaper trucks and the bakery vans. She'd found the house where the Torino was registered. She and Rousseau, the local, flashed lights around. He looked in a closet and said, "Uh-oh." Mora followed him.

Pasted on the back wall of the closet was a collage of pictures and words. Yellowed newspaper photos of individuals—men, women and children—cut out and glued up. Someone had cut tiny white robes out of paper and stuck them on, so each head would have a robe. In another spot there burned a lake of fire made from cut paper and cellophane, with cartoon angels standing near it and flying overhead. The collage merged elements of order and frenzy, a dream depicted by a child who is both gifted and psychotic.

Rousseau's breaths came short. "What is it?" Mora asked. "Do you know these people?"

He said, "They were in the paper. The locals we lost in the fire."

"What fire?"

"Mount Carmel," he said, as if there were no other possibility. "Waco."

Mora got the Polaroid from her car and took shots of the closet wall. Then she started waking neighbors.

Judah was his name, a neighbor said. Big fella. He lived with Mrs. Sayles, like a son to her, taking care of the house and such. Been with her maybe two years.

Yes, Judah was one of them, a Branch Davidian. Judah Cavanaugh. No, he wasn't there when the ATF came in. No, I don't know why, but I can tell you who might.

Mora knew what most people knew about Waco. She knew they were a cult led by David Koresh, a charismatic leader, that they hoarded guns, and the ATF moved in on them. She knew that the Davidians refused to honor a search warrant and that the ATF botched the raid, which forced them to turn it over to the FBI. There was a standoff for fifty-one days, ending with a fire and eighty corpses, including about twenty children. There were those who claimed that the Davidians had started the fire, suicidally, like the Jews at Masada, rather than be taken prisoner. Whether it was the Davidians or the feds who started the fire remained a matter of much lively debate and a little lively violence.

Rousseau led Mora to the Adventist house, where Mora promised she would be polite and not ask too many questions. May Ellen Ory had stayed there since the fire, the neighbors said. Rousseau knew her. Everyone knew her. She'd spent her whole life in Mexia, raised as an Adventist. But the Branch Davidians broke from the Adventists, thought the Adventists weren't strict enough. They would draw recruits from the Adventists now and again, figuring Adventists were the best candidates. May Ellen never married. Her parents had long since passed on. She was alone in the world. She went.

Maybe, Mora wondered, Judah killed Mrs. Sayles. It looked like he'd killed Rolo. But there was more to the story.

When they drove up, a light went on upstairs. As Mora and Rousseau approached the door, it opened. May Ellen herself, big sad eyes framed in wrinkled beauty, clutching her robe with one barbecued hand.

She invited them in.

64.
ⅡⅠⅠⅠⅠ

It was still pitch black out with no sign of dawn as I walked into HQ, straightening my tie. I hadn't shaved, but they knew they woke me up. I considered possibilities.

Option one: Jake Lund had planned this out as some kind of elaborate gag.

I got up to the Fifth Floor. In the absence of a receptionist, I looked into the computer room. All dark. No light under Jake's office door. He was either gone or asleep.

Option two: They brought me in to grill me about my relationship with Vita Carballo. So what? I admitted we'd had sex, that we'd known each other for years. I had no wife, so it was a crime but not one anybody cared about. Still, if someone wanted to hold it against me professionally, they could.

Option three: They'd arrest me for Vita's murder.

I headed through two doors, propped open, to the inner sanctum, the doors leading to the offices of the assistant chiefs, and the one to the office of Chief Cronin. Only Cronin's had light showing under it.

Another option: Harland Clay. They wanted to question me about the Czerniak business, what Czerniak told me he saw Clay doing. Or Clay had something on me, maybe about Vita. Maybe they wanted to make a deal. Or kill me. I knocked. The door opened.

Inside, Assistant Chief Oliphant greeted me with a firm hand-shake, and another assistant chief gave me the same. There was a third suit, a thin man with close-cropped hair and taut features. No one bothered to introduce us. And behind the desk, with his Aryan complexion and graying blond hair around a shiny bald pate, his skin crumbling like stone, stepping from behind his desk to shake my hand and pat me on the shoulder, with a disturbing look of warmth in his normally soulless eyes, was Chief Charles Cronin.

Cronin told me to have a seat. He leaned on his desk, and the three others hovered around, nearly buzzing. I half expected them to offer me a cigar. He said, "Dan, how long have you been with the department?"

I looked around at the flunkies. "Am I being retired?"

They laughed hard at that. I looked back at Cronin. He had my file. I'd been there eighteen years, and he knew it to the day. So I didn't answer. I stared him down, thinking, You're gonna fire me? Prosecute me? Fine. I have as much on the department as you have on me. A lot I knew.

When Cronin finally looked like he was about to bust, he blurted out, "You're promoted. Congratulations, Lieutenant Reles!"

65.
||||||

At the big kitchen table, they sat. May Ellen made tea. Rousseau apologized for the intrusion.

"I was awake," she said. "I had a dream."

Mora asked, "The fire?"

She turned to Mora suddenly. "Is that what this is about?"

Mora handed May Ellen the Polaroids. She let May Ellen sip her tea and talk when she was ready.

"David Koresh was waiting for a message from God," May Ellen said. "The federals asked if he was coming out after Passover. He said he was. But he didn't say *right* after Passover. So they told everyone he lied. Well, Passover came and went and . . ." Her eyes teared up. "David foresaw all of it. The Fourth Seal."

"I don't understand."

"In Revelation. The Fourth Seal is Death. In the last days, David said that the Mount Carmel standoff was the siege described in Zechariah 14:2. The chariots with flaming torches, in Nahum 2:3, those were the tanks outside."

Rousseau said, "May Ellen, did you know a man named Judah?"

May Ellen stiffened, looked at Rousseau, then Mora. "What did he do?"

Mora said, "Could you tell us about him?"

May Ellen shook her head. "He was crazy. Fanatic. He was the one who talked David into getting all those guns. We were against it. Finally David sent him packing, but it was too late. Someone told the federals about the guns. That's what started everything."

The story seemed to keep looping back to the beginning. Mora said, "What about the robes?"

"You don't understand," she said. "They were there for fifty-one days. Guns and tanks. Just waiting. There was no way out. We were scared all the time. We hardly slept. The children were hysterical. And then the shooting started, and the fires. Not just in one place. The old building went up like kindling. The fire was everywhere. We couldn't get out. Babies screaming. I saw them die. . . ."

May Ellen's face reddened and her eyes teared, but she didn't quite break out into crying. There was no relief for her. She looked down, sad and broken.

"Judah was closest to David. Judah took care of him. Advised him. But he wanted to help with services, then he wanted to lead services. They had words. Terrible fights. And finally David told him to leave. I was worried. Then we started hearing about the investigation." Her nose reddened.

"Judah wanted to *be* David," May Ellen said. "And when David wouldn't let him, Judah got back at him."

"How?"

"It was Judah who brought in the guns. I can't prove it, but it was Judah who reported us to the government for having the guns. He knew David couldn't back down and still keep face. Do you know how children scream?" Mary Ellen glared at Mora. "Not when they're scared. When they're burning to death. I saw those babies die." She trembled. "And in the flames, as clear as I see you, I saw Judah's face. And he was laughing."

66.
▍▍▍▍▍▍

Before I knew it, I was up out of my chair, shaking hands, getting pats on the back from a slithering bunch of administrators and being grateful for it. Their comments rolled over me.

"About time, huh, guy?"

"Bet it feels great!"

Then Cronin said, "Effective immediately you are to take command of the Homicide Squad."

That shut me up. In the thrill of the moment, I forgot that a lieutenant has to be in charge of something. I would have asked for Organized Crime, but they hadn't let me on that squad since I helped create it, and they weren't about to put me in charge. Who cared? I could run Homicide the way I wanted. If that expanded into the rackets, as they developed in growing Austin, so it goes. They couldn't stop us from investigating murders.

I said, "What about Marks?" Marks headed Homicide, and he wouldn't take kindly to my displacing him.

"What *about* him?" the white assistant chief said, and we all laughed. My pals.

They just about had me hustled out the door when Cronin said, "I want you to come in tomorrow and start creating a conspicuous command presence."

"Yes, sir," I said. If he told me to set myself on fire, I'd have said the same.

And with a last pat on the back, he said, "Good. We're breaking the story on Monday," and closed the office door behind me.

I didn't get it till I was driving back home up I-35 in the cold darkness before first light. Break the story. Tell the newspapers. Former Homicide detective Dan Reles promoted to lieutenant and put in charge of Homicide. Why?

Friday morning I'd been on the news when Clay got pulled in by the FBI and pointed me out to the cameras, swearing revenge.

Bingo: The press had me as a whistle-blower. Czerniak was the real whistle-blower. But the press saw me. So now with all the scandals coming to a head, Mal Sueño and Salina Street, the department could point to me and say, "Look! We don't punish whistle-blowers! We promote them!"

Why not? They promoted dumber cops for less reason. As a lieutenant I'd have more money. We could get a bigger house. I'd answer fewer late-night calls. And I'd be better able to make the world a safer place for our son. I pulled up at home and slipped quietly into the front door, hoping to get to sleep for an hour or two before Rachel and Josh got up and the new day began. I'd break the good news over breakfast.

I started to fall asleep the second my head hit the pillow as I realized that Rachel wasn't on the couch when I came in. Maybe she was in the bathroom.

67.
||||||

Judah stood on trial.

They propped him up before everyone he knew. From Desert Storm. From the Davidians. David Koresh was there. And Violet Sayles. And Suzanne.

Suzanne stepped up to testify. And she looked at him, her dark eyes filled with compassion and love. He moved close to her. "Tell the truth," he whispered into her ear.

She nodded. Then, from a distance, she pointed to him and said, "He did it!"

The ground opened, and Judah was falling, and he jolted and was awake.

He sat up on his single bed, wiped the sweat off his face with a towel from his chair, wrapped it around his waist and walked down the hall, out of the servants' wing, into the fireplace room at the back.

With a stone fireplace six feet high and handmade diamond-pane windows looking out into the enclosed courtyard, the room always felt to Judah like a relic of an earlier century, though not in America. The stone floor did little to maintain heat in the drafty space. On a moderate night, the room held a graveyard chill.

Opposite the fireplace and the courtyard windows, the far wall—nearly all windows—opened onto the rear meadow. Suzanne stood against the glass in a soft white nightgown that reached the floor, staring out at the meadow, framed in moonlight like a ghost. He walked up behind her.

"They're taking it away," she said.

"Taking what away?"

"The party. They'll make it about money. It was never about that. It was about God."

He put his right arm around her. He could feel her curves under the thin cotton nightgown.

"Suzanne, we belong together."

"Sweet boy," she said, taking his hand and turning out of his embrace. "You're warm. Are you feverish?" She put a cool palm on his forehead. He took the hand and held it to his heart.

"Marry me, Suzanne."

She smiled and turned away. "Oh, Judah."

"We'd be together. We'd be happy. If we were married."

If they were married, he thought, she couldn't testify against him.

"But I'm with Paul. I'll always love you, in my way."

He wrapped his arms around her waist and pulled her close. Her toes barely touched the ground. "I won't wait any longer!"

"You're scaring me."

"I love you!" he blurted. "He doesn't love you. I do." Fear showed in her eyes. He lowered her to her feet, held her more loosely. "Look what I've done for you!"

"I'm grateful. If it's your salary—"

"No!" He couldn't walk away with a few dollars. Not after this. "I've done . . . I've taken risks for you. If something goes wrong, you'll be tied up in it."

"Judah," she said. "Tied up in what? What did you do?"

He leaned over her. The words came out sounding like an order. "Marry me."

Suzanne moved from him, backing away in a ladylike manner. "I think you should leave. I think it's time you left." She inched around toward the far door.

"Suzanne," he pleaded, "you don't understand."

"It's best for both of us."

He shouted, "Wait!" She froze. "You can't fire me. I know too much."

Suzanne's jaw hung open.

"Don't think I won't tell."

She said, "No . . . no one will listen. No one will believe you."

"You think I'm stupid! It doesn't have to stand up in court. I'll talk to the papers. I'll talk to your friends. I won't be sent away."

She stood silhouetted in the courtyard window. Judah approached her.

"Don't hurt me, Judah."

"Hurt you?" he said as his fingertips reached the delicate linen of her nightgown. "I love you."

And as he moved into her arms, her weak, submissive embrace, Judah saw in a flash, in the diamond windows leading out to the courtyard, a shadowed figure standing and watching.

|||||||||||||||||||||||||||||||||||||||||||||||||||||||||||||

Part Three

THE FIFTH SEAL

SUNDAY

I opened my eyes around seven-thirty out of habit and saw that I was alone in bed. I'd made lieutenant, in charge of Homicide. I could make a home for Rachel, and our son. I looked at the expanse of mattress next to me. Jessica had gone out to find some other soul to feed off.

I reached the living room and saw that Rachel still wasn't on the couch. I walked the rest of the house and saw no sign of her and no note. The door to what I had already come to think of as Josh's room was closed. I opened it. Josh, in his rocket ship pajamas, was still wrapped in a blanket. He blinked and looked at me.

"Where's Mommy?" he said.

"She stepped out for a little while. You want some breakfast?"

He wiped his face and nodded.

"Go wash up," I said.

I looked out the front window at the conspicuous absence of Rachel's rental car.

Josh emerged from the bedroom. I noticed his pajamas weren't wet, which I took as a limited good sign. He stood before the bathroom, confused. I helped him into the bathroom, got him out of his pajamas and overnight diapers. He used the toilet, and then I washed him up.

"Where's my mommy?" he said again, though this time he looked worried.

I said, "She had to run out to take care of some business."

He said, "What business?"

I said, "She'll explain when she gets back. What do you want for breakfast?"

I got him into clean clothes from his suitcase, and he followed me back to the kitchen and climbed up to a chair. I scoped the fridge and found one egg and some salami I wouldn't feed to a dog. Josh mentioned three brands of cereal I hadn't heard of. I checked the cabinet and saw an envelope that wasn't there yesterday. No address, no writing on it, not sealed. Inside, two neatly folded documents. Josh's birth certificate, naming Rachel and me as parents. And his immunization records.

Rachel was gone.

I said, "I think it's a good day to go out for breakfast. What do you think?"

"Okay."

I grabbed the phone book and went into my bedroom and closed the door. I called two car-rental places before I thought to phone the ones at the airport. There I talked to the people at Alamo Rental, who said she had a car, they weren't expecting it back for a few days, but no, they didn't know when she was flying out. I said, "This is Lieutenant Reles of APD Homicide. When you see her, I want you to stall her and call me at the department." Then I called the airlines and found out that she had an open return on Northwest, no date set. I pulled on some clothes and found Josh in the living room, watching TV.

It was the first time I remembered needing something that wasn't connected to the department. I ransacked my memory for people who might do me a personal favor and came up with two names, one I'd trust with a kid.

Jake Lund answered on the second ring.

I said, "Can you take care of my son today?"

He said, *"Your what?!"*

In fifteen minutes Jake and his girlfriend, Lynn the programmer, were standing at the door in matching bowling shirts, looking a lot more excited about playing house than Josh did. I pulled Jake into the kitchen.

"Take him out to breakfast, wherever he wants. Then take him to the movies or something. I don't know. What do kids like to do?"

He grinned. "We'll think of something."

I said, "Then take him to lunch. Then call me." I gave him an extra key to my house and tried to hand him a few twenties for expenses. He pushed them away.

"Get outta here," he said.

I found Josh standing in the living room looking worried. Lynn tried to engage him in conversation, but it wasn't happening.

I said, "You're gonna spend the morning with Uncle Jake."

"He not my uncle," Josh said.

"I know." I got down on one knee. "Listen, sport. I have to go take care of some things. I need you to do this. You might even have a good time. How about it?"

He knew enough to know he didn't have a choice, the condition of the life of children. He nodded, submitting. I gave him a squeeze on the shoulder.

I could see how he felt, getting shuffled from his drunk mother to his strange father to some crazy couple. He fought back tears. I gave him credit for fighting them.

He was three and a half, and each day brought a new, terrible surprise. I thought about grown-ups telling me, when I was a kid, that childhood years are the best years of your life. I silently promised that the next time I heard an adult say that, I'd punch the shit out of him.

When we stepped outside, I noticed a brown cardboard box about eight inches cubed, sitting in the dirt by the old dog dish. I waited till Jake, Lynn and Josh drove off before I ran for the phone.

"Austin Police."

"This is Reles with Homicide. Get me the Bomb Squad."

Given the circumstances—the threats, the rock in my exhaust pipe, the brick through the window—I was no fool to call the Bomb Squad. An hour later the Bomb Squad left, snickering, carrying an opened cardboard box containing a dead rat.

The symbolism didn't escape me. That the rat couldn't bite was a plus. But the rat was dead.

I'd talked to IA about Clay. His friends might kill me. They sure wanted me to think they would.

And I wanted to provide a safe home for Rachel and Josh. Now I couldn't. I'd have to change that.

It was no surprise that when I got to HQ, it being Sunday morning and, as the calendar reminded me, Easter, the squad room was barren. I grabbed the few items in what had been my desk for a few days, and headed for my new office. Pete Marks had slipped his nameplate out already, and when I opened the door, I discovered that he'd taken all his possessions and files. I wondered how much advance notice they gave him of the transfer, considering they'd only told me a few hours before. I guessed they put him in charge of Narco or Vice, someplace that would benefit from his warmth and natural leadership.

I called Dispatch and told them which office I now resided in. Then I told them to call the rest of the squad and have them round up in the briefing room at 9:00 A.M.

I called the car rental place back and got Rachel's California driver's license number, and the make, model and license of the car she was driving. It was a white two-door Plymouth Sundance. Spectacular in its averageness, it was one of hundreds of its kind in the city. For laughs I had Dispatch radio its description to all the cruisers on the street.

I started calling Los Angeles. It was two hours earlier on Easter morning in L.A., where Rachel had taken up residence, so it was no shock that I couldn't find anyone who could tell me anything about her. The police looked up her license and gave me her L.A. address. I called the car-rental place again and the airline and told them Rachel was wanted in Austin and that, when she showed up, they should have security detain her. I called airport security and told them the same, hazy on the details of Rachel's crime.

I'd often wondered about Rachel's past. I knew she was a wild party girl until she met Joey and straightened out. I knew that something terrible had happened back then in Houston, that a man had attacked her, that she killed him, that she wasn't charged but the incident plagued her even after she cleaned up and became a high-powered real estate broker. For all her professionalism and control, there was always something rattling just below the surface. It took another disaster to shake it loose, but that was my fault, and that was why she left me.

I knew that she didn't want me sniffing into her past. The last time I did it, she considered it a betrayal of relationship-ending proportions.

But she'd just dumped her own son without even leaving a note. All bets were off.

I called DPS records. All they had on her was that she didn't have a Texas license anymore. I knew her Social Security number, with its New York State prefix. I decided to call Albany.

The state government offices were closed, but I managed to get hold of the New York State Police. I put in a request for old driver's license info, birth certificate, whatever they had. When I hung up, I wondered if she was in trouble with the law, and I started calling around for her rap sheet—DPS, Houston, LAPD—and asking if she had any active warrants.

Then I wondered if someone was after her besides the police.

By then it was 9:05, and I sauntered into the briefing room. Highfill, LaMorte, Fuentes and Halvorsen were there, all grumbling, all in their hanging-around-the-house clothes except Fuentes, who'd managed a jacket and tie, though those might have been his Easter clothes. The grumbling stopped when I took the head of the table.

Highfill said, "What the hell's going on?"

I said, "As of five o'clock this morning, by order of Chief Cronin, I've taken command of the Homicide Squad." LaMorte and Highfill gaped. Halvorsen's jaw gripped, and his skull bulged at the temples. Fuentes registered shock in his eyes but I could hear his brain calculating.

"But—"

"Fuentes, what's going on with Vita Carballo?"

"Whuh . . ."

"Let's hear it."

He said, "We . . . uh, we took a cast of her skull. The lab is trying different brands of hammers to see if anything fits. A rounded tip. Whatever it was, he took it with him."

"Who else was at the scene when you got there?"

He said, "Some patrols. The medical examiner. Then, later, Torbett. And you."

"Not Clay?" I asked.

They looked at each other. Fuentes said, "No. I tracked her phone records for two weeks, except for the last few days. I'm still waiting for those. I talked to everyone she was in touch with. We questioned the males twice. Two confirmed johns. DNA tests on all the males, pending. They all have alibis. Not counting . . ."

"Me?" I said. "Right. You'll need a DNA sample. I'll leave one at DPS."

He said, "Where were you that night?"

I thought again of Mora, the fact that I was now her CO. "Not there," I said.

He was turning a brighter shade of red, and while he wasn't exactly shaking, I wouldn't have trusted him with delicate machinery. He said, "Should I take your word?"

I said, "You should do your job. Anyone else on anything hot?" There was a pause, and LaMorte opened his mouth. I jumped in. "By 'hot' I mean in the last month." LaMorte aborted his thought. "Good," I said. "LaMorte, you're with Fuentes now. You have forty-eight hours to rule me out or charge me. In the meantime, I want you to keep an eye out for other suspects, no matter what you think about me. Think you can handle that?"

Fuentes was holding something down that wanted to come up. He said, "Yes."

I added, "And I expect you to keep me posted on the details of the investigation, because I'm your CO. If you want, you can also report everything to Lieutenant Torbett in IA."

"I will."

"Good. If I get arrested, I want Torbett putting on my cuffs. Halvorsen, I want you working with Mora on the Ortiz case."

"Where is she?"

"I don't know. Find her. Highfill, you're with me." I slid him my notes on Rachel and the phone calls I'd made that morning. "Keep after those numbers. We need to find her before she leaves town." He nodded. One case was as good as another.

I addressed the group. "Now, if anybody has a problem with me being here, you can make a formal complaint to Lieutenant Torbett in IA. I won't take offense. Anything other than a formal complaint I'll consider a personal attack, and I won't take it lightly."

They were devoted to Marks, who I had replaced. Fuentes considered me the odds-on favorite for Vita's killer. LaMorte and Highfill were department boys, Clay's type. And I had fingered Clay to IA. Halvorsen just didn't like me. And their new boss, a Jew, was making them work on Easter.

I sent them off in different directions, wondering which of them might want me dead. When I got back to my office, the phone was ringing. It was the Fifth Floor. My presence was requested. Now.

69.
⦀

Judah sorted through Suzanne's dressers and closets, looking for papers, old letters, anything. He'd stayed home while Suzanne and Paul went to church. Suzanne was suspicious, but too frightened to do anything about it. At least for now.

He went into Paul's room. He searched the dresser, the closet. Paul's desk had one drawer of old files. Plenty to sort through in very little time.

Judah didn't have much to go on. A couple of vague rumors. Subjects brought up and immediately dropped. There was something, though. He hoped he would know it when he saw it.

He needed leverage on Suzanne, and he needed it fast. Also, he needed Paul out of the picture.

One way or another.

70.
|||||

I stood in Cronin's office, only this time it was just the two of us. And the excitement he showed while promoting me less than five hours earlier was missing.

"What's this?" I said, wasting my charismatic half smile on Cronin's grim deadpan. "The honeymoon's over?"

He handed me a slip of paper. "Go to this address and take command of the investigation of the body found there. You may assign one detective to the case, besides yourself. You are not to speak to anyone in the department or any other department regarding the identity of the resident. You are not to disclose the resident's involvement with this case under any circumstances. You are not to question the resident, nor anyone associated with him."

"And if I refuse?" I asked just to see what the stakes were.

He had the answer ready. "You'll be immediately fired and subject to arrest in the murder of Vita Carballo." I should have seen it coming. "Any other questions?"

"How the hell am I supposed to—"

He cut me off. "Be resourceful, Lieutenant. You're dismissed."

I drove out to West Lake Hills and found the address. One patrol was parked in front. The front door was unlocked. Just inside, mail piled high on an end table, all addressed to Winston Muller, lieutenant governor of Texas.

Now I knew who I was protecting.

I followed the stink into the bedroom. I held a sleeve over my mouth and nose, but it didn't help.

The victim's eyes stretched wide open, feeding maggots. His lips had turned pale, nearly white, and so had his fingernails. His hands were blue. By patriotic contrast his face and neck had grown a crimson red, but not so much as to hide the mark of the wire that had wrapped his neck and dug into the skin on the way to cutting off his breath for the last time.

And he had curly black hair. And he was less than five feet tall.

I stepped out of the room and closed the door, gasping for air.

I could tell Mora now that we had found Rolo Ortiz.

71.
||||||

"Don't go out, Mommy."

Joshua's mournful voice was drowned out by a jet engine flying overhead, growing to a roar and then quieting as it came in for a landing, and Rachel opened her eyes and she was alone. The light entered through her eyes and pounded into the back of her skull.

She'd relocated to the Airport Ramada. The other bed was made, floral duvet sweeping against the carpet. TV. Table for writing postcards. Dear Imaginary Friend. Having a wonderful time.

She stared at the stucco ceiling. A wave of nausea rolled in.

She hadn't slept a wink at Dan's. On her best day, she was way past the point that she could go to sleep without drinking. With no escape from Joshua, she'd sneaked sips of wine through the day and evening just to ward off the shakes. Dinner almost made her scream and run for the nearest bar.

She looked at the clock: 11:45 A.M. She reached for a cigarette and lit it, falling back on the pillow.

She'd tossed and turned, then left the house around four, just after Dan. Found the motel and pulled her suitcase and bottles from the trunk. Inside, she fumbled for a plastic-wrapped cup, half filled it with vodka and glugged it down. It burned as she waited for it to quiet the yearning. She poured another and drank it. It went down smoother, now that her taste buds were deadened. Good old vodka. It didn't make her happy, but it took off the edge.

She must have passed out by five.

That was the way things had been going. She needed to drink every day. Then earlier in the day. She'd tried to put a lid on it during the last, exitless months of her pregnancy, with limited success. When she got out of the hospital, she went on a three-day tear. On the fourth day, she'd gone back to collect the boy, to the suspicious hums of the nurses.

And she settled in L.A., where she knew nobody, talking her way into a real estate sales job and pulling it together for work each morning, painting over the heavy circles under her eyes, eyedrops to get the red out. The sales were few and far between. The job didn't last.

And with baby in tow, she watched her savings dwindle, moving to cheaper apartments and then furnished rooms, working her way down the socioeconomic scale.

Josh was three when she stopped bothering to get him a sitter.

The baby-sitters were dubious anyway, drunken widows and single hags who haunted the motels of L.A., a vast network of highways with clusters of dense population in between. She toilet trained him, more or less, and he could change channels on the TV and get food from the fridge. He was safer alone, Rachel told herself, than he was with the women she knew, who would sell him on the black market for a vial of crack. She'd promise him she'd be back in an hour.

She'd come home at dawn as he was stirring. And she'd make him breakfast. Then she'd pass out and sleep most of the day.

She had a few boyfriends, fewer as time went on. But they were only good for drinks or maybe some coke, which helped her stay up and drink longer. And which she was trying to stay away from. They never gave her gifts or money. She had just one or two boyfriends like that back when she was young. She'd sleep with them, and they'd give her pocket money and make jokes that she was a prostitute, and then sometime later they'd get together and do it again. Not so easy now.

And the dreams that plagued her sobriety didn't go away with drunkenness. Always she was in her bed, always half asleep. And always he was on top of her. She'd shudder and fight and wake with a screech, sometimes to Joshua crying.

She lost everything. Her clear head, her initiative. Once she had the fire to make money and get ahead. Once she made a dozen cold calls in an hour, pulled in clients, sold houses in the worst of markets. Commissions poured in like rain. Now she couldn't get out of bed unless she needed a drink.

She lost her body, turned to flab from childbearing and liquor. She lost her face, sagging on both sides, puffing white. She looked worse than the housewives she'd held in contempt back in the days of her aerobics and moneymaking. She had nothing left but digestive problems and self-loathing and a growing fear of going outside that kept her from leaving the house sober. And she was teaching all this to Joshua.

What was left? Go to rehab and let them try to make her believe in God? Good luck. She swore off the stuff when she was twelve.

Drag Josh back to L.A., or somewhere else? He was no good with other kids. He'd burst out crying or wet his pants and get laughed at. Soon he'd be in kindergarten, getting picked on by bullies. If she ever had any survival skills, she'd taught him the opposite.

Leave Josh with Dan.

It seemed like a good idea when she left the house. Dan had sense. He could take care of a boy. Raise him up, teach him to fight, to take care of himself. He'd go out a lot, and it would make Josh nervous. But Josh was already nervous. Dan couldn't do worse than she had.

She pushed herself up off the bed and poured out the last two fingers of vodka into a glass, wondering how much she must have struggled before to leave that for the morning. She downed it, not enough to calm her but enough to get her dressed and out.

No question. She'd made up her mind. She'd leave Josh with Dan. It would be best for everybody.

Then she'd crawl under a rock and die.

72.
ⅢⅢⅢ

"You don't discuss the case with anyone besides me," I explained to Mora in the lieutenant governor's living room. "You don't question him or any member of his staff. We don't go near the capitol building. His name is not to be mentioned in relation to this case."

"Or . . ."

"You'll be fired immediately with no chance for appeal." I couldn't threaten her with arrest, though I wouldn't put it past Cronin.

The LG, Cronin claimed, had returned to his Austin home late Friday night, discovered the boy's body and promptly retreated to his family in Beaumont before calling the police chief more than twenty-four hours later.

I'd assigned Halvorsen to help Mora with Rolo's case, help she could have used, but I had to send him home. Thanks, Cronin.

Mora looked green from seeing Rolo, and now she was turning angry red. "This is bullshit," she said. "We're here to protect the government?"

I said, "We *are* the government."

I read something once about the U.S. Navy in the nineteenth century. A sailing ship would house the officers, who lived well, and the sailors, who operated the ship and did all the work. In between they had the marines, heavily armed men who neither administrated nor operated the sails. It was their job to keep the sailors from killing the officers.

I felt like a marine.

"Nice sellout, Reles. How long you been lieutenant? A day?"

"Not yet, no."

"Marks trained me," she said, "and he didn't train me to be a lapdog to the Fifth Floor."

"Hey, that's terrific. You want me to put someone else on this?"

Her eyes rattled with three kinds of betrayal. We'd been partners, if only for a few days, and now I was giving her a shitty, impossible order. And I was threatening her. And she probably hadn't forgotten that, thirty-six hours before, we had locked in a sloppy wet drunken embrace.

Mora said, "We're supposed to believe that the LG came home and tripped on Rolo's body, with no idea what he was doing here?"

"Officially."

"And he went home to Beaumont and waited *a day* and *then* called us?" I didn't bother answering. "This is bullshit," she said again, but the spirit was gone.

I said, "Can you do it?"

She nodded and left.

If I disappointed Cronin, he could toss me to the DA or to the Family, who was ready to kill me already for ratting out Clay. Cronin was the closest thing I had to a powerful ally, and he didn't care if I lived or died.

A month earlier I didn't care either. But now I had a son. And, somewhere, his mother. And they needed me alive. I'd be ashamed to tell Rachel how I'd knuckled under. But I'd make a safe home for her and our son.

I just didn't know yet what that would take.

73.
|||||

Suzanne maintained silence in the back of the limo all the way home from church.

The sermon was something about who gets into heaven. The reverend talked a lot about generosity. It sounded very much to Paul like only Christians could get into heaven, and only Christians in a certain income bracket.

Outside, Paul shook hands with a few other church husbands. Suzanne chatted, building alliances with some of the better wives. Paul took the reverend's idea and ran with it.

"Of course *we'll* go to heaven," Paul said. "But what about the Hindus?"

"The Hindus?" Kurt Harrington asked.

Paul spoke with growing authority. "Sure! What have they given the world? Where are the endowments, the hospital wings? I say screw the Hindus! If they wanted to go to heaven, they should have believed in Jesus."

Suzanne sat beside him in the Lincoln, silent but for the grinding of her teeth. When they pulled up in front of the house, the driver opened her door and helped her up. She told the driver, "We'll be out in half an hour. Wait for us." Instead of opening Paul's door, the driver leaned on the hood and lit a cigarette. Paul rated no more than a drunk in the back of a taxi.

Inside, Suzanne passed through the foyer muttering words like "inexcusable" and "humiliated." Paul made it to the bar and poured a bourbon on the rocks. "Get changed," she said. "We're going to the conference."

"They won't let you in, Suzanne."

She climbed the stairs. "Don't be ridiculous."

"Why don't you take Judah?"

She halted midway on the steps, turned to him and said, "They don't want to see me with a man. They want to see me with you."

And before she turned again and headed upstairs, Paul felt a shift.

Straightforward hostility wasn't Suzanne's normal MO. She was more about lies, semitruths, affectation and backstabbing. But that one emasculating remark was a gift. Suddenly the universe had shifted. A great weight lifted from Paul's shoulders. He felt lighter, taller. And, contrary to Suzanne's belief, he was a man again. And he was angry.

Paul headed back to the fireplace room, turning on lights as he went. His footsteps landed hard on the stone floor.

And he passed through the fireplace room, down the servants' corridor, toward Judah's room.

74.
‖‖‖‖

As I walked through the first-floor reception area, I heard my name shouted. It was Torbett. He waved me into his office. Fuentes waited inside, and we stood in triangle formation. I was itching to get out, to deal with Mora and get back to finding Rachel.

"Sergeant Fuentes has a problem," Torbett said.

"Can't you help him with it?"

Fuentes said, "All the evidence leads to you."

I turned to Fuentes. "You haven't got any evidence. Why don't you get off your ass and find some!"

Fuentes persisted. "You had the opportunity. Repeated contact with the victim over a period of years, including this week."

I said, "How do you know that?"

Torbett said, "It would help if you told us where you were Friday night."

I said, "I don't want him getting lazy."

Fuentes fumed.

Torbett said, "You're dismissed, Fuentes."

Fuentes looked between us, then puffed out a lungful of air and stomped into the hall. If he suspected Torbett was covering for me, I couldn't blame him.

Torbett said, "If you think you got me over a barrel, you're wrong."

I said, "All I wanna know is, who said I was at Vita's on Thursday? It means I was followed or she was being watched."

"I can't give out that information."

"Give me *something*, Torbett."

He thought hard. "There's a lot of pressure on me, from above," he said. "I won't say they want me to fail—"

"But they want you to fail." I went on, "Cronin put me in charge of Homicide at five in the morning. Figure I'm supposed to solve a problem, too, take some heat off the department for Salina Street and for Clay."

Torbett nodded. "It makes you high-profile. Gives the press an easy target."

"Same as you," I said. "What do we do? Get jerked on the line and hope we live to see retirement?"

"I don't know," he said.

I moved for the door. "I have to take care of something."

He shouted at my back, "Where were you Friday night?"

As I headed out toward the lobby, I yelled back, "I told you. I was at home."

75.
||||||

Judah was too tall to lie down in the bathtub, but he leaned his back against the tiles and soaked, holding his hands under the warm, soapy water so he'd sweat more, cleansing his skin from the inside out. His long hair lay wet on his shoulders.

He rose early—it was Easter Sunday—and prayed and read his quarterly. There was no church for him. The Adventists had disappointed him, and then so did the Davidians. He'd start his own church. With Suzanne's money.

He had everything he needed to plan whatever she wanted. He could plant explosives, let her blame the Left and swoop in to save the day. She could pose for the cameras, sympathizing with the victims. The clock sets off the blasting cap that ignites the deta sheet, which is wrapped around the plastique. Bang bang boom.

And he sat in the tub looking over the triumph of his life, the long years of waiting, the unappreciated work for Koresh, meeting Suzanne and devoting his life to her and her money, waiting and finally joining with her in an act of perfect love, more or less. Certainly the best she'd had in a while. The muscles in his groin felt relaxed and soothed, and the warmth emanated out to his arms and legs. Each atom in his body glowed with peace. The apocalypse could come right now, and he'd slide into it blissfully. He felt the muscles in his back unwind as the doorknob turned and the bathroom door slowly opened.

"Suzanne?" he said, half opening his eyes. But instead it was her husband, Paul Wade.

Judah made no effort to get up. "Paul," he said, though until that moment it had been "Mr. Wade." "Paul, you're looking well." The hall behind him was dark.

Paul had, in fact, lost the color from his face, and Judah couldn't help thinking how small and impotent he looked, how powerless, though he was standing and dressed, while Judah sat nude in the warm bath. Still, something in the small man unnerved him.

"What is this?" Paul said, holding up a small object. It was a blasting cap. "I found it on your desk."

"Put that down. You'll hurt yourself."

"You're a servant," Paul said.

"Not your servant. God's."

"Suzanne is my wife."

"She's *my* wife." Judah sighed sleepily. "In the eyes of God. And soon enough in the eyes of the church."

Paul said, "I'll kill you."

Judah chuckled. "You'll pack your clothes and leave. This is Suzanne's house." Judah leaned way back and stretched his legs out, raising them and resting his ankles on the edge of the tub. "You're so stupid, Paul. I kept hearing the name Faith Copeland on the radio. 'Faith Copeland killed in Austin, child-star killer still at large.' I knew I'd heard the name before but I couldn't remember where."

Paul said, "Leave this place."

"I went through Suzanne's old letters, the ones she wrote you. Sweet. Southern women and their letters. She was pregnant in '79. And then she went away."

Paul seemed to rise in height. "I'm not afraid of you."

"How long did it take you to figure it out? That you weren't the father. That Russell Copeland was the father. That she left the baby with Copeland and his wife and sent them checks to keep quiet."

"You're a servant!" Paul said, shaking.

Judah shouted, "You went out Tuesday night! The phone rang, I heard you take the call, and you left. The news said Faith Copeland was raped and killed Tuesday night. I didn't tie it together until I found her checkbook in your dresser. You took Faith's checkbook. Trying to hide evidence? And you left it in your dresser! You're the stupidest killer in Texas."

Paul could barely remember the checkbook. He had grabbed it, pocketed it, brought it home and hidden it away. Why?

"Leave!" Paul yelled.

"You raped your wife's daughter. What was that? Some kind of sick revenge for your pathetic life?"

Paul grabbed for something to swing at Judah, and the only solid object he could find was the hair dryer sitting on the towels. He held it over his head.

Judah laughed. "What are you gonna do with that, Paul? It's a *hair dryer.*"

The fury in Paul's eyes suddenly froze and vanished as he switched the dryer on to "high."

76.
||||||

I'd barely settled in at my desk when Mora walked into my office, shut the door and sat opposite me.

"Listen," I said, "about this morning . . ."

She cut me off with a wave. Then she said, "I didn't tell you a few things."

Rolando Ortiz, she'd told me earlier, was picked up in a Torino station wagon at a Stop'N Go downtown by Judah Cavanaugh, Thursday night just after midnight. She handed me a five-by-seven blowup of Judah's driver's license photo. The wagon was registered to a Mrs. Violet Sayles, deceased, of Mexia, Texas, outside Waco. Judah moved in with her in 1993 when the Branch Davidians threw him out. Her address was on his driver's license.

The house had been sitting since Mrs. Sayles's death. The Sayles family knew Judah and let him stay in the house as caretaker until they sold it. But he left sometime back, without contacting them. "I went there last night," Mora said. "Everything was normal except for one closet. Inside, on the back wall, he'd taped up pictures of the Waco victims, in cutout white robes." She showed me Polaroids.

"That's the problem with Protestantism," she added. "Too much room for interpretation."

The fires at Waco had become a rallying cry for the far right. Every lunatic survivalist, religious yahoo, gun nut and a few people with some sense pointed to Waco as an example of the federal government's criminality. It was hard to argue.

She went on. "Judah was with the Branch Davidians, but he was gone by the raid. David Koresh threw him out months before. Too crazy for the Branch Davidians."

"Did you put out a BOLO on him?"

"On him, on the car. Highest priority. But if there's a connection between him and the LG, I have leads I can't follow . . . dead ends. I have to know. . . ."

If she was waiting for me to lift the chief's restriction, she'd have to keep waiting.

Mora said, "What I'm seeing is a dead boy, and I don't know why he died or if he was just one in a series. Oh, another thing. The Waco fire happened on April nineteenth. So if he's planning something crazy, he might just do it on the anniversary."

I checked the calendar. "Today's the sixteenth," I said.

She nodded.

77.
||||||

Judah tried to jump out of the tub, rising halfway and losing his foot-
ing on the soapy enamel. He fell hard with a splash just as Paul
dropped the hair dryer into the tub.

And with a loud buzzing and a crack, Judah was blasted out of the
tub and up, up into the clouds.

78.
||||||

Highfill came in, heading off whatever brilliant conclusion I was going
to get to next. Mora took off.

Highfill said, "I got hold of Records at Mercy Hospital in Albany.
Asked for birth certificate on Rachel Renier, born March 25, 1958."

"Yeah."

"If you didn't give me that date, she never woulda found it. The
doctor's name was Mickiewicz. The mother was Caitlin Renier. The
father was Marcel Gagnon." Highfill had trouble twisting his mouth
against the foreign names. I was pretty sure the last name rhymed
with "canyon." He went on. "So if this is the girl you're lookin' for,
her name is Gagnon, not Renier."

Renier was Rachel's maiden name, or so I thought. I asked if she
was born out of wedlock.

"The papers didn't say. But I can check with the courts tomorrow
and see if she changed it legally."

"Good job. Keep on it."

"Till when?"

"Till you find where she is this minute."

He left, and I began to wonder how many of her years Rachel had
spent traveling under a name she wasn't born with, and why.

But Rachel had another surprise for me.

79.
‖‖‖‖‖

Paul opened the bathroom window to let the smoke out. He caught his reflection in the mirror. The color had come back into his cheeks. For the first time since his hair fell out, he saw his own reflection and thought, Handsome. You handsome devil.

Paul found his drink, drifted weightlessly to the fireplace room at the back of the house and sat in Suzanne's great peaked wooden chair by the stone mantel. Sunlight sparkled in from the courtyard through the diamond-shaped window panes. The room was cool and dark in the early afternoon. Paul took a sip of bourbon and, as it reached out to his hands and feet, leaned against the back of the chair and felt a wave of peace.

He hadn't worked in years. But he couldn't remember being so relaxed. Not when he was in business, not in college. Once with Emily Holzmueller, his first, lying in bed with her, his body purged and exhausted from the inside out. That once he had felt such a complete peace. And not again from then until now.

Suzanne clomped into the room. She'd changed into something blue and more sporty than her church dress, and she was holding an earring. "What are you doing?" she asked. "You should be dressed."

He made it a point not to smile. "Honey, I'm a little beat. You'll have to make it without me."

"Don't be ridiculous. Clean yourself up. You'll go and you'll behave. That's your job."

"I thought for sure you'd replace me after today."

She barked a collection of consonants as she put in the earring. She needed him on her arm.

"Gee," he said. "You must really love me."

She said, "Get dressed," and turned for the door.

He called out the name, "Judah!"

She stopped. "What are you doing?"

"Judah?" He turned to her. "You *should* go with Judah today," he said dreamily. "He's so strong. He *loves* you." He raised his hand and gave a blessing. "Go with Judah."

"I've had about enough—"

"What are you gonna do, Suze? Toss me out? You need me standing by you when you talk about the sanctity of marriage."

He'd never spoken to her that way before. It felt good. Better still was her reaction, shaking on her heels, the sudden realization that she didn't have anything to hurt him with. Her lips pursed, her brow furrowed, and she almost took a final shot at him. But something got the better of her, and instead she called out, "Judah!"

Just off the fireplace room, they could both see the light shining from Judah's room into the hall. But he didn't answer.

"Gee," Paul said, "I wonder what's up with Jude."

Suzanne turned her gaze to Paul, then walked clipped steps toward Judah's room. She'd surely made the trip many times before. Paul leaned his head back on the wood and waited.

Her scream rolled down the hall. It flooded the fireplace room, rose to the tops of the walls, then rolled in like a wave and crashed. The splash of sound ran through him, through his skin to his heart. Triumph, he thought. She had been breaking him for years. Now she was broken.

He brought his drink with him as he rose and glided down the hall, following her echoing screams to Judah's bathroom.

80.
⁣⁣⁣⁣⁣⁣

I ran to Missing Persons and Dispatch and talked to Patrol, and it was after 1:00 P.M. when I got back to my office. Highfill had left some papers on my desk, including a note that said "Gone home—Highfill" and a two-page fax from Houston police of Rachel's old rap sheet, the only record of her wild youth. One drunk-driving arrest, one assault on a police officer, arrested, no charges filed. Then the November 1981 incident first indicated as a domestic disturbance. The phone rang.

"Reles."

"*You better get over here right now.*" It was Jake Lund. Josh was crying in the background.

"What's going on?"

"*I can't— Wait a second— Just come home.*" He hung up. I went back to the elevator and read the rest of the fax on the way down.

The second report described Rachel's 1981 incident as homicide *se defendendo,* a form of justifiable homicide that implies that killing the assailant was the only chance you had of walking away from him. I started reading the details, and something clicked.

I knew that Rachel was hiding something from me the whole time we were together, something worse than justifiable homicide. Out of love and guilt, I'd decided not to ask her what her lifelong secret was.

Now I knew.

81.
⫿⫿⫿⫿⫿

Paul Wade never called himself an artist, but he had to admire the image in front of him. The back of his wife, Suzanne Addison Wade, heiress to the Addison estate and the fortune therewith, her stout outline and bright blue dress, her nearly-black hair sprayed razor-wire stiff, as her body throbbed out screams one after another, in even lengths. Beyond her right shoulder, the great and powerful Judah, his damp locks pasted against his massive shoulders, upright in the bathtub with his back to the tile wall, a charred stripe over the edge of the tub where the hair dryer cord lay.

Paul sipped his drink.

Each time he looked at his handiwork, it had greater resonance. A Renaissance portrait of Christ lowered from the cross. Marat in his bath.

Paul sipped. "The truth?" he said. "I think I found my calling."

"What have you done?!" she screamed. Paul had never seen her show so much passion.

He said, "I say we have someone paint him just like that for the art show. A tribute to the wealthy women of West Lake and Barton Creek," he waxed poetic, "who control the word of God by their purse strings." He sipped, swallowed and added, "And use their free hands to yank down the zippers of servants and busboys."

"What have you done?" she shrieked. *"What have you done!"*

She collapsed against the bathroom wall and slid down to the floor, crying, with Judah staring past her. Finally she looked up.

Paul felt a sense of completion. He said, "Well, that's that." He drained the glass and headed toward the main house. "My work here is finished."

"Where are you going?" she shouted.

"To turn myself in."

"Don't!" she said.

Suzanne had surprised Paul many times in their years together, usually for the bad. But never was he so surprised, and impressed, as when she suddenly appeared behind him as he walked through the fireplace room, and tried to stop him from calling the police.

"I'm thinking of you, darling," he said. "I'll be gone, and you can start over. Find some nice Mexican boy, raise a family."

"I'll be ruined!" she said.

"I can't take care of you anymore." He turned and headed toward the door as she called him.

"Paul?"

And somehow, with her rumpled dress and her smearing makeup and her frenzy, she'd softened. Somehow she was looking at him as she had years ago, at least until they were married, at least in front of the cameras. A studied, rehearsed gaze of love.

"I can be different, Paul."

Again she'd topped herself. It was almost too much to ask. He was headed for a lethal injection, happily, and she was giving him one last surprise after another.

"We can start over," she said. "I'll be a good wife. Don't leave me."

He couldn't help but walk toward her, drawn to her like a magnet. And, solid in the knowledge that she was acting, that he'd seldom seen her do anything but act, he stepped close enough to her that all he managed was a flinch as she swung her hand up from behind her dress and the fireplace poker whipped through the air and cracked into his temple.

82.
||||||

I pulled up in front of my house and ran inside. Josh was crying, his pants conspicuously wet. Jake and Lynn were trying to talk him down.

I said, "What happened?"

Lynn said, "Your girlfriend called him to say goodbye. She's leaving."

I hit Star 69 and got, *"The number you are trying to call cannot be reached by that method. . . ."* I called Dispatch and asked them to track it. But it would take time, and I didn't have any. So I called Mueller Airport.

"Security."

"This is Lieutenant Reles, APD Homicide. I need you to stop a Rachel Renier. She's flying out on Northwest Airlines if she hasn't already. Put her in custody until I get there."

"What did she do?"

"No time to explain." I hung up and turned to Josh.

"Listen, sport, we're gonna go get your mom." He nodded, and I picked him up. His sobs settled down. We'd change our clothes later.

Jake said, "He's a mess."

I said, "He's my son." The words sounded strange from my mouth, but I realized that it was the only thing I'd ever said that meant anything. We headed for the car.

I opened the passenger side and buckled Josh in place. "You okay?"

He nodded, and I slammed the door. I walked around to my side and climbed in next to him. He was sniffling.

I looked at him, his nose-dripping profile. Half a Reles, half a Renier. The product of my love for Rachel. In his three and a half years, he'd had more sadness than anyone should in a lifetime. The person who was supposed to take care of him had disappointed him at every turn. And still he loved her more than anything.

And, like a fucking idiot, so did I.

I put the car in gear, hit the flashing lights and headed for the airport.

83.
||||||

Mrs. Ortiz screamed in terror when she heard the news of Rolo's death, screamed like she'd been attacked by a lion. She kept on screaming. She pushed past Mora on the stoop and knocked over a garbage can. She screamed as she wandered into the street, and Mora had to stop traffic and drag her to the sidewalk. She screamed as people crossed the street to avoid walking near her. She screamed as she fell to her knees and pounded her head against the concrete until Mora got her in a tight hold and yelled to a neighbor who'd emerged from her house to call an ambulance.

She screamed as they strapped her into a stretcher and cried out pathetically as the needle went into her arm to make her stop screaming, to take away the last remnant of life in her heart. She cried, in her dissipating strength, *"Why him? Why my baby? Why didn't you take me?"*

And Mora stayed with her in the emergency room, cooing in Spanish into the sedated woman's ear as if she were a beloved child, not a grown woman, an old woman at age thirty-eight, who'd had her greatest joy and greatest pain in the gift God chose to give her and then snatch away.

Mora stayed when they checked Mrs. Ortiz in to a private room, strapped down with padded restraints, and she promised to return.

And to herself as she left the hospital she promised to catch the bastard who'd strangled Rolo. And if she could find an excuse, she'd kill him.

She ran Judah's license through DPS for offenses. She checked him for arrests or involvement in other cases. She took his enlarged photo and ran it by the foster home, Child Services and Rolo's school. She showed it to the street kids on the Drag and downtown.

There was a connection between Judah and the lieutenant governor, and she wasn't allowed to check the LG's end of it.

Back at HQ she headed for the squad room and saw a patrol standing outside Reles's office, looking confused. He held a sheet of paper. His badge named him Scotto.

"Looking for someone, Scotto?" she asked.

"Sergeant Reles?"

She pounded on Reles's door, then opened it. "He's not here. What do you need?"

"I got these phone records for him from Faith Copeland's house, the last few days."

Mora grabbed the paper, saying, "I'll see that he gets it," and she scanned the numbers and names as she walked into the deserted squad room. She could spend days, weeks or months tracking Judah. She knew where the LG lived and where he worked.

And she could still hear Mrs. Ortiz's cries echoing in her ears.

"Fuck this," she said, then headed for her car and drove over to the capitol.

Parts of the capitol building stayed open in spite of the holiday, and she badged her way in, making sure they didn't catch her name. She trekked down the echoing halls looking like she was going somewhere until she passed a mousy little secretary type in a plain blue dress.

Mora giggled apologetically, the way she guessed the woman would. "I'm sorry, I'm *so* lost. I'm looking for the lieutenant governor's office."

"Oh, they're all gone today. They'll be back Tuesday."

"I should have known," Mora said, tapping her own skull. "Duh! Do you *know* him? I think he's wonderful. Oh, sorry." She put her hand out. "I'm Maureen Rogish. I work for Public Records. I'm new."

The woman shook Mora's hand. "Kathy Holtz. No need to apologize to me. I'm a big fan, too."

On a long shot, Mora showed Judah's photo. "Do you know *this* man?"

Kathy Holtz gave a slight gasp. "That's Judah. He works for Suzanne Wade. Not at her office, at her house."

"Really?"

"Yes, and don't ask me what he does." Kathy gave a pointed look and raised one eyebrow.

"No!"

"I'm not saying. All I know is he lives there and he works there and no one knows exactly what he's paid for."

"Is that the house out of town or the one over on . . . where is it again?"

In her car Mora picked up the mike. "Homicide 6 to Central, K."

"Go ahead, Homicide 6."

"I need an exact address for Paul and Suzanne Wade out by the Lost Creek Country Club. It'll be unlisted."

"Hold for that."

Mora knew she'd heard the name somewhere recently. She'd read it in the papers, probably more than once, without thinking about it. What did she care about politics? But somewhere else, recently.

She looked over the sheet Scotto had handed her. Eight phone numbers and times, from the last days of Faith Copeland's life. Calls in and out.

And the very last call, at 8:07 P.M. on Tuesday, was to the home of Paul and Suzanne Wade.

||||||||||||||||||

Suzanne Addison Wade sat on the padded bench before her makeup mirror, finishing her lipstick and humming. Her face was the subject of much discussion, the black eyeliner and mascara to go with her black hair, bold strokes of beauty. She deserved the attention.

She'd showered and dressed and sprayed her hair, one layer at a time. She looked very smart in her soft pink, just the right combination of optimism and seriousness for spring. She stood and turned before the mirror. She still had her figure.

And then she took her valise, her notes, everything she would need, and headed out the rear entrance. The driver extinguished his cigarette and opened the door for her, then took her gloved hand as she stepped delicately into the car.

All she needed was to get inside.

⫿⫿⫿⫿⫿⫿⫿⫿⫿⫿⫿⫿⫿⫿⫿⫿

It was midafternoon when I shot east on Thirty-eighth Street toward the airport, siren blaring as I weaved through the traffic, and heard a familiar voice on the radio call out, *"Homicide 1."* Then again after a while, *"Homicide 1."* It was dawning on me that "Homicide 1" meant the guy in charge of Homicide, just as I heard Mora's voice yell, *"Now, Reles!"*

I took the mike. "I'm busy."

She said, *"Judah Cavanaugh spotted at the estate of Suzanne Wade, THE Suzanne Wade, in Lost Creek. P.S., I got the last of Faith Cope- land's phone records. Her very last call was to the Wades."*

"Fuck!" I turned to Josh. He was engrossed in the traffic. Mora gave me the address. I said, "I'll get there when I can."

I pulled in front of the terminal with my lights flashing. I asked Josh, "Can you wait here?"

He responded with a resounding "No!" that I didn't question, so I unbuckled him and lifted him up. He locked his arms and legs around me, and I ran into the crowded terminal.

Suitcases wheeled across our path, following harried travelers. I muscled to the front of the Northwest check-in line.

"When's the next flight to L.A.?"

She said, "Five minutes, but you can't get that flight."

I showed my badge. "Is Rachel Renier on the plane?"

She hit some keys. "She's on standby. You'll have to check at the gate. C10."

We ran for the gates. I showed my badge to the X-ray tech. "Call C10 and have them stop Rachel Renier from getting on the plane."

"I can't do that," he said, then gestured to my holster. "And you can't take that gun past here."

"It's okay," an older guard said. "Follow him."

I barreled through the X-ray, holding Josh against me with one arm. The alarm whooped after me. The younger guard ran alongside Josh and me to the gate. When we got there, there were no other passengers, no Rachel, only the agent giving last instructions into a walkie-talkie. I ran into the jetway.

At the end, two men with fluorescent vests were just closing the door. "Wait!" I shouted. They didn't stop.

I boomed, "WAIT!" and raised my badge. They stopped.

I said, "Tell me which seat Rachel Renier is in."

The two men looked at each other. One headed into the plane, and I went in after him. He was talking to a flight attendant, a brittle woman with too much makeup. She saw me, the badge, the kid, and said, "Eighteen F," very quickly. "Eighteen F."

I said, "Hold this," and handed her Josh. She held him under his arms. He started wailing.

I made my way down the aisle. I saw Rachel leaning her head against the window. The yellow afternoon sunlight warmed her face. She'd been drinking.

"Buddy," I said to the man next to her. "Would you tap that woman?" People started connecting me with the fact that the engine had slowed. He tapped her shoulder. She opened her eyes at him with irritation and then turned to me.

"Oh, God!" she said.

"Could we talk?"

The captain emerged from the cockpit, assured himself of my credentials and retreated. Rachel and I stood in the rear of the plane, between the bathrooms. I kept my back to the staring passengers.

She said, "Where's Josh?"

I said, "Jeez, I don't know. He was behind me, but I was moving pretty fast."

She said, "You left him alone?"

I said, "You got on a fuckin' plane!"

She covered her face.

I said, "Why are you doing this?"

She said, "It's better for Josh. You're better for him."

"Says who?"

"I'm drunk. I'm drunk all the time. I can't stop. I can't take care of him. I don't have a job. . . ."

"You have to say goodbye."

"I can't."

"Sure you can." I patted her shoulder, like a coach. "You're a grown-up. That's all I ask. Say goodbye to his face. Then you can ditch him like my mother ditched me."

I took her by the arm and led her up the aisle.

Just past first class, Josh stood, holding the hand of a frightened young flight attendant. Josh had run out of tears. He looked ashamed, of the mess in his pants, of the fact that his mother had tried to leave him. But when he saw her, he gasped and ran for her desperately, shouting the name she never planned on hearing again. "Mommy!"

He took a leap and wrapped himself around her. She nearly buckled under the weight. He was growing, and she was getting weak.

Josh had one ear pressed to her chest. He held on for dear life and squeezed his eyes closed. He was in his mother's arms, but I didn't see any sense of safety or assuredness. If she stayed, he would forever hold her like he was afraid she was going away.

For Rachel's part, she looked bone-weary. The weight of the boy, like the weight of the obligation, pulled her down. And she wasn't doing so great just taking care of herself. She tried to stand him on the ground.

"Stand up."

"No." He let his legs collapse.

She yelled, "Stand up!" He did. She said, "It's better for you to be with your father."

"I don't want to!"

The crew shifted around us. I led Rachel and Josh out into the jetway. The ground crew closed the airplane door.

She said, "He can take care of you. I . . . I'm a mess. I can't do anything."

"You're not a mess, Mommy. I'll take care of *you*."

I took out my key ring and peeled off the key to my house. "Listen," I said. "Could we just take a few days and talk it over?"

She didn't agree, but she didn't argue. I gave her the key.

"Go to my house," I said. "I'll be home in a while."

She said, "Then what?"

"Do you trust me?"

She kicked it around, then nodded.

"Good," I said. Then I leaned close and whispered to her, "He trusts you."

She nodded again, lost a tear.

I said, "Just don't sneak out. Please."

I didn't trust her, but I didn't have a choice. I headed out to find Mora.

||||||||||||||||||

Mora pulled up in front of the Wade estate and rang the bell, an impressive pull-and-release contraption that seemed to predate electricity. Then she headed around the side of the house. The first thing she noticed was a gray Ford Gran Torino wagon. Judah's car. The car that had picked up Rolo.

She knocked at the service entrance with no luck, then walked farther around the house looking for another way in. Just a few feet from the door, she found a small open window. She stood on her toes to peek in. Inside, a sink, a toilet and a large tub, its rim charred along the line of a hair dryer's cord. The dryer floated in the water, keeping company with one longhaired, naked, very large dead man.

|||||||||||||||||

In the parking lot of the Executive Business Park on West Tenth Street, Mrs. Suzanne Addison Wade donned sunglasses as she reached her linen-gloved hand into the palm of her driver and stepped from her limousine with the valise. She left the driver behind, entered the front door and scanned the directory. Austin Area Reclamation Organization. Fourth Floor.

"They gone."

She turned to the voice. An elderly black man in security uniform. "Excuse me?"

"Them AARO people. They all gone to the hotel. You can't get up there. Elevator door won't open."

"Oh."

He must have seen her disappointment. He said, "They over at the Washington on Seventh. You know where it is?"

|||||||||||||||||

There's such a thing as too much money.

I followed Mora's directions out west of town, through increasingly affluent suburbs, as the houses grew bigger and fewer and more obscured by tall hedges and distance, treading deeper into the fertile crescent of the Hill Country. I finally reached a private road leading out to an expanse of acreage that would have been suitable for an oil field and probably *was* an oil field once. Sporting spectacular mountain views and an expanse of sky you'd only expect to see from an airplane stood what Mora called the Addison mansion, the palatial digs of Paul and Suzanne Wade.

I pulled up in a circular driveway at the front. Twelve-foot windows marked the first of three stories. I expected a British butler to greet me at the door and hold out a silver tray for my calling card. Instead Mora opened it, letting me into a marble-floored foyer the size of my house. She led me through a succession of hallways.

"There's a ballroom above us that could double as a basketball court," she said. "I spent twenty minutes running the halls, and I can't tell you if there's anyone else in the house or not. I haven't seen half of it." She handed me the phone records from Faith's last days. Her final call, with a margin of several hours, was to the Wade estate.

Mora led me toward what had to be the rear of the house, explaining that Mrs. Wade was one of the people trying to bring Jesus into state government. "It's an insult to government," Mora said. "And it's an insult to Jesus." We reached a stone room with a medieval look. Through that to a hallway, and off the hallway Mora led me to a humble bedroom with a single bed, a bookcase and a desk. The room had its own bathroom. In its tub sat the body of Judah Cavanaugh, the man who Mora determined had picked up Rolo Ortiz the night Rolo was killed. Cavanaugh was dead, apparently by electrocution.

She said, "I saw him from the bathroom window. It was open. I hope that qualifies as probable cause."

Back in the bedroom, in the closet, Mora pointed me to a collage he had begun on the wall, not a great artistic leap from the closet collage in Mexia. Mora pointed to one figure that even I recognized as Jesus rising from the grave. She said, "The Resurrection. It's Easter today."

"Makes you wonder if something's in the works," I said.

"Look under his bed."

I looked underneath. Hand grenades. Guns. An AK-47. Bullets. Wires. Green deta flex sheets, the kind of explosive paper used in letter bombs. Blasting caps. All prominently shoved to the right and left. There was a space in the middle. Something had been taken.

Mora said, "None of the servants' quarters are in use. They must have a staff to keep the place in order, but no live-ins except for Samson here."

"Suspects?"

She showed me a framed color photo of a chubby, balding man with his lacquered wife.

"They did this?"

"Someone did."

And someone had left the house. Maybe with explosives. Maybe with a lot of explosives.

I ran for the phone.

||||||||||||||||||||

Suzanne blotted the perspiration from her chin with a lace handkerchief while holding the valise in her free hand as she stepped away from the car. Roman columns framed the hotel entrance to look like the White House. Inside, the lobby ceiling rose what must have been the full ten stories of the building. Her heels landed on dark marble, and even the regal front desk gave the impression of being part of a national monument rather than of a hotel. She stopped to get her bearings. A uniformed employee greeted her.

"Can I help you, ma'am?"

She spoke haltingly. "I'm . . . looking for the . . . AARO . . ."

"Right that way, ma'am. They're just starting."

She headed toward the great double doors to her left. From the corner of her eye, she thought she saw someone looking at her, a small Latin woman dressed in black, like a maid. Dark skin and curly black hair. But when she turned around, the woman was gone.

Beyond the double doors, well dressed young men and women checked lists and talked busily behind a table. Two Secret Service men flanked the inner door. Both wore sunglasses and earphones. She thought she knew one of them from the governor's staff, and she nodded politely. A tall, fair-haired young man stood leaning over a woman's shoulder as she sat at the table, giggling at the private joke he whispered into her ear.

The young woman spotted Suzanne.

The young man said, "What?" She whispered to him. He didn't hear her. "What?" he repeated.

She hissed. "Suzanne Wade!"

He looked up, amazed and amused, his open mouth curling into a smile. He tapped the shoulder of the man next to him, who looked up and saw Suzanne also. Soon the five of them at the table were watching Suzanne. She rose to her full height, lifted her chin and waited.

The tall young man who had been whispering into the girl's ear stood straight. "Mrs. Wade," he said. "What a pleasure. I'm John Oliver."

"Of course you are. Thank you, John." She offered her hand, and he took it. Suzanne noticed that his right wrist was badly scarred. "May I come in?"

One of the young people snorted, stifling laughter. John's handsome eyes sparkled.

"You understand this is a membership conference."

She felt herself perspire. "I'm aware of that."

He added, "And it's a secular organization. You see that we're meeting on Easter."

She said, "Don't you think I would be welcome? As party chair?"

He looked at his young cohorts, grinning at the spectacle. They were laughing at her, she thought. He said, "Technically, this group has no political affiliation. We're a coalition of community leaders who advise the state legislature on matters that—" He stopped. "Mrs. Wade, you're the subject of today's closing discussion."

The sweat seemed to cool from her face. She said, "All the more reason I should be present." She gripped the valise tighter.

He said he'd be right back, then disappeared through the doors. Others passed into the area, waved to the young people at the desk, showed IDs to the Secret Service men and continued on through. Suzanne stood proudly, not hiding from the awkward glances of the staff. Of course the conference was about her. They were planning a secular future for the party. If she could just get inside, just have a chance to speak, why, she could bring the moneylenders to Jesus.

John returned, somber. "I'm sorry, Mrs. Wade. I can't let you in."

"I'd like to speak to the management."

He said, "This is very embarrassing. That's who I just spoke to. The management. My father said he and any member of the board would be pleased to meet with you this week. But not today."

One of the young men at the table chuckled.

Blushing so hard her face burned, Suzanne turned her back and pushed out into the lobby, still gripping the valise, laughter echoing behind her, though she could have imagined that.

She weaved uncertainly through the lobby as a torrent of girls and mothers rolled through. Past the elevators she spotted Paul in the suit he'd been wearing earlier. She called to him but he didn't hear her, and he disappeared into an elevator before she could reach him.

A bellhop rolled by her with a cart holding a case of Moët.

"Excuse me," she said. "Is that for the AARO conference?"

"Yes, ma'am," he said, and proceeded, she guessed, toward the kitchen.

She followed.

|||||||||||||||||||

I tore up the Wade house looking for paperwork while Mora called DPS. There were four cars registered to the house: two BMWs, a Saturn and a black Lincoln Town Car limo. All in the garage except the limo. We alerted APD, DPS, the sheriff's office and the Bomb Squad. We called for a helicopter to scope the town. How hard could it be to find one black limousine?

|||||||||||||||||||

Suzanne followed the champagne to the kitchen, bright and expansive, filled with the bustle of a hundred Hispanics—cooks and bakers—and white managers barking directions. Lobsters dropped into pots of boiling water. Pans steamed and smoked. And with all the struggling to synchronize, to please the next-higher level, no one questioned a white woman in her very nice soft pink Easter dress as she crossed through with authority, and found the swinging double doors to the banquet hall.

She peeked through the windows.

At a hundred linen-swathed tables sat the biggest men in the party. Everyone she knew, everyone who had been at her soirée: senators, judges, CEOs. And the governor himself with his beady eyes and smug half smile. And the ex-president. And others she didn't know.

At the stage, Bill Oliver stepped to the podium. He held many pages of a speech in front of him.

A waiter stood near her. "Excuse me," she asked. "I'm supposed to hand something to that man. How can I get to the stage?"

He pointed to the door.

"No," she said, pointing. "I need to be back behind the curtains."

"Oh," he said. "This way."

‖‖‖‖‖‖‖‖‖‖‖‖‖‖

We were standing around at the Wade house waiting for word from Dispatch. Something was moving, progressing, but we didn't know where.

The phone rang. I grabbed it.

"Hello?"

"Reles? This is Dispatch."

"Yeah. Whattya got?"

"Fifty limos outside the Washington Hotel on Seventh. Some kind of business conference. Rich-people business."

I told them to send the Bomb Squad.

‖‖‖‖‖‖‖‖‖‖‖‖‖‖

Suzanne stood waiting in the wings, behind the curtains, opposite Bill Oliver. She had to time it just right, interrupt his speech at just the perfect moment.

". . . opportunities for growth . . ." he babbled on.

It had to seem as if she were there by design, by Bill Oliver's design.

". . . run the government like a business . . ."

Soon, soon.

Suzanne gathered her thoughts. It would be her best speech yet. And her most memorable.

‖‖‖‖‖‖‖‖‖‖‖‖‖‖

Mora floored it, her little Honda blasting at ninety up Bee Caves Road to MoPac and across the middle of town, weaving in and out of traffic and through intersections with the lights flashing and the siren screaming.

When we screeched to a halt in front of the hotel's ivory columns, we saw we were the first ones there, save a pair of patrols who looked like tourists at the White House, wondering what the hell they were doing there. Mora and I ran inside with Mrs. Wade's color portrait. We shook up a crowd in the cavernous lobby. The frightened desk clerk hadn't seen her.

"Is she registered?"

Click-click on the keyboard. "No."

Mora said, "Who are all these people?"

"It's a conference or something. Something political."

I said, "Where?"

She pointed to the double doors across the lobby. We ran for them.

Inside the double doors, two young women sat at a table. A couple of Secret Service men guarded another pair of doors. I showed my badge and the photo.

One woman said, "Mrs. Wade? She was here, but we didn't let her in."

"When?"

"Twenty minutes, maybe?"

I turned to the Secret Service men. "Is there another way in?" They didn't answer. I couldn't tell if they were being coy or just stupid. One of the advantages of wearing sunglasses in a dark room.

Mora said, "I'll find it," and disappeared out into the lobby.

I said, "You Secret Service guys, you don't work with the local law enforcement?"

No answer. I turned back to the girls. "Who the hell is in there?"

I made for the doors. The feds moved together, blocking me. One said, "We can't let you pass."

I said, "Listen, dickhead. I don't know who you're protecting.

But I just came from Mrs. Wade's house, and what she left there was one very large fucking corpse and enough plastic explosive to flatten the Hill Country. So maybe this would be a good time to change your plan and stop the lady with the fuckin' bomb. Unless you want to be responsible for cashing in this very nice new hotel *and everyone in it! Are you with me?*"

‖‖‖‖‖‖‖‖‖‖‖‖‖‖‖

Suzanne broke from the wings on the words "God-given right" and glided—magnificently, she thought—across the stage toward Bill Oliver as if she'd been introduced. There were a few gasps, some giggles and, finally, polite applause that rippled through the banquet hall until it was universal. Gate-crasher or no, she was Suzanne Addison Wade.

Oliver caught her in the corner of his eye and did a double take. "Suzanne!" he said. She moved close to him, lifting her head and turning so that he had to kiss her on the cheek. Then, as the applause settled, he asked, "What are you doing here?"

"You mentioned the Lord," she said with a twinkle. "I thought you'd forgotten Him." She scanned the audience with her smile. She was making a joke at her own expense. Like saying, "Everyone knows what a pain I am, talking to businessmen about God." Several voices went "Ah!" and then settled into chuckles. She'd broken in.

‖‖‖‖‖‖‖‖‖‖‖‖‖‖‖

We slipped into the back of the banquet hall. University president Bill Oliver now shared the stage with a jovial Mrs. Wade, her briefcase holding unknown contents. The feds fanned out, whispering into their shoulder mikes. I scanned a sea of tailored suits made of cloth that cost more than the town I grew up in. They wrapped politicos I'd seen on TV and in the papers. Businessmen. And the governor. And one former president.

The lieutenant governor, old Win Muller, was nowhere around.

The feds looked agitated. They had no word but mine that the responsible, prominent Suzanne Wade might be about to remove the movers and shakers of Texas from their bodies. The feds didn't rush to empty the room, but I could tell they wanted to.

Mrs. Wade and Oliver traded quips. She said something like, "Separation of church and state is nowhere in the Constitution."

He said, with a sparkle, "'Congress shall make no law respecting an establishment of religion, or prohibiting the free exercise thereof . . .'"

Popping banter. It was like Donny and Marie without the songs.

And just as he was conceding not that she was right but that she wasn't going away, and he uttered the words, "Okay, Suzanne, let's hear it," a short, balding man looking very much like the guy in the photo with Suzanne, appeared from the wings, swooped in behind her and grabbed her in an embrace.

"Get a room, you two," Oliver uttered with a nervous smile. Suzanne had jolted at the surprise, realized it was her husband and tried without luck to squirm from his grasp. A bouquet of Band-Aids attached to Paul's left temple did little to halt the stream of blood trickling down the side of his face.

I saw the feds move into formation. Four circled the ex-president, two stood by the governor, and two inched toward the stage.

Paul Wade yelled, "Stop where you are! I'll kill you all!"

I realized that Paul had the explosives, not Suzanne. She'd showed up to make a scene. He was there to become immortal.

Some of the feds reached for their guns. I waved and yelled from the back of the tables.

"Whoa-ho, hey, Paul, no rush, huh? It's Dan over here. I'm Dan."

Every eye in the room turned to me. Just now I rated more inter-esting than the guy with the bomb.

It goes without saying that Secret Service men, agents of the fed-eral government, should know more than APD does about stopping a lunatic packed with plastique. But the federal government was in charge at Waco.

All I knew was I needed to get him talking, about anything, and keep him talking. I hoped the Bomb Squad was on its way and that the rat incident in my house wasn't keeping them from responding to my call.

"Whatcha got there, Paul?"

He said, "It's a mixture of organic compounds, RDX and PETN. Wrapped in a deta sheet. The blasting cap will ignite the deta sheet and the deta sheet will set off the mixture. Bang, boom, pow!"

His left hand gripped a small plunger attached to wires that led into his jacket.

The feds grabbed the governor and the ex-prez.

"Nobody moves!" Paul said. He stood behind the podium, still embracing Suzanne with one arm, and spoke into the microphone. "I have enough to blow up this whole room."

"Good, good, good," I said, loud enough that he could hear me but not so harsh as to startle him. Nobody interrupted me. Probably they figured I knew what I was doing, or I had as good a chance of talking him down as anyone did, or maybe they just couldn't think of anything better to say.

"No rush," I said. "Who's that lady with you?"

He looked for words and finally came up with, "My wife."

"You don't want to hurt her."

"Yes. I do."

Paul looked at Suzanne's terrified face. Then he spoke right into the mike. He wanted everyone to hear.

"She said was two months pregnant. She was having a hard pregnancy." He licked his lips. He wasn't accustomed to public speaking. "She went to stay with family. She wouldn't let me visit. Five months later she came back, she said she'd had a miscarriage."

"I did!" she cried.

I wouldn't have advised her interruption, but he quieted her very gently. "She moved to her own bedroom. But she wasn't pregnant two months when she told me," he turned to her. "She was pregnant *four* months."

"No," she said, weeping.

"When she found out she was two months pregnant, we hadn't had sex in a year. She took me to bed one last time. In two months she told me I was gonna be a daddy. She slept with me for cover. And she gave the child away so no one would know."

Chatter around the room. Ear whispering. Nodding. The shifting of power.

Mrs. Wade choked, "I gave her to her father."

"But she wanted you. She called. Just this week. You weren't home."

"What?"

Paul said, "You wonder how she found you. But people figure things out if you give them enough time. I figured out you had a daughter. She figured out you were her mother. Maybe she saw letters from you in her father's house, or checks. And she was alone. She called, she needed her mommy. Nobody loved her. So I loved her."

Mrs. Wade seemed to be holding back dry heaves.

Bill Oliver, only a few paces away, turned on his charm and set it on simmer. "We're all friends here, Paul. . . ."

Paul held up the plunger with his free hand again. He barked, "Yeah?!" Everybody in the room jolted. "Who's my friend here? You oil guys? I lost everything, and you mocked me." He turned to the crowd. "There's so much insult a man can take. Then one day he just can't *take* any more."

He seemed so clear and lucid when he said it that I figured he was about to make a move. He raised his plunger hand slowly. Still no sign of the Bomb Squad. I said, "Paul, it's me, Dan, over here." I moved back and forth to draw his attention. "I'm a city cop. I make less than the guy who drives Bill Oliver's car. You can walk out of here with me right now. These guys are assholes."

Paul almost smiled. I could feel the heat rise in the room.

"What?"

"Assholes. Those oil guys. That judge. I know him. And Bill Oliver? What a fucking asshole! And a thief. Tell him, Bill."

Oliver raised an eyebrow, not one to lose his composure, even in the face of eternity. "Excuse me?"

"Tell him you're an asshole and a thief. We're waiting."

Oliver opened his mouth, closed it, then tried again. "I'm an asshole and a thief."

"And the governor? Holy crap! Stupidest guy in the state, am I right?" There was a general murmur of assent. "Paul, there's only one smart way out of this. That's you and me walk through this back door and get the fuck out of here."

He thought hard, then said, "But what about Suzanne?"

I said, "What about her?"

"If I leave her here, she'll have public schools sponsored by churches, isn't that right, Suzanne?" She looked mortified, humiliated more than scared. "And sectarian prayers on the Senate floor. How long before an official religion? I won't be responsible for that."

Suzanne blurted out, "Jesus wants you on His side!"

Paul considered this briefly, then said, "He should have thought of that before."

And as he raised his plunger hand again, and two feds pointlessly rushed the stage, one drawing his weapon, maybe hoping to pull off a shot that would sacrifice Suzanne but save everyone else, when a handgun shot blasted out of nowhere and a healthy chunk of Paul Wade's skull landed on Bill Oliver's very nice suit.

Suzanne, splattered with blood and still in Paul's one-armed embrace, shrieked and in an instant, retreated a solid ten feet from Paul before he toppled forward and landed on his fist, compressing the plunger, which set off the blasting cap, which ignited the deta sheet, which detonated a mixture of RDX and PETN just as Paul had promised: bang, boom, POW!

I hiked the somber hall of the Hite-Wallis Funeral Home on Lamar, toward the benches by the East Chapel. A practical woman, Vita Carballo had long ago made arrangements for her burial. The guests numbered six: A gaunt young white couple in black motorcycle leather. A housewife, maybe a neighbor. Sergeant Fuentes. Sergeant LaMorte. Me.

Fuentes had made all efforts to contact Vita's family, with no success. He and LaMorte were still working on Vita's murder. I was still the primary suspect.

I was stalling on giving a DNA sample and wouldn't do it until someone forced me to. I'd owned up to visiting Vita's house, and if push came to shove I'd own up to the details. But the novelty of DNA testing made everything bigger than life. Scientific evidence of sexual congress would be misinterpreted as evidence of murder. I didn't want such a concrete piece of misleading evidence to enter the discussion.

An attendant opened the doors to the chapel. We moseyed on in, and I drifted to the casket. Vita looked handsome and dignified. They had tied her hair back, hiding the red tips and the stitches on her battered skull. Fuentes sidled up next to me and crossed himself.

He said, "The indictment's coming down tomorrow. Might be a good time to tell us where you were that night. Sir."

I said, "What night?"

I wanted to give Vita something, but it was too late. She gave me comfort when no one else did.

I heard her voice say, "You were paying for it."

I said, "It was worth it."

Fuentes said, "What was?"

I drove straight from there to the memorial at the Convention Center, Fuentes and LaMorte in my rearview the whole way.

Looking back, we should have seen the explosion coming, and not just a few minutes ahead. In the aftermath of Waco, we'd seen attacks on embassies, a rise in vigilante groups and a callousness toward capital punishment, all evidence of a very different attitude toward life and death than what some of us considered standard.

Paul Wade didn't lie about having explosives, but he lied about the quantity. A skilled engineer, he knew exactly what he was carrying: not enough to end southwestern civilization as we knew it but plenty to blow a hole in himself and anyone he embraced, humiliating her in the process if he could.

Cate Mora's father taught her to shoot when she was a kid. She would have no problem clipping the lid off Paul Wade's skull at fifty feet while his wife was an inch away if only the wife would hold still. Mora finally made her shot. Mrs. Wade recoiled and pulled away as her husband fell on his plunger. While I dove for cover, there was a muffled burst of noise and light as a puff of flesh and blood blew out of Paul's back, expanded in a red cloud that filled the room, hung in the air over the paralyzed captains of industry and finance and settled on them like confetti.

Suzanne Wade bore the worst of the explosion. She escaped death, but her body was penetrated by parts of Paul (for the first time in years, servants testified). Surgeons managed to remove these, except for a few bits of Paul's ribs, which would remain in her like shrapnel. Now, a week later, she was just able to walk. Not willing to pass up a key photo op, she arrived—against doctors' orders, bless her heart— to speak at the memorial for those who'd died at Waco, and for those who followed them just this week on the anniversary of Waco, departing this earth from a government building in Oklahoma City. Suzanne's recovery was miraculous if the injuries were as serious as we'd heard.

I made it to the Convention Center in time to hear Lieutenant Governor Win Muller speak about Suzanne's heroism, about her warmth and concern for the well-being of the state, especially children, about putting aside partisan differences. He also said that the governor was the best the state had ever had and that, though it was years away, he'd cross party lines and back him for reelection. Muller's endorsement would make all the difference.

Win Muller had been reined in.

The governor took the podium. He talked about Suzanne bringing spirituality to the capitol, then something about the sanctity of marriage and the sanctity of human life. Earlier that week he'd bragged about shortening his evaluation time on execution appeals from thirty minutes to fifteen.

He mentioned God three times, a record for his brief career. I took it for Mrs. Wade's influence.

Suzanne mounted the stage to floor-rumbling applause. She

started small, waved the flag a little, then complained about the efforts of certain individuals to shift God out of daily life.

The lieutenant governor nodded prominently. So did Bill Oliver.

The political tide of the nation gently shifted.

A birth certificate, a series of letters and a collection of testimonies confirmed that Suzanne Wade was Faith Copeland's mother and Russell Copeland was Faith's natural father. Lucille Copeland testified that she herself had never been pregnant, that on Russell's insistence they'd adopted Faith. If I'm any judge of scrapbook photos, Russell developed a hankering for his beautiful daughter that was less than paternal and deferred parenting to Faith's stepmother, Lucille, for the girl's own good. Lucille suspected that Faith was Russ's real daughter, but she kept her mouth shut while it yielded a paycheck and bailed once it didn't.

We interviewed servants and ex-servants from the Wade estate on the subject of Suzanne's brief affair with Russell Copeland, and they generally dismissed it: Russell Copeland was Paul Wade without money. The two men even looked alike. Why would she bother? When pressed with proof of the affair, one maid conjectured that Suzanne must have wanted the real evidence (that is, Faith) out of her house. As to why she cheated on her husband with his double, the maid suggested that maybe her lover reminded her of her husband before their love went south. I wanted to lay the question on Suzanne myself, but city cops don't question important people like Suzanne Wade.

The Monday after the AARO conference, I told Chief Cronin everything I'd learned about Faith Copeland, the Wades and the events leading to the explosion. Cronin said no, the incendiary device was planted by Judah Cavanaugh, who later killed himself. Paul Wade died in an attempt to save his beloved wife. Suzanne Wade's husband was not a murderer. I pointed out that Judah had croaked in his tub before the Wades hit the hotel, and he must have been on pretty intimate terms with Paul Wade to set the bomb on Paul's person without Paul knowing. I added that a whole lot of evidence would need to be buried to maintain the chief's theory, the kind of evidence that tended to pop up later in the most conspicuous of places, such as newspapers.

Cronin blasted at me, something about questioning his authority. He reminded me of my pending indictment for the murder of a prostitute and suggested strongly that I toe the line. He reminded me that I had a family now.

I skulked out of his office, conquered. I was a lieutenant and a free man as long as I maintained the official word on Paul Wade's virgin death.

What could I do? I had a family now.

The memorial broke up after Suzanne Wade's speech, and I went outside the Convention Center for air. A young detective who'd threatened me the day the feds brought Clay in spotted me and took a few steps to shake my hand.

"I'm glad they made you lieutenant," he said. "Congratulations. And hey, I'm sorry I ribbed you about that Clay thing."

"You said, 'Why don't you die?' "

"Well . . . yeah."

Torbett said something to a black patrolman. I walked over to him as the patrol stepped away.

He said, "You ever notice how these things don't happen without TV cameras?"

I asked him how IA was treating him.

He looked around to make sure no one was close enough to hear. Then he leaned close and said, "Everyone's afraid to talk, I knew that. But the you-know-what pulls the strings. I only see what they want me to see. And I can't pin them because I can't prove they exist." He shook his head. "I thought I could build a second Family, an honest one. I'd probably get them all killed."

For the bad blood that had passed between us, I was grateful he confided in me. I said, "I'll join."

"You're a murder suspect. Where were you the night Vita was killed?"

I said, "Who spotted me there the night before?"

He walked away.

I saw the unmistakable thick black hair at the back of Mora's head. She wore a formal-looking blazer, black, with blue pants, and her hair hung loose and gleaming. Then I saw a hand appear in her hair. Someone, not her, was running his fingers through. I thought for sure she was about to haul off and deck him. Instead she leaned into the caress. I slipped through the crowd to get a better look. The hand belonged to the man I'd replaced as head of Homicide, Lieutenant Pete Marks.

Bang, boom, POW!

Mora said that she was "dating" someone. I heard that the some-one was married and lived in Pflugerville.

The night I kissed her, the curtain on her living room window stayed open. Someone saw us. I'd made an enemy.

But that wasn't the first time he saw us. People had seen us to-gether, word got out. He'd had me followed. He knew where I'd been. And he sent word to Torbett that I'd been at Vita's.

And when he saw me kiss Mora, he took bigger action.

Once Mora moved away from Marks, I worked my way around the crowd until I got close to him. His face was granite-hard, wrinkles like cracks. His cheekbones rose slightly as he spotted me.

"Ain't seen you around, Marks."

"They put me in charge of Organized Crime."

I nodded.

He said, "They wanted you. They figured you knew more about it." He showed his yellow teeth. It was common knowledge that my father had worked in the Mafia.

I said, "Hope you're not gonna steal any of my good people. Fuentes. Mora."

I saw a slight shift in his features, or maybe just a ceasing of movement. I looked him up and down. Stony complexion, square jaw, thin tie, badge and gun on his belt. I noticed that the gun a was Colt with a rubber grip and a rounded handle.

Think hard, Reles.

Vita Carballo was bludgeoned with something round-tipped, maybe a ball-peen hammer.

I turned my back to Marks. Cameras from the different TV stations grabbed some final footage of the crowd and pulled interviews. I thought of Torbett's comment, about these events not happening without the cameras. Like we were playing for them. I found Fuentes and tapped him on the shoulder. "Follow me." He followed me to where Torbett was standing. I leaned close to both of them and said, "Watch me. And watch Marks."

The crowd was spreading out and dissipating. Mora had her car keys in hand like she was readying to go. Half a dozen people stood between her and Marks. I ran up to her.

"Kiss me," I said.

"What? Forget it, Reles. It was just a thing."

I said, "If I told you that by making out with me right now, you could catch a killer, would you believe me?"

Her eyes flicked right and left, searching mine. She stopped searching me and turned, I guessed, to see if her boyfriend was watching. I put up a hand to distract her.

"If you believe me," I said, "do it."

She caught the message that she wasn't allowed to turn around first, to check if her boyfriend was watching. She said, "This better be for real, Reles."

She put her arms around my neck and planted her lips on mine. I held her by her narrow waist. I had one eye half open, and I could sense the patrols shifting around us, surely the first time they'd seen two plainclothes cops making out at a public memorial. Mora tightened. She wasn't comfortable. She was acting under orders. Then I saw Marks lunging for me.

I broke the liplock just as Marks, his face red with fury, roared and pounced on me. He knocked me with a left cross that I rolled with rather than blocking. I wanted him to look worse for attacking me. He clamped his arm around my neck. Torbett and Fuentes grabbed him, and the four of us crashed to the pavement. Marks writhed and growled like an epileptic. I climbed to my feet as he screamed, "Son of a bitch! Jew bastard!"

Torbett and Fuentes held him down. Torbett got his knee on Marks's chest.

I said, "Pete Marks killed Vita Carballo."

Marks yelled, "Bastard!"

Torbett said, "Why?"

I spoke to Marks. "You knew I was hanging around with Mora. You got jealous, so you followed me. You saw me go into Vita Carballo's house, and you told Torbett about it. Am I right, Torbett?"

Torbett nodded. I said, "When you saw me in Mora's apartment, you went crazy. You went back to Vita's. You didn't plan to kill her, but it happened. And you figured out you could frame me for it."

Fuentes said, "Can you prove any of this?"

I said, "His Colt has a rounded grip. He didn't go into Vita's house with a plan. He got the idea to shoot her and realized he couldn't leave a bullet. So he bludgeoned her with the butt of the Colt. It'll match the cast. I bet you find blood traces on the grip. What do you say, Marks?"

He didn't deny it. He had the right to remain silent.

I bent over Marks and slipped the Colt from his belt holster.

"You killed her with this," I said. "She had her back turned, and you bashed her brains in."

That Marks didn't argue wouldn't stand up as a confession.

Torbett got in his face. "Marks," he said. "Tell me he's wrong." No answer.

They got Marks to his feet, cuffed him and moved him into the back of a cruiser. Mora watched him go, shock spreading across her face.

"You okay?" I asked. She turned to me. I'd used her to catch her lover. He'd killed an innocent woman. I wondered, would Mora seek revenge? Where was her loyalty?

She straightened her spine and raised her chin. "I can take it," she said, adding, "boss."

The cameras pounced on me, the new head of Homicide. Reporters asked what I thought of the arrest. Just then I realized that the Family would bury Marks's actions and he'd walk. And I would keep my mouth shut, as Cronin had warned me, because I had a family.

The cameras still rolled. "Sir?" the reporter prodded.

Something clicked, and I spoke with great confidence and professionalism.

"I hope this puts to rest any rumors about 'the Family.'" I made the quotey motion with my fingers.

The interviewer asked, "What family?"

"Oh, you know. The rumor that there's an affiliation of influential men in the department who control promotions and discipline, protect their own. As you can see, the department holds its own members to the same standards as any other citizens. Higher. Watch Pete Marks's case go to trial, and see if that doesn't bear me out."

No one had ever mentioned the Family to their mothers before, let alone to the press. As soon as the cameras turned away, Cronin cornered me, veins bulging from his forehead. He hissed, "What the hell are you doing?"

I said, "You told me to create a command presence."

"I could fry you for this."

"For what? I said there was no Family. Did I lie?"

"You don't know what you've done!"

I noticed a camera over his shoulder, focused on us. I looked at it and said, "Smile." He turned to the camera. Then he twisted his grimace into a smile and waved. I put my arm around his shoulder and smiled big. "You can't hurt me, Chief," I said through the side of my mouth. "I'm a TV star."

Judah Cavanaugh would have been charged in the death of Rolando Ortiz, and Paul Wade would have been charged in the death of Faith Copeland, if Judah and Paul weren't already dead. Foster parents Chuck and Elizabeth Leitch were cleared in the accidental death of Joyce Graaf. According to Child Services, they can still take in children. Lots of kids fall through the cracks, they say. So many kids. So many cracks.

But I knew one kid I could help.

‖‖‖‖‖‖

That evening Josh sprawled on the carpet with a coloring book while Rachel and I sat on the couch watching the evening news. Rachel nursed a glass of wine. The news anchors congratulated themselves for being at the scene when a twenty-year police detective, the head of the Organized Crime division, got arrested for murder. They showed my interview.

Rachel said to Josh, "Look, honey. Daddy's on TV."

Josh looked at the screen, then at me. "It's you," he said. Then he went back to his coloring.

I told Josh he could call me Dad if he wanted to, or just Dan. He didn't call me anything. We got him a soft plastic sheet for the futon in the extra bedroom, just in case. I offered Rachel my room. She preferred the couch, she said, where Josh could find her if he had a bad dream, which he pretty much always had. And she slept better that way, too.

In the yard of what would be his kindergarten if he stuck around a while, Josh approached a very small set of monkey bars. If he fell, he'd only drop about two feet, but I kept wondering if I should go help him. He waved to Rachel where she stood, a foot or so from me. It was a sunny spring day, nearing sunset, and there were only a few kids around. He kept them at a distance.

Rachel and I both waved back. Josh smiled at Rachel, looked at me and returned to his business.

We watched him climb the monkey bars. I said, "I think you should stay."

"No room," she said. She smoked steadily, her free hand wrapped around her waist as if it were cold out. She was wearing baggy khakis and a loose knit shirt.

I said, "We'll get a bigger place. Or we could live near each other, close enough that Josh could walk from one house to another when he's a little older. He could have two parents. I'm administration now, so it wouldn't be so crazy. Or you could . . . stay with me. We wouldn't have to be lovers. You could . . . you know, you could see other guys, have your own life, but we'd all be together. Look out for each other."

I thought I saw her eyes tear up. She was still watching Josh, and I pretended I was, too.

I didn't imagine that Josh would warm up to me anytime soon. Or that I was going to have an easy time with Rachel. But I'd grown to believe I could do something for them, that for once in my life I could put someone else first. I didn't know if it would make me happy, but I knew it would make a difference. And in spite of what the department believed, I decided that "family" could mean something besides a partnership in malice and greed.

Rachel said, "I smoke all the time. And I drink. I have a big wobbly ass."

"I like a big wobbly ass," I said. "I'm a big wobbly ass man."

"I'm a mess," she said.

"We could be happy. I'll *make* you happy."

"Why would you want me?"

I said, "Because I love you. There's nothing you can say that would make me not love you."

Her chin seemed to shake. She said, "I killed a man."

I said, "I know."

Long silence. She was trying to decide whether to tell me something. Then she said, "It was my father."

I said, "I know that, too."

The name of the father on Rachel's birth certificate, Marcel Gagnon, matched the name of the deceased on the police report from the night in 1981 that an intruder entered her house and she killed

him. She'd been attacked by her father, and she defended herself. I
didn't know what else he did to her through the years. I knew it was
enough to keep her from traveling under his last name.

Six times out of ten, if you go through the victim's belongings,
you'll find a photo of the killer and the victim with their arms around
each other. In my wallet I had a snapshot of Rachel and her dad
together, when she was five. From what I'd seen over the last week,
there was a lot people would do to kids. I guessed he got what he
deserved.

Some other kids approached the monkey bars, and Josh quickly
dismounted and headed for the slide. It was low, only four steps to the
top, but I kept thinking Rachel should go over and help him, or I
should. Unaided, he climbed the steep steps.

Rachel slipped her hand into mine. It was the first time we'd
touched since she came back. I felt it down to my shoes.

Josh got to the top to the steps, sat, waved back at his mother, at
us, and began his slide.